ENDANGERED

By the Author

Mercy

Unexpected Partners

Endangered

ENDANGERED

by
Michelle Larkin

2019

ENDANGERED

ISBN 13: 978-1-63555-377-2

THIS TRADE PAPERBACK ORIGINAL IS PUBLISHED BY
BOLD STROKES BOOKS, INC.
P.O. BOX 249
VALLEY FALLS, NY 12185

FIRST EDITION: JULY 2019

CREDITS
EDITOR: RUTH STERNGLANTZ
PRODUCTION DESIGN: SUSAN RAMUNDO
COVER DESIGN BY TAMMY SEIDICK

Acknowledgments

Heartfelt gratitude to my editor, Ruth Sternglantz, whose guidance, feedback, and unbridled honesty is always welcomed and very much appreciated.

Thank you to Sandy Lowe for working her magic on the book blurb.

Sincere thanks, once again, to Tammy Seidick for her artistic insight with regards to designing this incredible cover.

Thanks also to my mom, Ruthie, and her longtime best friend, Donna, for keeping me company on this adventure while Aspen and Tora sorted things out.

And, as always, the biggest round of applause goes to the very loud and boisterous superhero duo, Levi and Jett, who also happen to be my sons AND my very favorite people on the planet.

Dedication

With eternal gratitude for your friendship
and unconditional love, this one is for you, Chloe.
My sweet baby girl. I miss you so.

Chapter One

Officer Aspen Wolfe hurried out of the cramped stairwell and stepped onto the building's rooftop, her gaze darting to the kid precariously balanced on the concrete ledge.

The kid peered down on Boston's busy Tremont Street with a look of wonder, fear, and longing. Winds from an approaching storm swiped the kid's gray hood. Shaggy brown hair darted from side to side.

Hard to tell if this one was male or female. Aspen's money was on female, but she'd been wrong before. Taking a careful step forward, she listened to the sounds of passing traffic on the city street below. She was keenly aware of how high they were. She hated heights. Always had. The feel of solid ground beneath her feet was definitely preferable to being up here.

"Don't come any closer." The kid glanced over one shoulder. "I swear, I'll jump."

With nine years under her belt as a Boston beat cop, Aspen's unconventional methods had earned her begrudging respect from fellow officers over the years. Due in large part to her success, dispatch usually saddled her with all the crazies.

She studied the kid and pulled her hair into a ponytail with the elastic from her wrist. Couldn't be more than twelve. Thirteen at most. Black eye, bruised cheek, split lip. She had no other information. Not even a name.

"Tell you what," she said, putting her hands up in a gesture of surrender. "I'll stay right here until you give me permission to come and sit with you. I've been on my feet all day and could really use the break." She reached into her pocket and pulled out the two Snickers candy bars she'd grabbed from her patrol car on her way to the call. She spent a small fortune on candy bars each year, but they'd gotten her out of more than a few dicey situations. Who could resist chocolate? A candy bar took down the defenses. Instant friend maker. She was considering starting a class at the academy on how to use chocolate as a defense tactic in law enforcement.

"You hungry?" she asked, tearing the wrapper and taking a bite.

The kid pulled up the hoodie and looked back at her like she was nuts.

"If you're gonna jump"—she held up the extra candy bar—"you might as well go down with some chocolate in your mouth."

"I hate Snickers."

"Copy that." Aspen tossed the Snickers on the ground and reached into her other pocket, still munching. The more she studied the kid, the more convinced she became this was a girl. "Butterfinger?"

The kid shook her head.

She dug around in the cargo pocket of her pants. "Kit Kat?"

The kid turned away, resuming her scan of the busy street below.

"Not a chocolate fan. Okay. That's cool." She was running out of pockets. Last chance. She pulled out a Skittles bag and gazed at it longingly before holding it up.

The girl turned. "Toss it here."

Just her luck this kid would pick the one she'd been saving for end-of-shift paperwork. She sighed. "Do me a favor and step down, just for a minute—long enough to enjoy your last bag of Skittles. Then you can climb back up there if you want. But every person deserves a decent last meal."

This elicited a small smile. "You're not like any cop I met before," she said, finally meeting Aspen's gaze.

"And you're not like any kid I've met before. People who think about taking the plunge into rush-hour traffic are usually older, grayer, and fatter than you." Suicide was no joke, but she had the kid's attention, and snark seemed the way to hold it. She took another bite of the Snickers. "You're a few decades too early, kid."

She held her breath as the girl spun around and effortlessly hopped from the ledge down to the roof. True to her word, Aspen tossed her the bag of Skittles.

She tore the bag open and popped a few in her mouth, eyeing her suspiciously. "Officer Wolfe," she said, studying the nameplate on the breast pocket of her uniform. "Cool name."

"Mind if we sit?" Aspen lowered her body to the ground and rested her back against the rooftop wall. They sat there and snacked together in silence. Savoring the last chocolaty mouthful, she crumpled the Snickers wrapper and tossed it aside.

The kid stopped chewing and stared at her. "You're littering."

"What do you care? You were on your way out."

"But you're a cop. Don't you arrest people for littering?"

"Cops aren't perfect," she said, rising to retrieve the offending wrapper before joining her once again. "By the way, I was saving those for later," she admitted, casting a glance at the bag of Skittles. "Came from my personal stash. Care to share?"

The girl handed her the bag. "Your dentist must love you."

She poured some into her palm and handed them back, digging into another pocket to pull out a travel-sized toothbrush. "Good oral hygiene is important."

"You're weird."

"Want to talk about what's going on?"

"I know the drill. You ask me my name and age and all that. When I refuse to tell you, you haul me down to the station, call Child Protective Service, and send me off to another crappy foster home."

Aspen studied the girl as she talked. Her red high-top sneakers were obviously too big. Her jeans were torn and filthy. The gray hoodie was sized for a much larger person and fell almost to her knees, its thin material providing little protection on this chilly November day. She was pale and gaunt—probably hadn't eaten a decent meal in ages. Looked like she was living on the streets.

Aspen remembered those days from her own youth all too well. "You like pancakes?"

"Do you think about anything besides food?" She looked right at Aspen—through her—her bright green gaze piercing and curious. "Whoa, your eyes are—"

"The windows to my soul," Aspen finished, well aware they perfectly matched her raven hair. She knew little about her parents, but her Native American heritage came through loud and clear.

"They're so...dark," the girl said, staring. "They're beautiful. You're pretty. For a cop," she added quickly.

Aspen sensed there was something special about this kid. And not just because the girl had complimented her, though that did score her some extra points. She couldn't put her finger on what it was exactly, but she was sure of it. Trusting her instincts had paid off more than once on the job. She checked her watch. Her shift was ending soon. "How about we grab some dinner at IHOP? My treat."

"How come you're not fat?" the girl asked, looking genuinely baffled.

Aspen smiled. "Fast metabolism."

"Fast what?" She shook her head. "Forget it. You're trying to trick me. I go with you, and we end up at the station instead of eating pancakes."

Aspen sighed, deciding to come clean. "I got my ass kicked today by a drunk who was twice my age. The guys at the precinct will never let me live it down." She stood, brushed the dirt from her pants, and extended a hand. "Believe me, I'm not in any big hurry to get back."

To her surprise, the girl reached up and grabbed hold with a firm grip. Time slowed the moment their hands connected. The kid faded from view like smoky wisps as the image of a huge white owl, wings spread wide, appeared before her. Aspen drew in a sharp breath. The owl had the girl's unmistakable bright green eyes.

She let go of the girl's hand, squeezed her eyes shut, and opened them again. The kid was now standing where the owl had been.

The girl took a step back, a look of surprise on her face. "You're a panther."

"Come again?"

"I'm an owl. You're a pan—" She shook her head. "Never mind." She lifted her red backpack from the ground and slung it over one shoulder. "Can we go eat? I'm starving."

An owl? Aspen stood speechless as she watched the girl hurry off toward the rooftop door. Did she say *owl*? She couldn't remember the last time she was rendered speechless. There was one thing about herself she knew she could always count on, regardless of the situation: she carried a well-stocked arsenal of clever quips and candy bars wherever she went. What good was one without the other?

The kid swung open the rooftop door and glanced back over her shoulder. "You coming or what?"

Aspen ordered the usual and handed her menu to the waitress, watching as the kid did the same. She had taken her regular booth in the back corner and requested that the surrounding tables remain unoccupied so she and the girl could talk. "So?" she finally asked as their waitress sauntered away.

The girl stared at her blankly.

"Chocolate-chip pancakes for a name. That was the deal."

"Fine. It's Skye. I'm thirteen," she said, her shoulders sagging in defeat. "Lots of people think I'm a boy, but I'm a girl."

Aspen gave herself a mental high five. "You cut your hair to look like a boy so no one'll mess with you on the streets."

Skye looked up, a mix of emotions spreading across her face.

"You're smart, resourceful. I admire that." She studied Skye's black eye, bruised cheek, and split lip. "What happened to your face?"

"Some homeless dude wanted my high-tops."

Aspen glanced under the table. "And?"

"And I said no." The girl met her gaze defiantly.

She thought for a moment, suddenly concerned for the homeless dude. "How badly did you hurt him?"

"I kicked him—hard—in the nuts. Told him I'd cut them off if he bothered me again."

"Okay." Aspen shook her head. She couldn't help herself and smiled. "Aside from your face, how's the rest of you?"

"Fine."

"Do you have any other injuries?"

Skye shook her head.

Just to be safe, she'd take the girl to the hospital for an exam and get her statement as soon as they were finished here. Skye had obviously perfected a tough exterior, but her underlying fear was palpable. "I bounced between foster homes and lived on the streets for a while when I was a kid." Aspen stood and went to the other side of the booth to sit beside the girl. "I got my ass kicked more than a few times. Made me think I always needed to look tough and be on guard with everyone. But deep down, I was really scared inside." She sighed. "It's okay to be scared, you know."

They sat together in silence. Skye wiped the tears from her cheeks with the back of one sleeve. "Did you make that up just to… you know…relate?"

"It's all true. I swear on my entire collection of candy."

The girl smiled and looked up. "How'd you end up in a foster home? Where were your parents?"

"They died when I was six. I didn't have any other family." She thought back, remembering the feeling of disbelief upon learning of her parents' death. The hardest part to grasp at that age was the permanence of their passing. She remembered waking up each morning, believing with all her heart and soul that they had magically returned in the middle of the night and were asleep in the next room. It had taken her a whole year to figure out that *dead* meant never coming back.

Aspen realized most people went through life fighting like hell to avoid revisiting the painful memories of the past. She made a point of regularly running her fingers over the old scars in her life to keep herself resilient and strong. "What about you?" she asked, returning to the opposite side of the booth. "Where are your parents?"

Skye looked at her for a long moment before answering. "Dead."

It took Aspen a few beats to put two and two together. She thought back to the moment their hands touched on the rooftop. This girl must be a Shroud—a shapeshifter. More precisely, an owl. But how had she figured out the girl's animal? Aside from a blood test, there was only one way to discern humans from Shrouds: actually *seeing* them shapeshift. She'd seen Shrouds shift many times over the years, both on and off the job. But this girl hadn't shifted in the usual sense. It was as if Skye had removed a mask, her human body, when their hands connected. Aspen had shaken hands with countless Shrouds over the years. Never once had that happened before.

She suddenly found herself with more questions than answers but refrained from asking the girl about it. Skye had lost her parents. She'd bet anything they were targeted and murdered simply because they were Shrouds. Aspen put her arms on the table and leaned forward. "You're a Shroud," she whispered, careful not to draw attention.

Nodding, the girl bit her lip uncertainly. She pushed up the cuff of her sweatshirt to reveal the mark on her right hand.

"Okay." Relations between humans and Shrouds were tenuous, at best. When President Decker took office three years ago, he'd wasted no time before playing to his base of racist supporters. He spread lies about Shrouds on a daily basis, exacerbating the tension between the two species and amplifying humans' distrust of Shrouds to a degree unprecedented in the history of human/Shroud coexistence. Aspen had seen the effects of Decker's toxic influence firsthand. She despised him and everything he stood for.

She pierced the girl with a steady gaze. "What happened to your parents?"

"A man in a suit knocked on our door a few months ago. He said he worked with my dad, so I let him in. He shot my dad with a gun, and then he shot Mom. He fired at me, too, but he missed. I escaped through the back kitchen door and..." Skye hesitated. "I ran as fast as I could to the police station. The police went to my house but never found my parents. They said they found suitcases on the bed. Looked like my parents had packed up all their clothes and took off without me. But my parents would never do that. They loved me." She shook her head as fresh tears welled up in her eyes. "I *saw* what he did to them. But the cops didn't care."

Aspen thought for a moment, unnerved by the similarity in their stories. She was six when her parents were murdered. They, too, were Shrouds. The only difference between her story and Skye's was that Aspen was human. She was adopted by Shroud parents, which is why she'd been spared.

She looked at the girl. Aspen could smell an omission a mile away. "There's something you're not telling me, Skye. What is it?"

The girl averted her gaze and shifted uncomfortably in her seat. "When the man in the black suit shot at my parents, they…shifted. My dad shifted into a black bear, and my mom shifted into an owl. Before my mom shifted, she yelled at me to fly away and trust my instincts. But I just stood there. I couldn't believe she'd said that."

President Decker had signed an executive order last year, making it unlawful for Shrouds to shift. Aspen had never arrested a Shroud for shifting—she refused—but she knew lots of other cops who had.

Skye opened her mouth to go on but thought better of it and looked down. Suddenly quiet, she fidgeted with the zipper on her sweatshirt.

"It's okay." Aspen reached across the table reassuringly. "You won't get into trouble with me for shifting."

Skye looked up, her expression doubtful. "Promise?"

"Promise."

"When the man shot at me and missed, I bolted out the kitchen door. You know that expression, fight or flight?"

Aspen nodded.

"Well, I flew. Literally. I turned into a white owl, just like my mom, and I flew into the sky. That's how I got away. He couldn't chase me up there."

"That was a smart thing to do."

"But how can you say that? You're a cop. Shifting is against the law."

Aspen shrugged. "It's a stupid law," she said honestly.

"My dad raised me *never* to shift—even before it was against the law. He did everything he could to make me as human as possible. He said it was too dangerous to embrace Shroud culture, that there were too many Shroud haters out there."

Aspen said nothing as the waitress returned and set their plates on the table. "What were you doing on the roof?" she asked as soon as they were alone again. The girl watched, seemingly mesmerized as she drowned her pancakes in as much syrup as humanly possible.

"You are seriously addicted to sugar."

"I know. I've been looking for a good support group. Haven't found one yet." She stuffed a large forkful of pancakes into her mouth, relishing their buttery sweetness. Syrup ran down her chin and onto the napkin she'd tucked into the collar of her uniform. "So?"

Skye stabbed a fork into her own stack. "I was going to jump."

"To fall or fly?"

"Fall." Skye took a modest bite, chewed, and swallowed. "I just didn't want to be here anymore."

Aspen set down her fork, wiped her chin, and took a sip of coffee. "Do you feel that way now?"

"No." Skye took a much larger bite this time, returning Aspen's gaze with confidence.

"Good. What's changed?"

The girl grinned around a mouthful of pancakes. "I met *you*."

Chapter Two

President Timothy Decker set his hands on his hips and stared out over the South Lawn from the window inside the Oval Office. "Have the SEA troops been mobilized?"

"Yes, Mr. President. Dispatched to every state and all major cities. Last unit touched down about an hour ago."

"And this still hasn't hit the news?"

"No, sir."

"Then it's time we got started." Tim took a deep cleansing breath. "Tell them the mission's a go."

His secretary of defense remained glued in place on the Oval Office rug.

The president turned and cast a stern glance at Finkleman. "Do it," he ordered. "Now."

"But wouldn't it be best to wait until morning, Mr. President?"

"I want to implement these changes before the media catches wind of this." Tim stepped away from the window and casually leaned over the leather chair behind the Oval Office desk—*his* desk, he reminded himself proudly. He checked his Rolex. "Most Shrouds are probably leaving their jobs right about now, scurrying home to their little fur families. Time to round them up and dispose of them like the vermin they are."

❖

It was closing in on seven p.m. by the time Aspen parked her patrol car in the hospital parking lot. She cut the engine and turned to Skye. "Just a quick checkup with the ER doc to make sure you're okay. No big thing."

"You plan on dumping me here?"

She cut the engine and turned to Skye. "Not at all."

"You're off the clock now." A palpable sadness crept into Skye's green eyes. "You'll call CPS, and then you'll be done with me. Right?"

Aspen thought for a moment. The kid was right. Protocol dictated that's exactly what she was supposed to do. But there was something inside that urged her not to follow the rules this time. She wasn't sure why. There was no denying she felt connected to this kid. But there was something else, too. Something she couldn't quite put her finger on.

Sighing, she reached inside the collar of her uniform and pulled out the pendant that had come to feel like a part of her body. She unclasped the chain and gave the pendant one last rub between thumb and forefinger. "Someone gave this to me when I was your age," she said, handing it to Skye. "It's the symbol of the phoenix." She watched as the girl studied the pendant's gold face. "When her old life is over, she rises from the ashes into a new life, emerging even more powerful and made even more beautiful by her newfound strength. Eventually, with time, that's what will happen to you. I see it in you, Skye, so I know it's there. Someday, you'll see it in yourself, too. And when you do, it'll be time to pass this on to someone else." She retrieved the necklace from Skye's hands, draped it around the girl's neck, and clasped it securely in place. "From now on, just know you're never alone."

Skye looked at her, the tears flowing freely down her cheeks.

Blinking back her own tears, Aspen offered a reassuring smile. "Oh, and one more thing." Unable to keep from breaking the tension, she put on her best serious-cop face. "You're not going to turn into an owl in the exam room, are you?"

Skye laughed. It was the first real laugh she'd heard from the girl since they'd met. "No. I promise I won't do that."

"Good. Let's go get you medically cleared."

Skye hesitated, carefully tucking the pendant inside the collar of her red hoodie. "Then what?" she asked.

Aspen shrugged. "I don't know. But we'll figure it out... together."

❖

The doctor rounded the corner and almost collided with Aspen in front of the vending machine.

"All set," she said, eyeing the pile of candy inside the barf bucket Aspen had confiscated and was now holding under one arm.

Aspen reluctantly turned away from the Payday dangling precariously inside the machine to give the doctor her undivided attention. "She okay?"

"She's a bit malnourished. Has some bruises and scratches but otherwise appears in good health. I'll finish my report and fax it over. You can go into the room and wait there. Skye's taking a shower now. I gave her a fresh pair of scrubs to wear." The doctor's eyes kept returning to the Reese's Peanut Butter Cups inside the barf bucket. "You've made quite an impression on her, Officer Wolfe. She trusts you."

The doctor's eyes were the most unique and beautiful shade of amber-gold she'd ever seen. Unruly curly blond hair was braided loosely down her back. Several locks had broken free and were tucked behind one ear. Aspen withdrew the Reese's from the pile and handed it to her.

She accepted the candy and extended her hand. "Tora Madigan."

Captivated by her eyes, Aspen returned the handshake but immediately wished she hadn't. Time came to a screeching halt. As the doctor faded from view, a lioness assumed her place with those incredible amber-gold eyes. Rippling with power, nobility, and self-control, the lioness held its tail high as it stalked around her in a full circle.

The hair on the back of Aspen's neck stood up. Her instincts told her she was being evaluated. As she turned to face the lioness, they squared off like two alphas vying for dominance. She felt her own primal instincts kick in, begging to take over. She shook her head to snap herself out of it. *What the hell?* How could this happen twice in one day? She released the doctor's hand and took a step back.

The doctor was now standing where the lioness had been. Exactly as it had happened with Skye and the owl.

Their eyes locked as they stood in silence for long seconds. The doctor observed her with a calm, quiet confidence that Aspen was unaccustomed to seeing. Most people were at least a smidgeon intimidated by an armed police officer in uniform.

The doctor was the first to break the silence. "Did you skip breakfast, lunch, *and* dinner?" she asked with an amused grin, glancing at the candy-filled barf bucket. "For a week?"

Aspen switched the bucket to her other arm a little self-consciously. It was getting heavy. "This is just an after-dinner snack."

Tora closed the distance between them and studied her intently. "I've never seen eyes so…dark. They're quite beautiful."

The alluring scent of Tora's perfume wafted over her, a little intoxicating. "Ditto," was all Aspen could think to say. "But minus the dark part," she added quickly. "They remind me a little of—"

"A lion's eyes?" Tora finished, an impish grin tugging at the corners of her mouth. She returned Aspen's gaze with the forthright and unwavering confidence of a leader.

It was a little unnerving. "Nice to meet you, Doc. Thanks for taking care of Skye," Aspen said, already heading down the corridor. She turned the corner and glanced back, relieved to see she wasn't being followed by a hungry predator.

Tora watched, mesmerized, as Aspen made a hasty retreat. Those eyes. Had she really seen what she thought she saw? Was it even possible? She squinted, following the cop's lithe figure as she disappeared around the corner and vanished from sight.

It was almost as if Aspen was unaware of her own gifts—ignorant to who and what she was. How could that be? Surely, she would have come to terms with her identity by now. But if that was the case, why would she be out in public, unprotected? What Shroud in their right mind would let someone as indispensable as Aspen roam around the city streets, fighting crime?

Her stomach growled as she gazed down at the Reese's in her hand. She hadn't taken the time to eat today and felt grateful for this small energy boost. She tore open the orange wrapper and peeled the brown paper from each peanut butter cup. She ate them quickly, her mind on Aspen.

Aspen knocked on the door and stepped inside the exam room. The door to the bathroom was closed. She heard water running in the shower. She sat in the only chair and set the barf bucket in her lap, unwrapping a Twix as she thought back to the day she met Oscar.

At twelve years old, she'd just bolted from another nightmare of a foster home. Living on the streets was an improvement to being bullied, beaten, and starved by a family who took her in for the sole purpose of getting a modest monthly stipend from the state. Convinced she could take better care of herself, she wasted no time in establishing a dependable routine.

She'd started each morning with a brisk walk to the local Dunkin' Donuts, scavenging what she could from the dumpster. They always discarded the previous day's unsold food before opening their doors at five a.m., so there was usually a plentiful buffet of baked goods from which to pick. From there, she headed to a spot along the Charles River to feed the ducks. Determined to continue her academic studies, she then made her way to the Boston Public Library, where she would disappear in the vast array of bookshelves and spend each day reading everything she could get her hands on. At three p.m., when students were released from Boston public schools, she took the bus to the local YMCA to shower, brush her teeth, and change into fresh clothes. Each night, she stopped by the Laundromat to wash her clothes in the sink, remove someone else's from the dryer, and steal a few minutes of their time until her clothes were dry enough to wear again the following day.

Her routine had continued, uninterrupted for months, until fall turned into winter. She had nowhere to go to keep warm. That was when she realized nobody cared about her. She didn't have any family. No friends to speak of. When it came down to it, no one gave a crap if she lived or died. Humans considered her tainted because she'd been adopted and raised by Shrouds.

Knowing her circumstances were unlikely to change, Aspen decided to take her own life. It was certainly better than freezing to death overnight on the park bench where she usually slept. She stole a knife from the local grocery store and stabbed herself repeatedly in the stomach in the middle of the night.

A local beat cop happened upon her as she lay in a pool of her own blood. He'd scooped her up and carried her in his arms all the way to the emergency room. She still remembered looking up at him and feeling the sting of his hot tears on her face. Looking back, she knew she was lucky to have survived without any long-term effects from such serious injuries.

In a bittersweet twist of fate, she ended up finding a home with that cop. He'd saved her life in more ways than one. By the time she turned thirteen, her second adoption was official. It didn't take her long to realize she felt safe and loved in Oscar Wolfe's presence. He was a man of integrity, honor, and intense loyalty, never far whenever she needed him. He was a Shroud—just like her parents had been. But she didn't mind in the least. Despite the fact that most humans were either intensely distrustful of Shrouds or downright hateful toward them, she believed Shrouds were inherently good. Not a popular opinion in this day and age, but it was one she vehemently defended.

Hard to believe eighteen years had passed since that fateful night. She'd come a long way since then.

Aspen spent her teenage years listening to stories about Oscar's time on the streets as a beat cop. His Shroud status prevented him from rising through the ranks, but that never seemed to bother him. He loved his job and saw it as his chance to change humans' misconceptions about Shrouds.

Shrouds were required to register with the Shroud database and be marked with a branding iron on their right hand before they reached their second birthday. Since Shrouds were prohibited from wearing gloves—no matter how cold it was outside—every human Oscar encountered on the job knew he was a Shroud. That, of course, created challenges on a daily basis for him as a cop, but it sure made for some interesting stories—stories he was always more than happy to share over dinner.

Aspen had lived vicariously through him and grew up knowing there was only one thing she wanted to do with her life: follow in her hero's footsteps. She applied for a spot on the BPD at twenty-one and never looked back. She was made for this job.

The sound of running water stopped. Skye emerged a few minutes later in green scrubs that made her eyes blindingly brighter. Freshly washed and still wet, her short hair was now a darker shade of brown. The color in her cheeks had finally returned. She smelled soapy clean.

Relieved to set eyes on the girl again, Aspen sighed. Was this how it happened for Oscar? Some kid hijacked your heart when you least expected it, and there was no turning back? She suddenly found herself wanting nothing more than to be there for Skye like Oscar had been there for her.

Skye exited from the bathroom, shut off the light, and glanced at the bucket in her lap. She sat on the bed across from Aspen, her brow furrowed in genuine concern. "I was just joking before, but I think you might have a real problem."

Aspen looked down to find she'd already polished off the Twix, a Hershey's bar with almonds, two York Peppermint Patties, and a bag of Peanut M&M's. The empty wrappers stared up at her. "I know how it looks, but this candy isn't mine," she said, wiping some chocolate from her chin.

"Nice try." Skye frowned. "I'm pretty sure denial is the first sign of a problem."

The kid had a point. She set the bucket on the floor. "How're you feeling?"

"Fine." The girl yawned. "I'm glad you're still here."

Aspen checked her watch. It was already nine p.m. "You've had a long day. Let's head to the station. You can sleep there tonight."

Skye sat up straighter, a worried look in her eyes. "Are you going home after you drop me off at the station?"

"Depends."

"On what?" Skye asked, leaning forward.

"Have you ever played Boggle?"

The girl was quiet as she thought for a moment. "The word game?" she guessed, looking up.

Aspen nodded.

"My parents and I used to play that all the time. It's only my favorite game in the entire universe. Why?"

If she needed a sign that she was supposed to stay in the kid's life, this had to be it. "You any good?"

"Not to brag or anything, but I've won every tournament against my parents since I was, like, eleven."

"Well, kiddo"—Aspen narrowed her eyes—"looks like you've finally met your match."

Skye grinned knowingly. "Or maybe you've finally met yours."

"Touché. Hot cocoa and Boggle at the station?"

"Only if there's popcorn and you agree to stay the whole night."

"Deal."

They shook hands, and Skye's tense posture visibly relaxed. She rubbed the pendant around her neck. "Thanks, Officer Wolfe."

"Aspen," she corrected the girl. "Just call me Aspen."

CHAPTER THREE

With Skye beside her, Aspen exited the exam room, rounded the corner, and came face-to-face with Skye's doctor. The lion doctor, she reminded herself. They sized each other up once again.

"There's been a complication," Tora said. "Follow me." Glancing nervously over her shoulder, she led the way back to the exam room.

The hair on the back of Aspen's neck stood up as she stepped inside. She set her hands on her hips, the weight of her gun belt reassuring. "What's up?"

Tora took one last look up and down the corridor, closed the door quietly, and turned to face them. "The president just made an announcement. He signed and enacted a worldwide treaty authorizing any and all humans to…" She trailed off, her eyes on Skye.

"To what?" Aspen pressed.

Tora sighed, turning her attention to Aspen. "To execute Shrouds."

"*Execute* Shrouds? You're kidding me, right?"

The doctor shook her head, her amber-gold eyes focused solely on Aspen. "He set up a government fund to compensate humans for every successful execution."

Skye edged closer to Aspen. "Humans will get paid for killing us?"

"Over my dead body." Aspen draped her arm protectively around Skye as a red-hot rage boiled within.

"There's more." Tora took a breath, her gaze penetrating and strong. "He created a new branch of military, the SEA—Shifter Eradication Agency. They'll start rounding up Shrouds to begin the extermination process."

"When?" She needed to know how much time she had to come up with a plan and get Skye to safety.

"They've already been deployed to every major city around the US. He said extermination troops are being released all over the world as we speak."

Aspen glanced down at Tora's hand and realized she didn't have the mark. But that didn't make any sense. She saw Tora as a lion, clear as day. "You're a Shroud, but you don't have the mark."

"Neither do you," Tora said, her gaze darting to Aspen's hand.

"I don't have it because I'm human."

"Lie to humans all you want." Tora stepped forward. "But don't you *dare* lie to me."

"What the hell's that supposed to mean?" she shot back, confused. Was Tora under the impression that she was one of them? She thought back to something Skye had said on the roof. *I'm an owl. You're a panther.* No way. Not possible. How could she be a Shroud her whole life and not know it? "First off, I don't lie. Second, if I did, I could lie to anyone I wanted. You included." Who the hell did this doctor think she was, anyway?

Skye cleared her throat. "Neither of you has the mark, but I do." She held up her hand. "If you get me to the roof, I can jump."

Aspen turned to the girl, pushing everything else from her mind. "I am *not* letting you jump off the roof, no matter how bad things get. I thought we already went over this."

Skye rolled her eyes. "Did you forget? I'm an owl. I can *fly*."

"Oh." Aspen scratched the side of her head. "Well, when you put it that way, it sounds like a pretty good plan. I guess we'll need access to the roof." She pointed to the badge that was clipped to the pocket of Tora's white lab coat. "Can I borrow that?" She knew from experience that the door to the hospital's rooftop was locked.

"No."

"No?" Aspen turned to Skye. "Did she just say no to an angry woman with a gun?"

Skye's eyes grew wide.

"The badge stays with me," Tora said firmly. "I'll take you to the roof myself."

This was a piss-poor time for a power struggle over a stupid badge, but whatever. If Tora insisted on tagging along, that was fine with her as long as she stayed out of the way.

"Take Skye to the elevator. Go to the fifth floor. I'll meet you there. We'll take the employee stairwell to the roof."

"Wait a minute." Aspen grabbed Tora's arm as she turned to leave. "Why can't we all go together?"

"SEA is already in the building. It'll look suspicious."

"Copy that." She set her hands over Skye's shoulders. "You're now my prisoner."

"I am? For real?"

"Of course not."

"Good. Because you sounded pretty convincing."

They exited the exam room together and set out in opposite directions. She and Skye were making their way down a long corridor toward the elevator when two SEA soldiers rounded the corner, coming face to face with Skye. With neon orange SEA patches on each sleeve, their black and green fatigues were badass.

The shorter of the two grabbed Skye by the wrist and held up her hand for inspection. "Got one!" he shouted, yanking the girl closer as he reached for the cuffs on his belt.

Every muscle in Aspen's body went on high alert. There was no way she was losing this kid. Not after what the girl had been through. "Lay off. She's mine." She held up her own hand. "Human," she said before the other soldier could even think about putting hands on her. "I found her, and I intend to collect my money."

The soldiers exchanged a glance, but the tall one held firm to Skye's arm.

"C'mon, man," she pleaded. "They pay Boston's Finest shit wages. I need the extra cash."

"Fine. You can have her." He released Skye with a vicious shove that sent her careening into the wall with an audible *thump*. "Just do us all a favor and throw a pair of cuffs on her before she does anything stupid."

It took every ounce of willpower not to draw her weapon and shoot the racist bastards in the face. "Will do," Aspen said with a forced smile, reaching for her cuffs.

"And be sure to do it in the garage. We have a cleanup crew on standby. No muss, no fuss," he said, wiping his hands.

"Copy that." She slapped the metal cuffs around Skye's slender wrists.

"When you're done with her, come back and find us," the shorter of the two soldiers added. "We'll give you a few more to fatten your paycheck. Adult males are worth the most. We'll save them for you."

"That'd be great, guys. Thanks. I owe you one." The elevator doors opened. Sick to her stomach, she led Skye inside and pushed the button for the fifth floor.

"Ouch," Skye said as soon as the doors slid shut.

"Cuffs too tight?"

"No." Skye brought her hands out from behind her and handed the cuffs to Aspen. "You left them loose enough for an elephant to escape." The girl winced as she rubbed the side of her head. "I have a huge goose egg, courtesy of soldier ass-face."

"Very observant. His face did resemble an ass, didn't it?" He had one of those long chins with a sizable cleft in the center that made it look like a tiny butt.

The doors parted on the fifth floor. Tora was already there waiting for them. She led them to an employee stairwell and unlocked the door with her beloved badge. They sandwiched the girl in an unspoken alliance to keep her safe. By the time they reached the tenth floor, they were all breathing heavily—Aspen guessed as much from fear as from physical exertion.

A small window set high in the door looked onto a vast rooftop and then out to the city beyond. Tora swiped her badge and jiggled the handle. The door didn't open. She inserted her badge a second time.

Aspen sighed impatiently. "What's taking so long?"

"My badge isn't working."

Had the SEA already put the hospital on lockdown?

They all froze at the sound of a door banging open below them, followed by the distant echoing of heavy footsteps in the stairwell.

If she wasn't mistaken, it sounded like those boots were marching *up* the stairs, not down. She peered over the metal railing just as soldier ass-face did the same. The good news: he was on the second floor, eight stories below. The bad news: they were like sitting ducks up here.

Aspen considered winding her way back through the hospital, but she didn't want to risk getting ambushed. She also couldn't, in all good conscience, risk the lives of hospital staff and patients if things got ugly. The safest bet was to get on the roof and let Skye escape—assuming she could really fly, of course. But this wasn't the time for second-guessing. Now was the time to trust her instincts. They had never let her down in the past.

Aspen couldn't shoot the lock and risk the bullet ricocheting around the stairwell—too dangerous. She holstered her gun, withdrew her baton, and started striking the door's lockbox again and again as hard as she could. The metal box didn't budge. Not even a dent.

They were trapped.

"You keep working on the door," the doctor said. "I'll stall our friend below."

Aspen gave the box another hard blow. "And just how do you plan on doing that?" she asked, knowing she was the one with the gun. If anyone was going to confront him, it should be her. She hated the thought of leaving Skye's side. But she would, if it came to that.

❖

Tora's mind raced through likely scenarios as she contemplated shifting there in the stairwell. If she went through with this, she could never return to work here—or in any hospital, for that matter.

From this day forward, she would forever be on the government's radar.

It took her a few heartbeats to wrap her mind around what she was giving up. Resuming her career as a physician would never be an option. Everything she had worked her whole life to achieve would be cast aside in the blink of an eye.

Still, she didn't flinch. Knowing there were other things much more important, she shifted into the lioness that felt more familiar to her than her human body. Now she was ready to wage war on anyone who posed a threat to Aspen.

She knew it was her duty to keep Aspen safe, even though Aspen seemed oblivious to who and what she was. Did she really believe she was human? The smartass cop was about to get the biggest wake-up call of her life. Not only was she a Shroud, but she was also the most important Shroud alive right now—the one who could save them all. And it would be up to Tora to show her how.

When the doctor didn't answer, Aspen turned to discover a formidable lioness standing in the stairwell behind her, tail flicking agitatedly from side to side. She dropped her baton, reached for her gun, and put an arm across Skye to push the girl behind her.

The lioness turned and descended an entire set of stairs in one graceful leap to land silently on the floor below. She glanced up at Aspen with those amber-gold eyes before resuming her stealthy descent.

"She's beautiful," Skye said, her eyes glued to the empty landing below.

Aspen holstered her gun and let out a lungful of air. "If by beautiful you mean terrifying and dangerous, then…yes, she is," she said, bending to retrieve the baton. "Pretty sure I peed my pants a little."

Skye set a hand over her mouth to stifle a case of the giggles.

Blow by blow, she kept hammering at the lock. A deep, guttural roar reverberated through the stairwell, making Aspen work faster to get the hell out of there as quickly as possible. A man's bloodcurdling scream was cut short by a loud *crunch*. The sound made her feel sick to her stomach. Maybe she shouldn't have eaten all that candy.

The door behind them suddenly flew open as the second soldier from their earlier encounter rushed inside the stairwell. In desperation, Aspen gave the lockbox one final blow. It disintegrated in slivers on the floor at her feet. Chucking her baton at the soldier's head, she reached for the handle, grabbed Skye, and shoved her through the doorway to the rooftop.

She needed to buy the girl some time, so she held the door shut with all her might, digging her boots into the ground as the man pummeled it with his body from the other side.

"Go!" she shouted.

"What about you?" Skye cried.

She didn't know how much longer she'd be able to hold him back. Felt like there was an NFL defensive tackle on the other side. "I'll be fine. Go!" The door finally gave way. She was knocked to the ground. The gun slipped from her grasp and skidded across the rooftop.

Aspen scrambled along the ground and reached for her weapon as a shiny black boot stomped hard on the back of her hand, pinning her to the ground. She looked up to find a dart gun pointed at her face. In that moment, she knew she would die for the girl without giving it a second thought.

"Where is she?" he asked.

She didn't like his tone. His mother had obviously neglected to teach him how to properly address an officer of the law. "There's an angry lioness on her way up the stairs right now—"

"Where's the girl?" he asked through clenched teeth.

Wincing as he crushed her hand harder under the sole of his combat boot, she decided to take the higher road and offer some friendly advice. "I'd seriously reevaluate my escape plan if I were you." As those words fell from her lips, an enormous white owl swooped in on silent wings, wrapped long talons around the dart gun, and effortlessly plucked it right out of his hand.

The lioness she had warned him about was now standing behind him. His face contorted into an expression of stark terror as he spun around. He opened his mouth to scream but didn't have time as the lioness sprang up and clamped powerful jaws around his throat. Aspen turned away as the lioness finished him off. When she turned back, his lifeless eyes were staring into the dark night sky.

The lioness collapsed near his body, drawing shallow, rapid breaths. An orange-tipped syringe protruded from the big cat's thigh muscle.

"You were hit," she said, unsure if the lioness could understand her. The lioness stared her down with flattened ears as she reached over and carefully withdrew the syringe.

An owl swooped in, landing beside them. Skye was back— not that she'd ever left, Aspen reminded herself. She watched in amazement as the owl shifted into a thirteen-year-old girl.

Skye bent down to hold the big cat's head and peer into her eyes. "Thanks for protecting us, Dr. Madigan." She stood and turned to Aspen. "She can't turn back into herself now because she was darted. I've heard about this happening to other Shrouds. We need to get her to a doctor, or she'll die."

Aspen knew the girl was right. The BPD had recently added the dart guns to their arsenal against Shrouds. As of next month, they'd be standard issue for every cop on the street. "Can Tora understand us like this?"

Skye nodded.

"Okay. New plan." Aspen retrieved her gun from the ground and stood guard by the door as she talked. "Are you strong enough to fly across town and find someone for me?"

Skye nodded. "I could fly forever."

"His name is Oscar. He's a wolf, and I trust him. You can trust him, too. Tell him what happened here tonight. Show him the necklace I gave you. Tell him you're in danger, and you need his protection until I can get there. I'll meet up with the two of you as soon as I can."

"Where are you going?" Skye asked, nervously rubbing the pendant around her neck.

Aspen looked at the lioness. The lioness held her gaze. She couldn't abandon the doctor. Not after the doctor had risked her life to help them. "I'll be busy smuggling a three-hundred-pound ass-kicking predator out of the hospital."

Skye grinned. "Copy that."

She recited Oscar's address and made the girl repeat it back to her. "Will you be able to find it?"

"Duh, I'm an owl. We have a great sense of direction. Having me around is better than GPS."

"One more thing." Aspen picked up the dart gun Skye had stolen. "Take this to Oscar. Tell him we need to have it analyzed ASAP. Maybe we can get an antidote to whatever's inside this thing."

The girl ran over and gave her a long hug.

"Just be careful," Aspen said, determined not to get choked up. "And stay high so no one can track you from the ground."

"You can trust me, Aspen." Without another word, the girl jogged along the roof, broke into a full sprint, and leaped high into the air. Her arms elongated into huge, gorgeous white wings as the rest of her body followed suit. She reminded Aspen of an angel. Her transformation was instantaneous and breathtaking to watch. Even the lioness seemed momentarily transfixed as Skye swooped back in to snatch the dart gun from Aspen's hand as she held it aloft.

Chapter Four

With Skye en route to Oscar's, she turned her attention to the lioness. "Thanks for your help tonight, Doc. We need to get out of here. Can you walk?"

The lioness rose with great effort until she was standing on all four paws.

"For obvious reasons, we'll stick to the stairs." Aspen held the rooftop door open. "I'd offer to carry you, but you outweigh me by at least two hundred pounds. No offense," she added, on the heels of a disgruntled growl.

Side by side, they began their slow descent. Aspen pinched herself repeatedly to make sure she was awake. She felt dwarfed by the lioness's hulking form and suddenly found herself wondering what it would feel like to shapeshift into such a powerful animal. If she really was a Shroud, why hadn't she ever shifted?

The lioness stopped abruptly in front of the door on the eighth-floor landing. Her amber-gold eyes were like laser beams as she peered intently back and forth between Aspen and the doorknob.

"It's subtle, but I'm getting the feeling you want me to open this door." She could only imagine how frustrating it was to be stuck in this form without the ability to communicate. "I don't think that's such a hot idea, Doc."

The lioness growled deep in her throat.

"Don't you growl at me."

The lioness flattened her ears but stopped growling.

"That's better," Aspen said. "A little respect goes a long way."

The lioness clamped her jaws over the doorknob and tugged, popping the metal doorknob off like a dandelion head. She spit out the doorknob, hooked one long, sharp claw from an enormous paw into the resultant hole, and pulled the door all the way open. She looked up at Aspen expectantly.

The doctor obviously wasn't taking no for an answer. "Fine, I'll go first and see if the coast is clear." She pointed her finger at the lioness. "Stay," she ordered, grinning.

The lioness peeled her lips back to expose four-inch canines.

"Intimidation won't work with me. Can't you take a joke?"

With another low growl, the lioness pushed past her into the eighth-floor corridor.

Despite her conviction to see this through, Tora now had doubts about her decision to put everything on the line for Aspen. She already couldn't stand her. Joking when so much was at stake was irresponsible and just plain reckless. Humor in the midst of a crisis was akin to fingernails on a chalkboard.

She thought back to the question Aspen had asked Skye on the rooftop—about whether or not Tora could understand their words while in lioness form. How could Aspen not have known the answer to that? Tora circled back to her earlier theory. Maybe Aspen really didn't know what she was. If that rang true, then it was reasonable to assume Aspen had also never shapeshifted.

But was that even possible? She studied Aspen through lion's eyes and guessed her to be somewhere in the ballpark of thirty. How could Aspen have gotten through thirty years without shifting? She'd never heard of such a thing happening. By nature's very design, their bodies were programmed to shift well before adolescence. The scientist in her wondered what it was about Aspen that made her an exception to that rule.

The eighth floor of the hospital was dark and eerily quiet. Aspen followed the lioness who had no sense of humor. As far as she could tell, they were the only two up here. Silver nameplates on the doors suggested this floor was used for offices. She glanced at her watch: 10:33 p.m. Looked like everyone had gone home for the day.

She paused at the vending machine halfway down the corridor, marveling at the vast array of candy options. This vending machine was way better than what they had on the patient floors below. Her stomach growled in agreement.

She was nearly yanked off her feet when the lioness sank her teeth into the pocket of her cargo pants and started dragging her along. "Okay, okay," Aspen said, struggling to break free from the viselike grip. "I'm coming."

But the lioness didn't let go until she had dragged her all the way to the door with a nameplate that read: *Dr. Tora Madigan.* The lioness stared at the doorknob.

"We've been down this road," Aspen admitted. "Please, allow me." She turned the doorknob and held the door open for Tora.

Aspen stepped inside the office, shut the door, and drew the blinds as the lioness moved past her to a large mahogany desk. She watched as the lioness carefully withdrew a gold pen from a cup with her front teeth before using it to peck at the computer keyboard. She pierced Aspen with a predatory gaze.

Maybe have antidote for dart was typed across the screen.

What did she mean by *maybe*? Either she had it or she didn't. Before she could ask for clarification, the lioness added the word *experimental.*

"Okay, I'm with you." The experimental part made her raise an eyebrow, but this was a step in the right direction. "Who has it?"

The lioness pecked at the keyboard with surprising speed and accuracy. *Me.*

"Where is it?"

Fridge. The lioness glanced at the stainless steel minifridge in the corner.

"Is it safe to try? You said it was experimental."

Nothing to lose.

"Right." Doc was a goner for sure without it. "How can I help?"

Open fridge.

Would it kill her to say please? She went to the minifridge and knelt on one knee. There was a thermal fingerprint scanner to the right of the handle. "Um, Doc?"

The lioness was busily pecking at the keyboard. *Need to take fridge with us.*

It occurred to her that the antidote was in the refrigerator for a reason. "Does the antidote need to stay cold?" she asked.

Yes. Can be unplugged 60 mins max.

She wanted to be sure she understood correctly. "So, it'll expire after an hour if it doesn't stay refrigerated?"

Yes.

Aspen mentally reviewed her new to-do list: sneak a large predator out of the hospital, carry a refrigerator down eight flights of stairs, and make sure they arrived at Oscar's in sixty minutes or less to plug it back in. Just another day on the job. She set the timer on her watch. "Anything else I should know before I start the countdown?"

The lioness thought for a moment before typing. *Fridge heavy.*

Aspen couldn't tell for sure, but she could swear the lioness was smirking at her. She started the timer, unplugged the minifridge, and lifted it from the ground with substantial effort. Having to use both hands to carry it meant she couldn't reach for her gun in a pinch.

Feeling more than a little vulnerable, she followed the lioness out of the office, down the corridor, and into the stairwell once again. Stepping over the dead soldier's body on level four proved a little tricky. The smell hit her hard and made her gag. It was only a matter of time before someone used this stairwell and found the body. They'd been lucky so far, but she knew luck always ran out sooner or later.

As if she had tempted fate with the very thought, someone chose that precise moment to swipe their badge and enter the stairwell on level two. Fortunately, the dead guy was two floors up and the smell of him wasn't ripe enough yet to travel this far. The white-coated doctor looked up from his medical tablet as the door banged shut behind him. His eyes met Aspen's before darting to the lioness on her right. He dropped his tablet and backed up against the door with an inaudible scream.

Tora did her best to look as nonthreatening as possible. Dr. Prandlepin stared at her, his terror palpable. The chief of cardiothoracic surgery, his nasal voice, pencil-thin neck, and supersized ego had always gotten on her nerves. She glanced at his hospital scrubs as a telltale stain spread across his pant leg. Grimacing at the pungent smell of urine, she had half a mind to put him out of his misery. But taking innocent human life was against her code of honor. Besides, she was starting to feel the effects of the dart and needed to conserve every precious bit of energy.

She took a few steps back and sat down, deciding this was as good a test as any to gauge Aspen's skill set.

❖

"Everything's okay," Aspen assured him, setting the minifridge down on the landing. She'd had six flights of stairs to come up with a convincing story to prepare for this little hiccup. "The lioness is tame. You've heard of police K-9s?"

The doctor nodded, refusing to take his eyes from the lioness.

"We've started using police *felines* at the Boston PD to help us with different aspects of the job. For instance"—Aspen gestured to the minifridge—"Fluffy here sniffed out a large stash of illegal drugs in this refrigerator, which is why I'm confiscating it for evidence."

The doctor's eyes remained on the lioness. "You named it *Fluffy?*" he asked in disbelief.

"There's nothing to be afraid of." Aspen extended her hand to the lioness. "Fluffy, come."

The lioness glowered at her with murderous intent as she begrudgingly joined her.

"Fluffy, sit."

Amazingly, and without protest, she sat her furry rump on the floor beside Aspen.

"See?" Aspen turned to the terrified doctor. "Harmless."

But the whites of his eyes were still showing. "I'd like to leave now, please."

When Aspen bent over to retrieve his tablet from the floor, the lioness shoved her from behind with a paw the size of a dinner plate. She lurched forward, banged her head against the door with a loud *thump*, and winced as razor-sharp claws poked through the fabric of her pants on her rear end. Massaging the goose egg that was already beginning to form, she stood and handed the doctor his tablet. "She could probably use a little more training."

Tablet in hand, the doctor made a hasty retreat to the other side of the door.

Aspen felt her heart pick up speed as she parked the patrol car in Oscar's driveway. She hoped Skye had made it here safely. It took all the willpower she had not to call Oscar on the drive over to find out. She was being extra cautious in case the SEA was monitoring her cell.

She checked the timer on her watch and called out through the clear bulletproof partition. "We're here, Doc. Made it with six minutes to spare."

The lioness was crouched in the back seat. So far, no one had spotted them. The cover of darkness and empty roads had definitely helped. At seven feet long, her grumpy companion wasn't exactly inconspicuous back there.

Aspen cut the engine and stepped out of the car as the front door of Oscar's house opened wide. Oscar was there, a sight for sore eyes. With one hand on the door and the other on the gun at his hip, she could tell from his body language he was expecting her. She took a deep breath and let it out into the chilly nighttime air. Relief washed over her. Skye had made it.

She opened the patrol car's rear door to free the lioness from her cramped quarters. A warm, tingly sensation crept down the back of her neck and spine. They were being watched. She was sure of it. Her hand wandered to the holster on her hip as she caught sight of several pairs of glowing eyes in the dark recesses around Oscar's home. She froze, looking more closely. Wolves. One by one, they stepped forward and acknowledged her with a nod. She got the feeling they were letting her know they were there for her protection.

The lioness eased her body down from the car. Aspen could see she wasn't doing well. Panting heavily now, her movements were slow and exaggerated. "Let's get you inside." She walked around the car, lifted the minifridge from the passenger's seat, and followed the lioness to the house. They both stepped inside the living room as Oscar locked the door behind them.

"Oscar, this is Dr. Tora Madigan. Doc, meet Oscar. She says the antidote is in here, but it's locked. Do you have a crowbar?" she asked as she made her way to the kitchen. She set the minifridge on the tile floor and checked her watch. "We have four minutes until the antidote is no good."

Oscar made a beeline for the basement. "One crowbar coming up."

Skye stood from the kitchen table and ran to greet Aspen with a hug.

"Good to see you, too, kiddo." Aspen let her gaze surf the kitchen: empty plates and bowls on the table, dirty pots and pans of all sizes on the stove, empty plastic containers on the counter. It looked like she'd missed a championship cook-off. "Did you save anything for me?"

"Flying makes me hungry," Skye admitted guiltily. "I think I ate everything he had. Oscar's a really good cook." The girl sat cross-legged on the floor and held one of the lioness's giant paws between her hands. "She's burning up. You really have the antidote for what was in the dart?"

Oscar returned with a crowbar and set to work on the minifridge.

"Doc said the antidote is experimental." Aspen checked her watch again. Three minutes remaining. She turned her attention to Oscar. "The pack's outside?"

"Yep." He glanced up and met her gaze as he pried the minifridge open. "Figured it couldn't hurt to have a little backup."

The lioness was sprawled across the tile floor. Her chest heaved with each intake of breath. She had obviously used up the last of her energy to carry herself from the car to the house.

Aspen went to the minifridge and withdrew a plastic tray with foam holes and about a dozen small vials inside. She lifted one and handed the tray to Oscar before turning to the lioness. "Are you supposed to swallow this?"

All the lioness could manage was a snort.

"I think that's a yes," Skye said, her eyes glued to the lioness and full of concern. "I can help by holding your head up." The girl rose to her knees and lifted the big cat's head. Aspen removed the vial's rubber tip and poured a clear liquid down her throat. As the lioness swallowed, Skye gently lowered her head back down to the floor.

They all stared at the lioness in silence. The kitchen clock ticked loudly behind them.

"What now?" Oscar finally asked.

Aspen shrugged. "We wait."

"How will we know if it's working?"

"If she's not dead, then…it worked."

Still sprawled on the floor, the lioness summoned enough energy to growl in protest at that last comment.

"Skye, stay here with the grumpy doctor. Oscar and I will be in the other room."

Aware that her life was hanging in the balance as she struggled for air, Tora followed Aspen and Oscar with her eyes as they walked out of the kitchen. If Aspen made one more wisecrack, Tora decided she was going to save the SEA the cost of a bullet and kill Aspen herself.

She closed her eyes and willed the antidote to work as Skye knelt beside her and held her paw in supportive silence. Tora prided herself on her ability to keep everyone at arm's length. She never let sentimentality cloud her judgment, but Skye was knocking her off balance. She found herself liking this girl more and more. Skye's only apparent flaw was her lapse in judgment when it came to trusting Aspen. The two obviously shared a bond that was beyond Tora's comprehension.

She tried to flick her tail in agitation and suddenly realized her body was no longer responding to the synapses firing off in her brain. Feeling the end draw near, she hurriedly reviewed her checklist for the sanctuary. Everything was in order. Provisions had already been made for sanctuary members in the event of her demise.

Unable to lift even her eyelids, she felt her consciousness slipping away against her will. Her final thoughts were of Aspen. She only hoped the wisecracking cop could get it together long enough to be the leader their people so desperately needed.

CHAPTER FIVE

Oscar led the way to the living room, peeking through the blinds to take a quick scan of the backyard. "Been quiet so far. Doesn't look like you were followed." Years on the job as a beat cop had kept him in shape. He looked strong, fit, and in charge.

"I made about a million unnecessary turns. Would've spotted a tail."

He gestured to the love seat across from him and settled in his favorite armchair, its dark leather worn sandy brown in all the places that mattered most. "There's something you need to know, kid." Sitting in the dimly lit living room in a black T-shirt and sweatpants, Oscar's dark African complexion was perfectly camouflaged against the armchair. Pearl-white teeth blew his cover—a stark contrast to the rest of him. He sighed. "I knew your father."

The feeling of betrayal reared its ugly head. Oscar had come into her life eighteen years ago. Never once had he mentioned that he knew her dad. When it came down to it, the thing she valued most about their relationship was honesty. She always knew where she stood with Oscar, and he with her. There were no games, no guessing matches, no pretending. Just total unbridled brutal honesty. It was there from the moment they'd met. "Why'd you wait so long to tell me?"

His eyes revealed a sadness that took her off guard. "I was trying to protect you." He regarded her for a long moment. "Your father and I were part of the same brotherhood. We ran with the same pack. He was a wolf, like me. He was our alpha."

"My adoptive father," she corrected him. "I know he was a wolf. I remember."

"Your mother and father didn't adopt you, Aspen."

She leaned forward. "Are you saying they *stole* me?"

He shook his head. "They were your real parents. Your biological parents."

The sting of betrayal lashed out again like a hard slap in the face. She held her tongue and waited for him to go on.

"Before you were born, the world already hated Shrouds. Your father was convinced it would one day come to this—that humans would decide we were too much of a threat and either jail us or wipe us out of existence. More than anything, he wanted to protect you from humans. He knew the only way to do that was to make you one of them.

"There were rumors that a vaccine had been developed by one of our kind. It could be given to an infant just after birth to effectively thwart their ability to shapeshift. There was conflicting data as to the vaccine's effectiveness. For some, it lasted months. For others, years. The one thing we knew for sure was that it always wore off, eventually. Your parents didn't want to take any risks, so they sought out this vaccine and gave it to you each year until your fifth birthday."

That would explain how she'd made it through three decades of her life without shapeshifting. Aspen listened intently, hanging on his every word.

"You have to understand," he went on, "it was a very volatile time in Shroud history. Humans would go on killing sprees just for the hell of it and wipe out entire Shroud families. Your father made all of us in the pack promise not to interfere if something happened to him. He made us swear not to take you in if you were orphaned. He saw each of us in the pack as a liability for you. He didn't want you on the government's radar at all. That's why he had false adoption papers drawn up, claiming you were human."

She thought for a moment, struggling to connect the dots. Her parents were murdered when she was six, and she spent the next six years in and out of foster homes. "But you broke your promise and took me in when I was twelve. Why the hell did you wait so long to come and get me?"

"There was little I could do for you without attracting unwanted attention, so I kept tabs on you from afar for six years. When I saw the vaccine seemed to be working, I maintained my distance. But watching you bounce from one foster home to the next was more than I could bear. I informed my pack that I was breaking the oath I'd made to your father. No one stood in my way. That was the night you ran away from your last foster home. I looked everywhere for you. The whole pack did, and none of us could find you. I was convinced you were dead…until that morning when I found you in the park."

They were both pensive for a long moment. Aspen was filled with a profound sadness at the thought of never being able to shapeshift. Her ability to do so was taken away without her consent. "So I really *am* human?"

"That's what I was beginning to think until Skye showed up here and told me about you. When she took your hand, she said she saw a panther."

"So?"

"When we meet one of our own kind and shake hands, the shroud drops away. We see one another for what we truly are: the animal beneath the shroud. You and I have touched hands countless times since you were twelve. I've never seen a panther. Here," he said, reaching over. "Take my hand."

Aspen drew in a quick breath as a large wolf appeared before her with fur as black as the darkest night sky. The only thing that betrayed Oscar's nighttime cover were pearl-white canines, which protruded menacingly from both sides of his muzzle. He circled her slowly, sniffing the air around her as he moved.

She couldn't take her eyes off him. Seeing Oscar in this form was magical for her. Instincts told her he was the pack leader. She'd be willing to bet anything the wolves outside took orders from him. Until now, this was Oscar's world—a world he'd kept private.

He sat in front of her and peered into her eyes intently. Returning his gaze, she recognized Oscar's eyes at once. A warm shade of chestnut brown, they could be loving and tender with her or guarded and unyielding on the job. Long seconds ticked by. She got the feeling he was studying her. Feeling suddenly self-conscious, she wondered if something was wrong and drew back, breaking their connection.

Back in human form, he stared at her, mouth agape.

"What's wrong?" she asked. "You were looking at me funny."

He leaned back in the armchair.

"Do I have a giant panther pimple or something?"

"You're definitely a panther," he said, rubbing his chin in thought. "But your eyes...they're the brightest yellow I've ever seen."

She failed to see the problem. "Don't panthers have yellow eyes?"

"Maybe. Probably." He waved a dismissive hand in the air. "That's not the point. When we shift, we always keep our human eye color, regardless of our animal."

"So what does that mean?" She scooted forward on the love seat. "Can I shoot laser beams from my eyes?" she asked jokingly, trying to break the tension.

"I can't believe this," he said, standing from the armchair. He started to pace around the living room. "All this time...I never knew."

"Guess that makes two of us." She tried to be patient, waiting as he paced. "Care to clue me in?"

He sat beside her and set a hand on her shoulder. "It means you're a Myriad, Aspen."

"Let me get this straight. I was born a Shroud, but my parents gave me a shot for the first five years of my life that made me a temporary human, and now I'm a Myriad?" She looked up, thoroughly confused. "What the hell is a Myriad?"

"It's a very special kind of Shroud. Myriads were thought to be extinct. Humans hunted them down all over the world and killed them off over a century ago. Yet here you are," he said, shaking his head. "Your parents must have known about you. That explains why they fought so hard to keep you off the radar. They knew how valuable you were." He rose from the sofa and resumed pacing.

"They were hoping the vaccine would suppress your shapeshifting ability until you were fully mature and at the peak of your power." He stopped pacing and turned to her. "Your parents were brilliant. I should've known they had something up their sleeves. Can't believe it took me this long to put it all together."

At the peak of what power? Aspen had so many questions, but her instincts told her not to interrupt Oscar's train of thought. She had never seen him excited like this before.

"Myriads always assume the animal of the mother. In your case, your primary animal is a panther, but you can shapeshift into *any* animal at will. The telltale sign of a Myriad is bright yellow eyes, markedly different than the eyes you have in human form. Myriads also possess unique…" He paused, studying her. "Abilities."

She could tell Oscar was choosing his words carefully, which wasn't like him at all. Alarm bells went off inside her head. "What do you mean by *abilities*?" Processing all this new information was making her hungry.

"With each Myriad, it's different," he explained. "You won't know until it happens."

"Are we talking superhero abilities? Or is it more like I wake up one morning to discover I have a hidden talent for knitting?"

"The abilities vary, from what I understand," he said vaguely. "Now that the vaccine seems to be wearing off, the important thing is to start paying attention and be on the lookout for certain… changes."

There it was again. That telltale pause. He made it sound like she was about to go through puberty all over again.

She'd grown up believing she was human. But she was actually a Shroud? How could this be happening? She was still reeling from the revelation that her adoptive parents were her real parents. They'd chosen to withhold the truth beyond their graves, even from her. A part of her felt angry with her parents and betrayed by Oscar. How could he let her go through life believing these lies?

In that instant, she realized there was a part of her that had always felt…different. She had felt a kinship with Shrouds her whole life, but she'd attributed that to being raised by Shrouds who loved her and treated her well. Had she felt that kinship from the outset because she was one? She wanted to believe she would have felt the same if she really was human. Believing it gave her hope that humans and Shrouds might, one day, overcome their differences enough to realize just how much they had in common and coexist peacefully.

Her next thought made her heart skip a beat. "Would you have taken me in if I *wasn't* a Shroud, if everything my parents told me was true?"

Oscar hung his head in thoughtful silence. He was quiet for so long that Aspen decided she didn't want to hear his answer. Knowing the truth might change her relationship with Oscar forever.

For the last eighteen years, he'd been her hero, a Shroud who opened his home and heart to a human. She'd always believed he possessed more integrity than every other human she'd ever met. But maybe Oscar wasn't the man she thought he was. She balled her hands into fists and shook her head, determined to stuff down the tears that were threatening to break free.

"Had that truly been the case, there's only one thing I would do different," he said, finally looking up. "I would have found you sooner. As a human raised by Shrouds, you would have faced endless ridicule. I would've wanted to save you from that."

There was the Oscar she knew. She searched familiar brown eyes and knew he was telling the truth. "But I *thought* I was human and I *did* face endless ridicule. So what's the difference?"

"The difference is, you're a Shroud, Aspen. I figured your shapeshifting abilities would manifest sooner or later, and if push came to shove, you'd be able to defend yourself. Placing you with humans was like hiding a lion among lambs."

"How can you say that when humans have been murdering Shrouds for centuries?" she asked, dumbfounded.

"Because Shrouds are stronger than humans. In here," he said, tapping a finger against his temple. "Always have been. Probably always will be."

There was a part of her that instantly sensed the truth in his words. The Shrouds she'd encountered in her life, both on and off the job, all seemed to possess a certain mental toughness, a resilience that she'd come to admire over the years.

"The morning I found you in the park was the best and worst day of my life. I felt like I had found my daughter. You may not be my blood, but it sure as hell felt like you were. Still does," he said with cheeks full of tears. "Shroud or human, I should have come for you sooner, kid. I'm sorry."

"You found me exactly when you were meant to," she assured him. "When I look back on that time in my life, there's nothing I would change about it. I believe all of it happened for a reason. You saved me that day. And you've been there for me ever since." She went to Oscar, sat on the armrest beside him, and wrapped her arm around him. "You're the person I trust most in this world. I've never said thank you, but I try to live my life in a way that honors you and everything you sacrificed for me."

"There were never any sacrifices. Raising you was a privilege. I was the lucky one."

She gave his shoulder a gentle squeeze, stood, and returned to the love seat with a sigh. "If you think getting all sappy and showering me with compliments lets you off the hook for withholding the truth for so long, you're wrong. I'm still mad."

"Copy that. You have every right to be."

Silence filled the space between them.

"Taking accountability and validating my anger is a good start," she said finally. "If you threw in pancakes at IHOP every Sunday for a year, I might be able to let this go."

"Just a year?"

Oscar was right. His eighteen-year omission was a serious offense and should be treated accordingly. "Make it three," she said. Out of habit, she reached up to rub the phoenix pendant between her thumb and forefinger. Remembering it was now in new hands made her smile. "And Skye comes, too."

"Already figured she was part of the deal. She showed me the necklace you gave her." Oscar had given Aspen that necklace the day after he found her in the park.

He laced his fingers together and lowered his head, pretending to give her demands serious thought. "Five years," he said at last, looking up with the no-nonsense expression he reserved for the job. "Final offer. And I'll throw in twenty boxes of those Girl Scout cookies you like."

"Thin Mints?"

He nodded.

"Done. All is forgiven," she said. They shook hands and then hugged, long and hard.

CHAPTER SIX

O scar returned to his armchair and leaned toward her, his body now visibly tense. "You need to be extremely careful, Aspen. If the SEA learns you're a Myriad, they'll come after you with everything they've got. You should know I'm now sworn to protect you. My pack, Skye, the doctor—all Shrouds—we're sworn to keep you safe, no matter the cost to our own lives."

Aspen cringed at the thought of someone risking their life for hers. Her life wasn't more important than anyone else's. No wonder the doctor was so grumpy. Tonight's events made sense now. Tora must have seen her yellow eyes when they shook hands in the hospital and figured out she was a Myriad. That's why Tora circled her when they met, just like Oscar had. That's probably also why she'd made the decision to help. It wasn't Skye she was protecting. It was Aspen.

"I'm no more important than you, Skye, Tora, or anyone else," she argued. "Besides, I don't need your protection. You know I can take care of myself."

"That's the law of our people, Aspen. You're one of us. And as a Myriad, you're the last of your kind and extremely valuable. You have a duty to every Shroud on this earth to do whatever it takes to stay alive."

"You're a Myriad?" Skye asked, stepping into the living room. "Like…whoa." She made the gesture—along with rather impressive sound effects—of her mind being blown.

"Let's not get ahead of ourselves. I don't even know how to shapeshift yet."

No longer confined to the body of a lioness, the doctor stepped forward. "You don't know how to shapeshift?" Tora was wearing the same blue hospital scrubs and charcoal gray Adidas sneakers from earlier. *Dr. Madigan* was stitched in black thread on the breast pocket of her white lab coat.

A new question arose in Aspen's mind. How did Skye and the doctor shift back into their clothes? "Welcome back from the dead. And thanks for *this*, by the way." Aspen pointed to the goose egg on her head. "Oscar here was just telling me I'm the chosen one. You're required by law to protect me, not give me a concussion."

Ignoring Aspen altogether, Tora directed her question to Oscar from across the room. "How can she be a Myriad if she's never even shapeshifted?"

Oscar briefed Tora and Skye on his recent revelations as they both settled on the sofa across from Aspen. She studied each of them as they sat in rapt attention.

Tora's posture was rigid as she listened with the expression of a professional poker player. Her hair was still braided down her back with several loose curls tucked behind one ear. Makeup-free, she was the embodiment of fresh-faced radiance and raw beauty. Amber-gold eyes were her most striking feature. Aspen let her eyes roam Tora's body. Her legs were crossed at the thigh, her arms folded protectively across her chest. Even in hospital scrubs, her lean frame and feminine curves were visible. She was both elegant and fierce, all in one breath.

Skye, on the other hand, was an open book as she leaned forward, her expression full of hope, innocence, and wonder. Watching the girl, Aspen was reminded of the feeling she had as they shared candy on the rooftop earlier that evening. There was something special about Skye, something that transcended their shared traumas and shapeshifting abilities. She couldn't put her finger on what it was exactly, but her instincts insisted it was there. She also felt strongly that *it*—whatever it was—would be revealed soon.

Aspen let her gaze fall away and return to Oscar as he finished relaying her story. The room grew quiet as they processed his words. Tora was the first to break the silence. "We need to relocate. Tonight."

"Why?" Aspen asked. "No one knows I came here."

"The SEA knows you have Skye. By now, they've figured out Oscar adopted you. They're following the trail and figuring out exactly who you are as we speak. This will be one of the first places they visit."

Oscar nodded in agreement. "She's right. They're coming for all of us, whether we like it or not. We need to get you someplace safe."

"I can take you to a sanctuary a few hours from here," Tora offered. "You'll be safe there. We should leave tonight."

"Fine. But where I go, Skye goes. She stays with me." Aspen couldn't explain it, but she was overcome with a powerful maternal instinct toward Skye. Like a lightning bolt illuminating the dark night sky, she saw her purpose clearly for the first time: she needed to protect the girl at all costs. Skye was not only special, but she was important somehow in the big picture.

Tora uncrossed her legs and leaned forward. "Now's not the time to let sentiment cloud your judgment."

Aspen met her fiery gaze head on. "I'm not."

"Then give me a reason for your request."

"It's not a request. And I don't need to give *you* a reason for anything." Aspen couldn't believe she'd willingly relinquished her Reese's Peanut Butter Cups to this woman.

They stared each other down. Neither she nor Tora budged.

Oscar cleared his throat. "What is it you're not telling us, Aspen?"

Good old Oscar. Giving her the benefit of the doubt, as usual. She broke the stare down and diverted her attention to him. "You said Myriads have unique abilities."

He nodded. "Go on."

"I know Skye's important. I don't know why yet, but I'm supposed to keep her with me. Protect her. That's my purpose. I've never been so sure of anything in my life." Those words would hit home with Oscar. He knew her better than anyone. She wasn't prone to irrational thinking. She approached everything in life with a combination of integrity, heart, and common sense. Some of that was innate, but most of it had been planted in her by Oscar's steady guidance over the years. He had unwittingly molded her in his image. She was proud to be the person he'd helped to create.

"Copy that," he said without hesitation. "Skye stays with you."

Skye stood from the sofa and joined Aspen on the love seat. "My mom started teaching me how to shift just before my eighth birthday. We kept it a secret from my dad—he didn't want us doing anything that would make us a target for humans. But your mom never got the chance to teach you." The girl looked to Oscar and then to Tora. "One of us has to teach her."

"On that note"—Oscar stood abruptly—"I need to check in with my pack." Obviously steering clear of the conversation, he made a clean getaway to the kitchen. Aspen heard the door slam shut as he exited abruptly from the house.

"Why do I get the feeling he doesn't want to teach me how to shapeshift?" Aspen asked, trying to figure out what was going on. "How hard can it be?"

Skye and Tora exchanged a knowing look.

"It's not that it's hard exactly," Skye volunteered. "Definitely takes a lot of practice. It's just that…"

"It's a very intimate experience," Tora finished for her. "Traditionally, a mother assumes all training for her daughter, and a father does the same for his son."

"What if there isn't a mother?" Aspen asked.

"Then it falls to an aunt or a grandmother."

"What if there isn't an aunt or a grandmother?"

"I'm not sure. I've never heard of such a thing happening."

"Well, I need to start somewhere." Aspen thought for a moment. "Can I teach myself? Maybe there's a book I can read."

"This can't be learned by reading a book," Tora explained. "It must be taught, skin to skin."

Aspen raised an eyebrow. "As in…naked?"

"Yes."

"Oh." Aspen was beginning to grasp the dilemma. "Is there another way I can learn how to shift? Without getting naked?"

Tora shook her head. "No. That's the only way." She turned to the girl with a sigh. "Skye, can you please give us a moment?"

"Don't worry, Aspen." Skye set a reassuring hand on her shoulder. "We'll figure something out."

She watched the girl disappear into the kitchen. "What are we talking here? Like, full-body naked or just down-to-your-undergarments naked?"

"Both teacher and student are fully disrobed."

"And what about the skin to skin part?" she asked suspiciously. "What parts are skin to skin?"

"Full body contact is required for each shapeshifting lesson," Tora said calmly. "It's a totally platonic experience."

Shapeshifting sounded a lot more complicated than she'd imagined. No wonder Oscar had bailed. She didn't blame him.

"I'll volunteer to take charge of your training. We'll start first thing tomorrow."

The sooner she got started, the better. Her people were being slaughtered. If there was something she could do to stop it, she was all in. She couldn't explain it, but she could *feel* their silent cries for mercy somewhere deep inside her own body. She centered her gaze on Tora. "Why you?" she asked.

"Oscar's a man, and Skye's too young. I'm the most logical choice," Tora said matter-of-factly.

She was about to vehemently protest that there must be another Shroud out there somewhere who could train her—she'd put an ad on craigslist if she had to—when the sound of a rapidly firing automatic weapon broke her train of thought.

Tora bolted from the sofa in a flash. She had already shifted into a lioness by the time Aspen had her weapon drawn.

"Skye!" Aspen shouted toward the kitchen as the sound of an automatic weapon continued to assault her ears in short consistent bursts.

"I'm okay!" Skye yelled back.

She thought of Oscar outside with his pack. As worried as she was for him, she knew he could take care of himself. Her main focus right now was getting the girl to safety. Staying low, she made her way to the kitchen and found Skye underneath the table. "Are you hurt?"

The girl shook her head.

Tora came up alongside them, still in lioness form.

Aspen crawled out from under the table to latch the dead bolt on the kitchen door. It wouldn't keep the bad guys out forever, but it would slow them down. She crawled back and looked from Tora to Skye. "There's a window in the attic. That's the highest and safest point in the house right now. I'll take you up there so you can fly out of this mess. Let's go." She grabbed Skye's forearm and started pulling her along.

"I can't," Skye said, not budging. "Our laws say I'm supposed to protect *you*."

Aspen glanced down at her uniform and thought for a moment. Who was she to argue about following the law? Rapid gunfire outside was suddenly interrupted by the heart-wrenching sound of a high-pitched yelp. One of the wolves had been hit. Her stomach somersaulted at the thought of losing Oscar.

"You're right," Aspen said, wiping a smudge of leftover whipped cream from Skye's chin. "New plan. Go upstairs and fly out from a window. Swoop down and take every weapon you can from the bad guys, just like you did with the dart gun. But be careful. At least one of their weapons is fully automatic. It's big and can do a lot of damage but less accurate when it comes to hitting a target." She turned to the lioness. "I'll take the front. You take the back. We take out as many bad guys as we can. Agreed?"

"But you can't shift yet," Skye protested.

"Maybe not. But as a police officer, *this* is my weapon of choice." The Glock felt solid and familiar in her hands. "Until I get my teeth and claws," she added, trying to muster a reassuring smile for the girl.

A longer spray of gunfire outside made her stomach do another series of flips. From what she could tell, there was only one automatic weapon at play. "Go for the largest gun first," she told Skye.

Skye followed her to the stairs leading to the second floor of the house. The girl fled up the stairs two at a time and vanished around the corner. Aspen looked back at the lioness with a check-in glance. The lioness nodded and headed off toward the kitchen at a gallop.

Aspen was poised to exit through the front door of the house. She hesitated. How would Tora manage to open the locked kitchen door to get outside? She considered going back to help her when she heard something large crash through one of the kitchen windows. Apparently, the doctor had already found a solution on her own... without the need for opposable thumbs.

Ducking down low, Aspen threw the door open and dove headfirst behind some bushes. Bullets sailed through the air around her before she even hit the ground. How many SEA soldiers were there? She had heard just one fully automatic weapon, but maybe that was a tactic to lure her outside and get her to think they stood a fighting chance of escaping alive.

Did these soldiers have every exit and window covered? She couldn't risk letting Skye open a window to find out. A white owl against the dark night sky would make an easy target. But she had no way of knowing which side of the house Skye would choose. Given the girl's loyalty and protective nature, she would probably choose the side of the house from which Aspen had exited.

Without giving it a second thought, she took a deep breath, rolled from the bushes, and sprinted across the front yard toward the source of the gunfire. A moving target was harder to hit than a sitting one. With any luck, she would draw the attention away from Skye and give her the precious few seconds she needed to escape.

Tora galloped across the kitchen, leaped up, and squeezed her eyes shut as she crashed through the window above the sink. Confident her thick fur would protect her from glass shards, she landed, unscathed, on the cold ground in pitch-black darkness. Her lioness eyes adjusted. Seeing at night had never been a problem for her.

Forced to assess her surroundings at lightning speed, she was on the move in microseconds as she evaded bullets aimed in her direction. She was intuitively aware of two wolves nearby. Fortunately, identifying friend versus foe was easy. Anyone in human form was now fair game.

She quickly honed in on the soldier shooting from the tree line and immediately recognized his weapon of choice: a Remington R-25 semiautomatic. She knew from experience this particular rifle was a favorite of humans because it was built to take down big game. Tora loathed this weapon. It had taken the lives of more than a few of her colleagues, friends, and family over the years.

She sensed the wolves were already stalking him from both sides. Tunnel vision kicked in as she charged at a full gallop. Covering thirty feet with every stride, she was on top of him in seconds.

The wolves arrived at the same time with calculated precision. They clamped powerful jaws around his forearms and bit down into his flesh. One on each side, the wolves held his arms away from his body as she reared up and tore into his throat.

Releasing his lifeless body, she was instantly aware of a second soldier who had taken up position behind the first, about ten yards out. Rifle cocked, he took aim at her and fired.

CHAPTER SEVEN

Bullets from at least three different sources rained down around Aspen. She kept running toward the one in the middle, finally deviating from her course when a bullet whizzed past and took part of her uniform sleeve with it. Suddenly, everything around her slowed. She became acutely aware of the cold air on her skin, the sound of her own heart thumping wildly in her ears, the taste of blood in her mouth. Still running, she zeroed in on three bodies hiding in the darkness as clear to her as if they were under bright spotlights, an impossible feat if she were merely human, but she realized her abilities were flexing their muscles now. She sensed two wolves moving in at Oscar's command. The man on the left and the man on the right, she suddenly knew, would be disposed of quickly.

The wolves were leaving the one in the middle for her.

She dove behind a large boulder and felt her mind reaching out to Skye's. Almost immediately, she sensed a large winged presence hovering somewhere above her in the darkness. Had she somehow instinctively called Skye to her? No time to think about that now. The important thing was that she *knew* Skye was there, watching and waiting for her signal. Without looking up for fear of giving away the girl's location, she darted out from behind the boulder to draw the soldiers' attention once again.

They fired on her repeatedly as she sprinted forward. She heard the sound of muffled screams on both sides as the wolves finally caught up with their quarry. Closing in on hers, she saw the panic in his eyes as a giant owl swooped in and plucked the weapon from his grasp with ease. Skye disappeared just as efficiently and silently. That girl had skill.

He was reaching for the gun at his hip when Aspen blew two holes in his chest, dead center. He went down hard, hitting the ground with an audible thud.

Everything went eerily quiet. The wolves approached her from both sides, blood still dripping from their muzzles. "Thanks for your help," she said. "Where's Oscar?"

They led her to the backyard. One wolf walked ahead while the other took her six and walked behind. Oscar had obviously shared the news that she was a Myriad. They were taking their allegiance of protection seriously.

Aspen sensed a somber feeling in the air. The wolf in front lowered his head, flattened his ears, and tucked his tail as they rounded the far corner of the house. Several wolves had already gathered in the backyard, their heads hanging low.

Her heart plummeted as she stepped between them to gaze down at Oscar. One of the wolves chuffed to get his attention. Sprawled on the ground in wolf form, Oscar lifted his head with great effort to peer into her eyes as she approached. She dropped to her knees and held his head between her hands. His thick black fur was soaked with blood, his body riddled with holes. She realized he was holding on only to say good-bye.

Despite her desire to be strong for him, she felt her eyes well up. Oscar meant everything to her. How could she ever say good-bye? "I'll make sure we win this war to save our people. You have my word."

He blinked and nodded ever so slightly.

Still holding his head up, she kissed his muzzle and peered into his eyes. "Love you, Pop." She had never called him that before. But he was as much her father as any man could be.

The tears spilled from his eyes now as he returned her gaze with such tenderness and love. Then, with one final breath, he was gone.

Aspen set his head gently on the ground. She laid a hand over the blood-soaked fur on his chest. He wasn't breathing. His heart had stopped beating. She ran her fingertips over his eyes to close them.

Tora stepped out from the shadows and knelt beside her. "He took those bullets for me," she said. "Oscar sacrificed himself to save my life. I'm so sorry."

Aspen shook her head. Dammit. Of all the people he could have died for here tonight, why'd it have to be her? "First, you get yourself darted. Then you get Oscar killed. Do you still think *you* should be the one to train me?"

Unfazed, Tora wrapped a hand around her arm. "Come on. We need to get you out of here."

Aspen jerked from her grasp and stood. "Get your hands off me!" She'd shouted louder than she intended. "That's my father. I'm not leaving him like this."

The wolves closed in around her. One by one, they tilted their heads and howled in unison into the nighttime sky. Her arms broke out in goose bumps as they bid their pack leader farewell with a hauntingly beautiful forlorn chorus.

Out of the corner of her eye, she saw the owl touch down. She watched as Skye approached. "He's dead?"

Aspen nodded, drying her eyes with the back of one sleeve.

Skye went to Oscar. She lifted her arms above her head as they shifted into the pure white wings of an owl. Amazingly, the rest of her body remained in human form. Aspen had no idea Shrouds could do that. Judging from the gasp that escaped Tora's lips, the doctor was just as surprised.

Everyone stood still. All eyes were glued to the girl in the center of their circle. The night itself seemed to hold its breath in anticipation of something magical.

This was the moment Aspen had sensed was coming—the moment when the girl would reveal why she was so important. Skye looked like an angel in the moonlight as she extended her wings and wrapped them around the wolf's body. She bent her head, as if in prayer, and sat motionless for long minutes. A warm light began to spread from the tip of each wing until every last feather was aglow. The light slowly enveloped her entire body, turning even her short hair a pure, radiant white.

Aspen found herself wishing for sunglasses. It hurt her eyes to stare directly, but she couldn't look away. After several minutes, the girl's light began to dim. She gracefully shifted her wings into human arms, stood, and stepped back.

Impossibly, Oscar's chest began to rise as he replenished his oxygen-starved body with a huge lungful of air. Aspen knelt beside him in the dirt as he lifted his wolf head—on his own this time—and blinked up at her. He rose on all fours, looking strong, robust, and healthy.

She didn't wait for Oscar to return to human form. Aspen threw her arms around him and hugged him as hard as she could. She felt him shapeshift in her arms as he hugged her back with equal ferocity.

"Thank God you came back. Now I don't have to pay for Sunday brunches at IHOP," she said, struggling to keep the tears to a minimum.

"My treat," he whispered. "As long as you keep calling me Pop." He reached out for Skye and draped an arm around her shoulder, giving her a squeeze. "Thanks, kid. You've earned free pancakes for life."

Skye grinned shyly. "I didn't even know I could do that."

The magic of what just happened was still sinking in. Curiosity got the best of Aspen. "Then how did you know what to do?" she asked.

The girl shrugged. "I just followed my instincts."

Skye's white hair remained—a ghostly reminder of tonight's brush with death. The color was made even more striking by her bright green eyes. She'd mentioned earlier that her mother was an owl. Aspen wondered if her mother possessed the same ability when she was alive. For all she knew, maybe every owl could bring someone back from the dead.

Oscar turned to his pack. "Anyone injured?"

A gray wolf stepped forward and shook his head.

"Thanks for your help tonight, boys. Conduct a perimeter check and report back." The wolves dispersed immediately, their lithe bodies disappearing into the shadows.

"I can do a perimeter check from overhead," Skye offered.

Oscar nodded. "Stay high."

"I will." Skye leaped into the air, shifting with a grace and speed that Aspen could see mesmerized even a seasoned Shroud like Oscar.

"Never heard of a Shroud who could bring someone back to life," he said as soon as Skye flew away. "You were right. There's something special about that kid. She'll make a hell of a cop someday."

"How do you feel?" Aspen asked.

"Better without all the holes," he said, patting his stomach and chest in disbelief.

"You were dead."

"I kind of figured that out already."

"Like, *really* dead."

"Did Beckett do a celebratory jig?" Oscar surveyed the shadows. "He's been after my position as alpha for years."

"Like, big *X*s over your eyes dead," she added.

"What about Miller? He's quiet about it, but I can feel him breathing down my neck for pack leader."

"Like, deader than lobster in butter sauce."

Oscar turned to face her. "Feels like you're rubbing this in just a little."

Aspen shrugged. "I've just never met a zombie before." She stared at him. "How long does it take for body parts to decompose and start falling off?"

With a slightly panicked expression, he checked his own wrist for a pulse. "Sorry to disappoint you, but I'm very much alive."

"Do you have a sudden craving for brains?" According to every horror flick she'd ever watched, brains were always a zombie's delicacy of choice.

Frowning, he looked past her to Tora. The doctor was sitting alone on the porch steps. "If I know you—which I do, and quite well

I might add—I'm guessing you said something to make her look all sad and lonely."

Aspen sighed. "Please don't make me go over there to make up with her."

"Great idea," he said, slapping her proudly on the shoulder. "You go do that, and I'll start packing up some food and supplies. We should get moving soon." He retreated to the house and promptly shut the door behind him, giving her the privacy she didn't want.

Tora kept playing it over and over in her mind. With a quick glance in the soldier's direction, Oscar had reacted faster than she could even think. Before she'd had time to process what was happening, Oscar had stepped in front of her to protect her from the onslaught of bullets. He'd stood stoically in place as the bullets pierced his wolf body, one right after another, his eyes on his pack members as he waited for them to put an end to the threat once and for all.

Tora had shifted back to human form and caught him as his legs gave out beneath him. They'd locked eyes as she cushioned his fall and held his head in her lap. She'd stroked the fur on his neck and shoulders, tears coursing down her cheeks. Too choked up to say anything at all, she hadn't even thanked him for saving her life.

She felt her face flush with embarrassment and shame as Aspen approached.

❖

Aspen took a deep breath, walked over, and sat beside the doctor. "You didn't deserve what I said tonight—"

"Apology accepted. No harm done."

"That wasn't an apology. But if it was going to turn into an apology, I wasn't finished with it yet."

"Well, whatever it was, I've already moved on and forgotten about it. I suggest you do the same." Tora stood and brushed lightly at her scrubs. "We need to leave. I'll meet you around front whenever you're ready." Without waiting for a reply, she shifted and disappeared around the corner of the house.

Unbelievable. Aspen shook her head. That woman had a hard candy shell, but she doubted there was anything chocolaty inside. More like an M&M stuffed with turnip.

Sudden movement in the tree line bordering the backyard caught her eye. Squinting into the shadows, she stood at full attention but didn't dare move a muscle.

Chapter Eight

"Pop?" Aspen had meant to shout, but it came out as a pathetic squeak. Feeling the heat rising in her cheeks, she cleared her throat and tried again. "Pop!" Out of the corner of her eye, she saw the storm door spring open.

Oscar poked his head out. "Taking the new name for a test drive?"

"Drove it. Happy with it. Old news," she said, never taking her eyes from the tree line. She felt his eyes shift to the tree line, too.

"Oh," was all he said.

"Is there a party you forgot to mention?"

He sidled up alongside her and whispered, "I may have asked Beckett to tell a few friends about you. Didn't expect this kind of turnout."

A tiger, a grizzly bear, a cheetah, a gorilla, a snow leopard, and a huge rhinoceros looked on from the safety of the trees. She felt more than a little intimidated. "Are they going to eat me?" she asked, only half joking.

Oscar stepped forward. "Enough gawking, everyone. You're making her nervous. Get your furry butts over here and say hello."

She watched as each of them emerged from the shadows and effortlessly shifted into human form. Seeing someone shapeshift was truly magical. It never got old for her.

"You know Hank," Oscar said, gesturing to his longtime friend, the fire chief, who never missed their Friday night poker games.

"Good to see you again, Aspen," he said, shaking her hand to reveal himself as a towering, ferocious-looking grizzly. "Welcome to the club," he said, stepping aside with a wink and a tip of his ball cap.

One by one, everyone approached and shook her hand, obviously wanting to see for themselves that there was a Myriad in their midst. As each made physical contact, they studied the panther inside her that even she wasn't yet acquainted with. They paid particular attention to her eyes, of course, uttering various animal sounds of surprise upon seeing them.

It had been awhile since she'd seen Tony—one of her favorite instructors at the police academy. An avid long-distance runner and cyclist, he was in his fifties and still looked fit enough to compete in an Ironman. A sight to behold, his shiny orange-and-black-striped coat rippled in the moonlight. The irony of his name didn't escape her. Frosted Flakes was her favorite cereal as a kid. "Always knew you'd make a name for yourself," he whispered with a sincere smile.

Pierre was a French pastry chef who owned the bakery she and Oscar had been frequenting for years. She was surprised to discover he was also a well-muscled silverback gorilla. "Bonjour, my friend," he said with a quick kiss on both cheeks. His handlebar moustache tickled her face.

Next in line was Detective Beckett's teenage son—she'd babysat Liam for years when she was a teenager. He was just ten the last time she saw him. He came up to her with a skateboard under his arm, blue hair in his eyes, and a pierced lower lip. As a cheetah, his long, lanky body was built for speed. "Cool," was all he said upon releasing her hand.

Caught off guard, Aspen reached out to return the hug from her high school chemistry teacher. "Mrs. Belarino?"

"Guilty as charged." Mrs. B adjusted the large black-rimmed glasses that dwarfed her face. "Please, call me Gladys."

Who knew this short round unassuming teacher was a hulking rhinoceros? She was the sole reason Aspen had made it through high school science and math. This gifted teacher not only tutored her when she was struggling to keep up her grades, but she was also an endless source of inspiration, encouragement, and hugs.

Helga was the last to step forward, looking just the same as Aspen remembered her—tall, voluptuous, and conservatively stunning with kind blue eyes and honey-colored hair that was just beginning to gray around the edges. Her thick German accent brought Aspen back to the year of therapy she underwent, at Oscar's request, to deal with the loss of her parents and her suicide attempt. "How wonderful it is to see you"—she reached up to cup Aspen's cheek—"so beautiful and strong."

Aspen hugged her. She would always have a special place in her heart for this woman. When their hands touched, Helga revealed herself as a snow leopard with a luxuriously thick and spotted coat. But Helga didn't study her yellow eyes like the others had. Instead, she simply sat and bowed her head to Aspen in an elegant and humbling display of acceptance.

"What are all of you doing here?" Aspen asked, stepping back. Even though she'd known these Shrouds for years, she had never before seen the animals beneath their human forms.

"What does it look like?" Mrs. B pushed her glasses up with one finger. "We've come to kick some ass."

Aspen smiled. "It means a lot that all of you came here tonight. But the fight's over." She slid her hands inside her pockets. "We're leaving. It's not safe here anymore."

"That was just the beginning," Pierre countered. "There are many more soldiers who will come for you."

"You're probably not familiar with our laws yet," Tony explained, "but we're sworn to protect you."

"And we're done hiding." Liam set his skateboard on the ground. "We're ready to fight."

Hank nodded, removing his ball cap. "There were always lots of reasons to fight, but we never dreamed in a million years that we'd actually have a chance of winning this war against humans."

"Until now," Helga added. "You have given us hope, Aspen. Historically, Myriads are very powerful creatures. You haven't yet realized the full extent of your gifts. We want to keep you safe so you have the chance to discover those gifts over time, at your own pace."

"So we're coming with you, whether you like it or not." Mrs. B crossed her arms. "And we won't take no for an answer."

Aspen studied this unlikely group and felt a sudden responsibility so profound it gave her butterflies. She looked up at the tree branch behind them and nodded at Skye. The girl had been perched and listening for the last few minutes. Skye flew over and landed beside her, her red high-top sneakers touching the ground as she shifted.

"I'll accept your terms on one condition," Aspen said, reaching an arm around the girl's shoulders. "Each of you must protect Skye at all costs. If it comes to choosing between me and her, choose her."

Their heads turned in unison to look questioningly at Oscar. He nodded. "Do what she says. Skye is important."

Skye turned to Oscar. "There are eight black Suburbans about ten miles out. I tracked them for a few miles. Looks like they're heading this way."

"Nice work," he said proudly. He turned to the group, counting aloud. "My pack and I make nine, plus Skye, Aspen, Tora, and the six of you—"

"Eighteen," Hank finished for him, grinning. "Good thing we splurged and got three."

"Three what?" Aspen asked.

"Beckett, Miller, and Johnston are getting them now," Oscar told Hank. "Should be back any minute."

Aspen watched them, confused. "Getting what?" she asked again.

Tora appeared in the backyard. "Transportation's here," she called out, returning to the front of the house.

The merry band of six ducked behind the tree line. One by one, they returned with military-issue duffel bags and hurried toward the front of the house.

There was a sudden and distinct change in the air—like ants from the same colony had just met in secret, and now everyone knew what they were supposed to do.

Intrigued, Aspen studied the efficiency with which everyone seemed to be working. "Why do I get the feeling everybody here has done this before?" she asked aloud, to no one in particular.

Still standing beside her, Skye set a reassuring hand on her shoulder. "We start training for this as soon as we're able to walk. All Shrouds do."

"Training for what?"

"We're taught humans could show up at any time of the day or night to kill us. We have to be ready to run on a moment's notice."

Aspen shook her head, grateful she hadn't grown up like that. The injustice of being hunted down and murdered by SEA soldiers at the direction of the president was beyond her comprehension. How could obliterating an entire species be allowed in this day and age in America—the land of the free and the home of the brave? A fundamental change *had* to happen. Something that would allow humans to see the error of their ways and realize Shrouds were people, too, who were just as deserving of equal rights.

With Skye beside her, Aspen followed the bustle of activity to the front of the house. Three brand-new black Hummer H1s were parked on the street. Beckett, Miller, and Johnston hopped out and began loading the vehicles with the equipment Oscar had already carried to the sidewalk. Five other pack members emerged from the shadows, shifted from wolf to human, and lent a helping hand. Skye joined in, too.

"Nice wheels, Pop," Aspen said as Oscar deposited another load on the sidewalk. She wondered how a cop and a fireman could afford this type of luxury.

"Poker night," Oscar replied as if reading her mind. "The guys and I played every week, but that was just for fun. This is where all our money really went," he said, nodding at the Hummers. "Poker was just a cover."

Ingenious. "What else have you been keeping from me?" she asked, incredulous.

"Helga and I are dating," he blurted.

Okay. She liked Helga. "How long have the two of you been—"

"Eleven years."

Apparently, Oscar had more secrets than he knew what to do with. This might take a little getting used to.

"Glad that's out of the way." He let out a breath. "I'd like your blessing so I can finally ask her to marry me."

"Why do you need my blessing now? You've been together for eleven years."

He shrugged. "Just figured it was the right thing to do, seeing as she was your therapist and all."

"Would've been nice if you'd asked me that eleven years ago." She sighed. "Can I have some time to think about it?"

He looked at her like she'd completely lost her mind. "No."

"Well...don't I get a moment to process the feelings I have about you dating my therapist?"

"Ex-therapist," he corrected her. "And that was, like, seventeen years ago." He tapped his foot impatiently.

"Then why'd you ask for my blessing?"

"I was being polite." Not wasting any time, he waved Helga over with boyish enthusiasm.

Aspen watched as Helga nodded and unzipped her duffel bag. She withdrew a small white pastry box before handing the duffel bag to Beckett for loading.

Helga strode over to them confidently. Without a word, she raised the box's lid and held it out to Aspen like an offering. There was one slice of chocolate lava cake inside. Helga reached into her coat pocket, pulled out a white napkin that had already been folded in half, and opened it to reveal a clear plastic fork.

Oscar and Helga had obviously conspired to manipulate her into accepting their relationship. They really should have given her more credit than this. Her approval could never be won with such a *tiny* offering. She reluctantly accepted the fork and reached in to sample the goods, taking a modest and noncommittal bite. *Oh. My. God.* There wasn't even a word for how good this tasted. She took a second bite—much bigger this time—just to be sure. "Did you bake this?" she asked, trying not to sound as if she'd just won the lottery.

Helga nodded. "Baking from scratch with chocolate as the primary ingredient is a passion of mine." She closed the lid and held the pastry box aloft with a knowing smile.

Unable to hold herself back any longer, Aspen accepted the box with a sigh. "Welcome to the family," she conceded around a mouthful of cake.

"Sorry to break up the reunion," Hank said, slapping Oscar on the back. "Everything's loaded and ready to go."

"Showtime, everyone!" Oscar bellowed. "Pick a vehicle and load up. We'll be on the road for at least a few hours, so make yourselves comfortable."

Aspen watched as Shrouds scattered, chose a Hummer, and climbed inside in absolute silence. No bickering about who was riding with whom. The doors were shut and the sidewalk bare in seconds. Shrouds took efficiency to a whole new level.

Oscar climbed behind the wheel of the first Hummer with Hank beside him in the passenger's seat. Aspen, Skye, and Helga settled into the back seat. Tora was already waiting inside.

Smiling politely as she took a seat beside Tora, Aspen couldn't imagine a better companion for this road trip.

Not.

Why couldn't the doctor have chosen a different Hummer? She could barely stand the thought of sitting next to Tora on the porch for a few minutes. How would they survive a few hours in this cramped space together? Thank God Skye and Helga were back here, too. She glanced down at the pastry box in her lap. The cake… thank God for the cake. She only wished she had more.

Tora leaned forward. "I've already added the sanctuary's address," she told Oscar, indicating the Hummer's GPS.

"Landgrove, Vermont," he said, glancing at the screen on the dash. "Never been." He put the Hummer in gear and started driving.

"It's pretty remote. Landgrove has fifteen miles of unpaved roads and a population of one hundred and fourteen."

"How many Shrouds live at the sanctuary?" Hank asked.

"Two hundred and thirty-six."

Hank turned in his seat. "And you've never been discovered?"

Tora shook her head. "We keep to ourselves and stay out of trouble. Members go through a rigorous interview and screening process before they're permitted entrance. I have pretty good radar for troublemakers." Tora locked eyes with Aspen and narrowed hers in silent accusation.

Aspen felt her grip tighten around the pastry box. Cake or no cake, this was going to be a long ride.

Chapter Nine

Finkleman rushed into the Oval Office and tripped on the edge of a round rug in the center of the room—an exquisitely designed blue-and-gold presidential seal. Tim Decker watched him make a perfect face-plant from the comfort of his leather chair behind the desk. The balding man's glasses, tablet, and phone skidded across the polished wood floor.

Why'd he pick such a louse as his secretary of defense? He shook his head, remembering he'd needed someone who would bend to his will. Someone who would allow him to initiate the population cleansing that this country—and the world—so desperately needed. Finkleman was irritating, yes, but Tim put up with him because he had just the right amount of spinelessness for the job.

Finkleman stood and retrieved his belongings. "Sorry, Mr. President."

"Do you have an update for me?"

"A rather disturbing one, I'm afraid." Finkleman stepped over, set the tablet on the desk, and swiped the screen.

A photo of a female police officer appeared. "What's this?"

"She's a Shroud, sir."

"Cop or no cop, they all must go. No exceptions, Finkleman. I thought I made that clear."

"That's not it, sir. She's listed as human. But we just received word she's a Myriad."

A Myriad? Damn. Those things were supposed to be extinct. Tim didn't know much about them, only that they were powerful and very dangerous. "How'd she slip through the cracks?"

"Her parents allegedly vaccinated her against shapeshifting and passed her off as human."

This was the first he'd heard of a vaccination to prevent a Shroud from shapeshifting. These things were getting smarter by the second. "Are there others?" he asked. "Others who were vaccinated and pretending to be human?" The possibility was more than a little disturbing.

"We're not sure about that yet, sir."

"Divert all available resources to finding the Myriad. She can't be allowed to survive."

"Sir, just moments ago, she and several other Shrouds killed a group of our soldiers."

"So? Send more."

"Our men were surveilling the house and caught wind of something called the sanctuary. That's where the other Shrouds are taking her right now."

Tim shook his head and sighed. His patience for this particular invertebrate was growing thin. "Intercept them. Take them out." He pushed the tablet away. "Shit, how hard can that be?"

"Another unit is en route to do that, sir."

"Good. Let me know when it's done."

Finkleman picked up the tablet and hesitated. "Actually, sir, I was wondering if you wanted me to call them off—"

"Now why the hell would I do that?" he shouted.

Finkleman took a step back. "One of our men darted the leader of the sanctuary, so we can track her by transmitter. The Myriad is with her."

"And?" Tim felt his patience giving way to a headache.

"I figured you might want to track them, wait until they reach their destination, and then take out the entire nest in one fell swoop."

Tim took a sip of bourbon from a crystal glass and ran his fingers over the presidential seal. Now *that* was a damn good idea. He finally stood, walked around his desk, and set a hand on the small man's shoulder with a smile. Maybe Finkleman wasn't such a nuisance after all.

❖

Aspen stepped down from the Hummer and stretched as Oscar cut the engine and headlights. When Beckett and Miller followed suit behind them, the darkness swallowed everything. She couldn't see her own breath in front of her face, but she was sure it hovered in the freezing air like barroom smoke. It was officially frigid in Landgrove, Vermont.

Feeling a little melancholy, she caressed the edges of the empty pastry box in her hand. She'd donated the rest of her cake to Skye, who was famished after the long stakeout flight back at Oscar's. Aspen was now just holding onto the box as a reminder of what heaven smelled like.

She was glad to be out of Tora's personal space. The doctor had been quiet for the duration of the trip but kept fidgeting uncomfortably on the seat beside her every time their legs or shoulders touched. The animosity radiating from her was palpable.

Aspen pressed the glow button on her watch to check the time: 3:47 a.m. She was exhausted. Skye was still asleep in the car. Wherever the hell they were was definitely remote. She couldn't remember the last time they'd passed a streetlamp, house, or any sign of civilization. She felt disoriented and a little angry that the SEA had ousted her from her home in Boston. What she wouldn't give to curl up in her own bed right now.

A porch light clicked on, illuminating a modest log cabin. The door to the cabin swung open as an old woman stepped outside. "All the rooms are ready, dear," she said, shuffling over in a bright pink bathrobe and fuzzy slippers to give Tora a warm embrace.

What was this? Aspen was intrigued. There was someone who willingly hugged the doctor and, judging from the genuine smile on her face, appeared to actually *like* her? Poor thing must be suffering from dementia.

"Thanks, Edna. You'll take care of the vehicles before daybreak?"

"Of course, dear," Edna replied, still smiling as she looked behind Tora and caught Aspen's eye. "Is that her? She's quite beautiful. You didn't mention that on the phone."

Edna stepped forward and wrapped thin arms around Aspen. "Welcome to the sanctuary, dear."

Oscar, Helga, and a sleepy-looking Skye joined them. The others trudged wearily from the Hummers toward the cabin.

"Thanks," Aspen said, grateful for the fleeting warmth of Edna's hug. Edna's arms might be thin, but that woman could hug. "We all appreciate that you're letting us stay." She watched as Tora disappeared inside the cabin.

"Oh, I'm just the welcome wagon, dear. This is Tora's sanctuary."

That explained a lot. Tora was obviously accustomed to calling the shots. Well, the doctor was about to get a wake-up call because Aspen took orders from no one. Did being a Myriad trump being the leader of a Shroud sanctuary?

"If everyone will follow me, I'll lead you to the tunnels."

"Tunnels?" Aspen asked, suddenly uneasy.

"Tora didn't tell you?" Edna patted Aspen's hands like a child's. "The sanctuary is all underground, dear."

Underground tunnels sounded less like a sanctuary and more like a dungeon.

"Savor that last breath of fresh air," Edna said, inhaling deeply. "You won't be coming back up to the surface for a while."

"What?" Aspen asked. "How long is a while?"

"New members are permitted to revisit the surface after one month."

This was sounding less like a dungeon and more like a cult. *Well played, Tora.* Instead of sharing that tidbit on the drive over, Tora's convenient disappearance had forced Edna to do her dirty work. She'd obviously assumed Aspen wouldn't dare argue with an old lady in fuzzy slippers. Frowning, Aspen was about to open her mouth anyway in outright defiance when Oscar grabbed her by the arm and yanked her aside.

"I know what you're thinking," he whispered. "But this is the safest place for you right now. Will you do me a favor and just go with the flow?"

"You don't fool me," she whispered back. "You're only saying that because you're a zombie."

Oscar stared at her in confusion. "What?"

"Zombies love dungeons. It's like a well-stocked cooler of buffet-a-la-brain down there."

He laughed in spite of himself. "We're in this together. I have your back, kid."

"Fine. But if they try to get me to wear one of those prairie dresses, I'm *so* leaving."

"Fair enough. For the record, though, I think you'd look nice with your hair in a bun."

Edna led everyone into the cabin with assurances that their equipment would be unloaded and brought down as soon as possible.

Hank called out from the back of the line. "What about our Hummers?"

"Not to worry," Edna replied as she led them through a quaint living space with an armchair, side table, and wood stove. Bookshelves were built into the walls and bursting at the seams with paperback novels. "They'll be stored safely in the hydraulic underground garage here on the property." Edna opened a door off a long hallway leading to the kitchen and pulled a silver chain to turn on the light. "Michael will meet you in the basement," she said, motioning for Aspen to step inside.

"You're not coming with us?" Aspen asked.

"No, dear. This is my post. I man the fort." Edna winked. "Just think of me as your personal bodyguard."

Very funny, Aspen thought, questioning Tora's leadership skills. The decision to post a little old lady as their most prominent line of defense was obviously a lapse in judgment. What was the plan here? Hug the bad guys until they surrendered?

When Aspen hesitated, Edna reached over to take her hand. A giant African elephant rose before her with tusks as long as the Hummers outside. She raised her long trunk and blasted Aspen with a ground-shaking trumpet, flapping her ears and swaying her massive head from side to side to show off her formidable size and strength.

She released Aspen's hand and patted it between bony, arthritic fingers. "There's nothing to worry about, dear," she said, ushering Aspen down the basement steps before she had a chance to respond.

An unnaturally large man greeted her at the bottom of the stairs. Sporting a full beard, jeans, red plaid shirt, and suspenders, he looked like a lumberjack. "Welcome. Name's Michael," he said, his timbre deep and gritty. He extended a beefy paw to Aspen.

The minute she closed her hand around his, he disappeared. She looked around, but Michael was nowhere to be found. Oscar hadn't said anything about Shrouds who could make themselves invisible. Dumbfounded, she was about to release her grip when a faint squeak from below caught her attention. There, on the basement floor, was a tiny brown field mouse. Balanced on hind legs, it gazed up at her with twitching whiskers and a cute pink nose.

Michael withdrew his hand from hers. "Everyone calls me Mouse."

It took every ounce of willpower for Aspen to keep a straight face. She wondered if the rest of the group struggled to do the same as he made his way down the line with introductions.

She took the opportunity to scan the basement. It was pretty barren—save for some stacked logs, gardening tools, and a green storage bin marked *Xmas Lights*. She wondered where they were going from here. There didn't appear to be a tunnel entrance anywhere in sight.

"Listen up," Mouse bellowed from the other end of the line. "Before we descend into the tunnels, all of you will need to relinquish your weapons. They'll be stored in the arsenal here at the sanctuary." He picked up a wicker basket from the floor and made his way down the line once again.

Aspen raised an eyebrow when he reached Oscar, who simply smiled in compliance as he added his Glock to the pile. Shaking her head and against her better judgment, she did the same. But without the smile.

Mouse set the basket down and reached for a wooden support beam overhead. The wall of logs slowly slid aside to reveal a darkened tunnel entrance. He stepped in, lifted a lantern from a hook on the wall, and pointed to a basket of flashlights on the floor. "Help yourselves," he said. "It's a long walk and a lot less scary if you have one of those."

Aspen withdrew the flashlight from her duty belt and switched it on. She couldn't wait to get this uniform off and into more comfortable clothes.

Eyeing her rechargeable SureFire R1 Lawman with IntelliBeam, Oscar plucked a plastic Rayovac flashlight from the basket. "Trade?" he asked, holding his flashlight out with a look of hope.

She didn't even dignify that with an answer. "When were these tunnels made?" she asked, jogging to catch up with Mouse as the others fell in place behind her.

"About thirty years ago. They're made from precut steel tubes and then covered in a thick layer of rock. Nearly indestructible," he said. "Doc Madigan built this place. Starting the sanctuary was his lifelong dream."

"Tora's father?"

Mouse nodded. "Best man I ever knew. Tora took over after a human got him. He was killed right in front of her. She was never the same after that. But she didn't waste time feeling sorry for herself. She stepped up, kept this place running in his absence." He glanced over his shoulder to make sure the rest of the group was keeping up. "Tora runs a pretty tight ship around here. A lot of people depend on her, and she's never let us down. Her dad would be proud."

She walked the rest of the way in silence, feeling like a giant jackass. No wonder Tora was so pensive when Oscar was brought back from the dead. Last night's events had probably stirred up Tora's memories of losing her own father. And Aspen had taken jackass to a whole new level by blaming Tora for Oscar's death. She sighed. Even a truckload of Reese's couldn't make up for that.

They walked for miles. The tunnels seemed to go on forever. Aspen did her best to keep a mental road map, but it was no use. Too many twists and turns with left and right passageways from which to choose. She'd need a bloodhound to find her way back through this maze.

They finally came to a heavy steel door illuminated by a single torch set high in the tunnel wall. Aspen studied the door more closely. There was no doorknob, handle, keyhole, keypad, or security scanner in or around the formidable-looking door. How in the world would they open this thing?

Mouse set the lantern down and turned to them. "Stay here. I'll be right back."

Aspen was just about to ask where the hell they would go when he shapeshifted and scurried inside a teeny tiny hole underneath the door. She had to hand it to them. Security was tight.

The sound of metal scraping against stone echoed through the tunnel as the steel door cranked ajar, inch by inch. Inside, there was a second door that slid open and disappeared into the rock wall. She had been looking for vulnerabilities since setting foot on the property. So far, this place seemed dauntingly impenetrable.

Mouse was restored to his lumberjack size on the other side of the threshold. He waved them in with a big smile. "Welcome to the sanctuary."

Chapter Ten

Expecting quarters similar to the cramped conditions of the tunnel, Aspen's jaw dropped as she stepped inside. A fifty-foot-high rounded rock ceiling towered above them. Exposed rock in natural hues of brown and gray comprised the walls, floors, and ceiling. There was a massive sofa in the shape of a circle built into the rock in the center of the room, invitingly cozy with more throw pillows than a department store. The sofa surrounded a huge gas fire pit, already ablaze and lending much-needed warmth to her fingers and toes.

"This is chamber one," Mouse explained. "Bedrooms are off tunnel one." He pointed to a tunnel behind him. "You've each been assigned a bedroom. Your name's on the door, and your personal belongings are already inside." He waved a hand in the air. "The rest of this chamber is easy to navigate. Take tunnel two for the kitchen, tunnel three for the library, tunnel four for the exercise room and indoor pool, tunnel five for the basketball and volleyball courts, tunnel six for the indoor track, and tunnel seven for the recreation room. The rec room has a bowling alley, arcade, air hockey, Ping-Pong, and pool tables."

Everyone stood in awe. The accommodations were magnificent, to say the least.

Aspen checked her watch: 4:53 a.m. This place was eerily quiet. "Is everyone asleep?"

"Members of the sanctuary are in a different, much larger chamber," Mouse replied. "You won't have access to that chamber, or to the rest of the Shroud population, until we finish our background checks on all of you."

"And how long does that take?" she asked, feeling antsy at the thought of being locked up for any amount of time, even if it was in the lap of luxury.

"About thirty days."

Giving her the eye before she could incite a rebellion, Oscar stepped forward to address the group. "We've all had a long night," he said, his voice commanding. "Let's get some sleep. We'll start fresh in the morning. Meet in the kitchen at ten hundred hours for breakfast." He turned to Mouse, his expression momentarily frozen in worry. "Is there coffee here?"

Aspen held her breath. Oscar without coffee was a short road to hell.

Mouse nodded. "The kitchen's fully stocked."

Visibly relieved, Oscar sighed as he turned back to the group. "Any questions?"

Mrs. B raised her hand. "Bathrooms?"

"Each bedroom has its own private bath," Mouse assured her. "I'll be leaving now," he said when the room fell silent. "If you need anything—anything at all—just pick up the phone in your bedroom. Someone will be on the other end to help you."

He wasn't kidding when he said Tora ran a tight ship. Was there anything they hadn't thought of?

Still uneasy at the thought of being locked in an underground chamber, she was too tired to do anything but find a bed and get some shut-eye. She waited for Skye as the rest of the group wandered off to tunnel one.

The girl was busy gazing up at the ceiling. "Do you miss it?" Skye asked as Aspen approached.

She mentally skimmed through the list of what Skye could be referring to: miss being aboveground...miss being human...miss having a career in law enforcement...miss her friends, colleagues, life, and home in Boston. "Miss what?"

"The cake," Skye said, taking her eyes from the ceiling to glance at the empty box Aspen was still clutching.

"I do," she admitted sadly. "Best cake I ever had."

There was a moment of silence in the lava cake's honor.

"We can ask Helga to bake another one tomorrow," Skye said at last, casting her eyes back to the ceiling.

Aspen watched her, thankful Skye accepted her for who she was, sugar addict and all. "What's up?" She could tell there was something on the girl's mind.

"This place is beautiful, and I'm grateful to be here with you and the others." Skye hesitated. "But now that I've had a real taste of flying, I don't know how I'll go without it for a whole month. These ceilings are high. They're just not high enough for me to go anywhere. Feels like I'm in a cage."

The girl had a point. In a way, they were all in a cage.

"I'll talk to Tora and try to work something out," she said, draping an arm around the girl's slender shoulders as they walked to tunnel one. "Maybe she'll make an exception and give you some flying time at the surface."

But a terrifying thought occurred to Aspen. What if they had just been captured and imprisoned here by the SEA without even realizing it?

Tora was glad to be back at the sanctuary. It had always felt like home to her. She'd spent the best years of her life here with her dad, planning the sanctuary's layout, building it, perfecting it. Getting this place up and running was his lifelong dream. She felt grateful for the time she got to spend with him making that dream come true. She only wished he was still around to see the difference he was making in the lives of his people. Shrouds were safe here. That's all he'd ever wanted.

She hopped inside the trolley, switched on the headlights, and sped through the maze of tunnels at top speed. She knew these rock tunnels inside and out, could navigate them with her eyes closed if she had to. She checked her watch: almost five a.m. No time to sleep. She had a lot to do in three hours.

She tried to remember the last time she'd slept. Was it two or three days ago? Shaking her head, she decided it didn't matter. There were more important things to think about right now.

Part of her still couldn't believe there was a Myriad here in the sanctuary. Granted, Tora wasn't crazy about this particular Myriad. So far, her assessment of Aspen left much to be desired. She was a smart-mouthed cop who was undisciplined, impulsive, and full of herself. Tora had her work cut out for her for sure.

❖

"Wake *up*!" Tora shouted.

Aspen sat up in bed, rubbing her eyes. "Who died and made *you* my alarm clock?"

"I've been calling you on the intercom for five minutes."

Aspen knew she was a heavy sleeper. She'd always thought of it as her eight hours of personal hibernation. She could fall sleep anywhere and sleep so deeply people often thought she was dead. "I locked the door. How'd you get in here?"

Tora held up a badge, looking all serious and annoyingly beautiful. "Get up." She tossed a change of workout clothes on the bed.

Brand new purple-and-black Nikes were lined up neatly on the floor beside the bed. They looked to be her size. Did the doctor come in and measure her feet while she was sleeping? This was getting creepy. She checked her watch. "I've only been asleep for three hours. What's the rush?"

"I told you last night. Your training starts this morning."

"I accept your proposal to train me." She sank back down to the pillow and threw an arm over her eyes to block out the overhead light. "*After* I get some sleep."

There was a long silence. She felt Tora's eyes drilling a hole in her head.

"You're the first Myriad to come along in over a century. There are Shrouds being slaughtered by the SEA as we speak. The longer we wait to train you, the more of your people will die. You really want that on your conscience?"

So much for her theory about being captured by the SEA, though she might prefer that if it meant she could sleep a little longer. "You really know how to insert a little sunshine in someone's day," she said, swinging her bare legs over the side of the bed. Since she'd never had the chance to stop by her house and pack before leaving, she was still wearing the plain white T-shirt from under her uniform. "I'll meet you in ten minutes. Out *there*," she said, pointing to the hallway beyond her bedroom door. "Unless you think I should also give up all bathroom and personal hygiene habits for the cause."

Seemingly satisfied, Tora went to the door and let herself out with her trusty break-in badge. What was it with that woman and badges?

Aspen brushed her teeth, showered, and dressed. She pulled her wet hair into a ponytail and laced up the new Nikes. A perfect fit. The black sports bra, gray running shorts, purple tank, and matching sweatshirt also fit her perfectly. Curious, she went to the dresser drawers and opened them. They were fully stocked with everything she needed in her size. Intrigued, she opened the closet doors. An entire wardrobe awaited her in her size and style of clothing. She hoped the same went for Skye in the adjacent room. They had both arrived here with only the clothes on their backs.

She stepped to the door and pushed the button on the side panel. The door slid open smoothly. Tora was standing in the hallway. "Here," she said, handing Aspen a stainless-steel thermos and brown paper bag.

"Doughnuts?" Aspen could smell them a mile away. She reached into the bag and pulled out a chocolate-frosted doughnut with sprinkles. "I take back everything bad I thought about you this morning," she said, taking an inhumanly large bite.

Watching her finish the doughnut with a mixture of disgust and curiosity, Tora handed her a napkin as Aspen reached inside the bag for doughnut number two: a chocolate-frosted Boston cream. Also gone in three seconds flat.

She'd saved the best for last. Reaching into the bag for the third and final doughnut, she held the chocolate glazed aloft for inspection before finishing it off in two bites. Satisfied for the moment, she wiped the chocolate from her mouth and took a sip of coffee.

"How long have you been eating like that?" Tora asked.

"As long as I can remember."

"Do you work out?"

"I run a few miles most mornings before work."

"Does your diet consist of mostly sugar?"

She nodded, bracing herself for the impending lecture on proper nutrition. She'd heard it all before and had tried it all before. Whenever she limited her sugar intake, she became so light-headed and lethargic she could barely function at all. Running on pure determination, she once went a whole week without any sweets and ended up in the hospital on a glucose IV for three days.

"I suspect your sugar cravings have something to do with the vaccine you were given to thwart your shapeshifting abilities."

That was an interesting theory. Sure would explain a lot.

"Your body is probably expending a lot of energy trying *not* to shapeshift. You may find yourself craving different foods once we start training your body to do what comes naturally."

"Did you put all those clothes in my room?"

Tora nodded. "I did the same for Skye. I know the two of you didn't have time to pack."

"Thanks." Maybe she'd been too quick to judge Tora. Looked like there was a softer side to the doctor, after all. "How long are we training today?" She didn't want Skye to wake up and wonder where she was.

"We'll be training from dawn until dusk every day," Tora replied. "Sometimes longer."

"Do you have a pen I could borrow?"

"A what?"

"A pen. You know, one of those ancient writing implements people used before computers and smartphones came along."

"I know what a pen is. Why do you need one?"

"I want to leave a note for Skye so she knows where I am."

Tora reached over and pressed a button to the right of Skye's bedroom door. "Skye, this is Dr. Madigan. Aspen and I are training.

We'll be gone all day." She released the button and turned to Aspen. "That message will play automatically as soon as the sensors detect movement in her bedroom."

Rolling her eyes, Aspen leaned over to press the same button. "Skye, this is Aspen. Sorry for the boring message from the robot doctor. Have fun today, eat lots of sugar, and kick Oscar's ass in air hockey. Aim for the right corner—that's his weak spot. Oh, and check your closet and dresser drawers. A little fairy paid you a visit in the middle of the night and brought you some cool stuff. Later, kiddo."

Tora frowned. "Follow me." She led Aspen to tunnel six. "We'll start on the track with a five-mile run to warm up." As they stepped inside, she waved her keycard to lock the door behind them. "All of our sessions will be done in private. If someone tries to get in, a message will play outside to let them know the room is occupied. It's important for you to know we'll never be interrupted."

Aspen unzipped her sweatshirt and hung it over the bleachers, waiting as Tora did the same. Wearing red shorts and a formfitting white V-neck, the doctor's toned, athletic body was clearly visible now. For the first time since they'd met, she noticed they were the same height and build. But that was where the similarities ended. Tora's fair skin, curly blond hair, and amber-gold eyes perfectly contrasted Aspen's olive skin, straight black hair, and dark eyes. They were like yin and yang, Aspen realized. In more ways than one.

"What's your pace?" Tora asked, stretching her quads.

"I do about an eight-minute mile, give or take. You?"

"Same."

They started out at a comfortable pace, side by side. Before long, Aspen found herself pushing forward a bit. She wasn't used to running with someone and found herself inadvertently quickening her pace, but Tora wasn't backing down. Barely breaking a sweat, Tora kept up with no problem.

Aspen's competitive streak started rearing its ugly head. Soon, they were in a full-out sprint on the final lap to the finish line. Neck and neck, their legs were pumping high and fast. Aspen pushed her body as hard as she could, but she just couldn't gain an inch. She suspected Tora was trying to do the same. They were too evenly matched. They crossed the finish line the same way they'd started—side by side.

Breathing too heavily to talk, they walked another lap around the track to cool down.

"Not bad for a bossy pants doctor," Aspen said as soon as she got her wind back.

"Not too shabby for a doughnut-eating cop."

Touché. "What's next? We're not doing that naked thing now, are we?"

Tora walked over to a stainless-steel refrigerator, opened it, and grabbed two water bottles. She tossed one to Aspen. "Let's hit the showers and then meet in the library."

"Please tell me we're not doing the naked thing in the library."

"It's called melding," Tora said, taking a long drink. "And no, we're not doing that in the library."

"Good." Aspen sighed with relief as she unscrewed the cap from her bottle.

"We're doing that in your bedroom after the library."

She started to choke on her water.

"Don't worry. We'll start with our clothes on first." Tora waved her keycard to open the door. "See you in twenty minutes."

Chapter Eleven

A spen returned to her room wondering how on earth she'd make it through melding. Even the word felt too…intimate. She wasn't afraid to be naked with another woman. Hell, she'd done that plenty of times before. There was just something about getting naked with *this* woman that made her uncharacteristically nervous.

She had come out to Oscar when she was fifteen and still remembered their chat over a bowl of Cocoa Puffs one morning before school. "I'm a lesbian. Just thought you should know."

He'd calmly set his spoon down on the edge of the bowl. "Are you sure?"

She'd nodded, still chewing.

"Thank *God*," he'd said, leaping up from his chair to hug her. "Pubescent boys showing up at my house to take you on a date is a level of stress I just can't handle." He'd wept with relief. "Please, Aspen—I beg of you—please don't change your mind about this. Boys are nothing but bad news until they turn sixty. If you change your mind at that point, I'd offer my begrudging support. For the record, my strong personal preference is that you remain a lesbian. But no pressure," he'd added quickly.

Months later, at a Pride festival he'd insisted they attend, he bought a bumper sticker that read *Proud father of a lesbian.* Faded and peeling, that sticker was still on the back bumper of his prized metallic blue '67 Ford Mustang.

Showered and dressed in jeans, a white V-neck T-shirt, and a zippered black Old Navy hoodie, she made her way to tunnel three and stepped inside the library. Tora was already sitting at a supersized rectangular oak table in the center of the room. Intricately carved and regal, it seated twenty and looked like it belonged in a castle. Tora removed her glasses, closed an ancient-looking book, and stood. She walked to Aspen and locked the door with a wave of her keycard. "You're late."

"By, like, three minutes," Aspen replied, checking her watch. She'd decided to take the extra time to shave her legs in case they did that melding thing later.

She looked around in wonder. Cherrywood bookshelves lined the walls from floor to ceiling. The rock ceiling in this room was at least fifteen feet high. A rolling ladder was affixed to each wall, allowing access to books on higher shelves. Brown leather armchairs with matching ottomans sat in all four corners of the room. Each had its own throw blanket, side table, and Tiffany lamp. A worn emerald-green Persian rug covered the rock floor, lending the room a distinguished but comfortable look.

"You'll have to give me the name of your decorator," Aspen said, thoroughly impressed. She'd bought her house three years ago and was still using the box her computer came in as her coffee table.

"I've gathered some textbooks with photos of panthers," Tora said, indicating a pile of books on the table. "I'd like you to flip through and study the photos."

"I don't need picture books. I already know what a panther looks like."

"But have you ever studied the photo of a panther? The shape of its ears, the width of its nose, the length of its tail? You need to submerge yourself in those details and feel them on your own body."

"How can I feel a detail? That doesn't make sense, Tora."

"It's called using your imagination."

"I don't have one of those."

"Of course you do. I'll prove it." Tora pulled up a chair alongside her. "Close your eyes and imagine you're just finishing a five-mile run."

"I don't have to imagine. We just did."

"Close your eyes and visualize it, please."

Sighing, Aspen closed her eyes. But her brain didn't go for a five-mile run. It was still right there in the library, sitting beside Tora.

"Now that you've completed your run, your body is hungry."

That wasn't much of a stretch. She *was* hungry.

"After you shower and dress, you decide to go to the kitchen for something to eat and bump into Helga. She's been in the kitchen all morning, baking."

"Is she baking something for me?" Aspen asked.

"Helga heard you were training today, and she wanted to surprise you with your very own chocolate lava cake."

Aspen's mouth was already beginning to water. She liked where this was heading.

"You sit at the kitchen table. She cuts a very large piece and carries it over to you on a white porcelain plate. She hands you a silver fork and smiles. The cake is still slightly warm. It smells rich and moist. You take your first bite of this chocolaty heaven, delighting in every last chocolate-filled mouthful, one after another, until not even a crumb is left behind. You wipe your mouth with a napkin and take a long drink from the glass of milk beside your plate—"

"I was with you until the milk."

"You don't like milk?"

"Nope."

"Then what do you drink with cake?"

"Orange soda."

"That's appalling. Who drinks orange soda with chocolate cake?"

"I do," Aspen said, opening her eyes.

"Fine. You can have some orange soda with your cake, if that's what you want."

"Is Helga really in the kitchen baking me a cake right now?"

Tora frowned. "No, Aspen. That was the point of this exercise: using your imagination to believe the story and *feel* the details."

"That was cruel. And now I'm really hungry. You're a terrible trainer."

A man's voice came over the library's intercom. "Tora, you there?"

The doctor stood abruptly, hurried to the door, and pressed the intercom button. "I'm here."

"Sophie's water broke. She's in active labor."

"I'm on my way." She turned to Aspen. "You should come with me."

"Someone's having a baby?"

Tora nodded and waved her keycard to open the door. "But Shroud births are very different from human births."

"I don't really have the stomach for that kind of thing. I should probably hang back and become one with my brethren," she said, reaching for a panther book.

"This is something you need to see. We don't have much time. Let's go."

❖

Tora led Aspen to her bedroom, waved the keycard, and stepped inside.

Aspen hesitated at the threshold. "I thought we were going to deliver a baby. Why'd you bring me here?"

"You'll see. Come on," Tora said impatiently.

But Aspen didn't budge. Something felt off. "Did you trick me into coming here to do the naked melding thing?"

Tora grabbed the front of Aspen's sweatshirt and, with surprising strength, yanked her into the bedroom before waving the keycard to lock the door behind her. "You cop types are unbelievable," she said, walking to the closet. "Always have to be in control."

"Sounds like you should have been a cop instead of a doctor."

Tora opened the closet door and stepped inside, glaring at her. "Get in here."

"There are a lot of things you could probably convince me to do, but this is where I put my foot down. As a proud gay woman, I am *not* going back in the closet." There, she'd said it. She needed that fact to be known before any nakedness happened between them.

With any luck, maybe Tora would decide to put her with someone else for that portion of her training.

"As a proud gay woman myself, I would never ask you to," Tora shot right back. "Just get in here before I shapeshift and drag you in with my teeth."

Against her better judgment, Aspen joined Tora in the closet. Apparently, her gaydar needed new batteries.

Tora shut the closet door and switched on a dim overhead light. "There's a back door in here that leads to the railway system." She ducked behind the hanging clothes, grabbed for Aspen's hand, and pulled her to the rear of the closet. "Yours is the only bedroom with access, which is why I assigned you here. Most of your training will be at the surface or in other parts of the sanctuary. We'll be using this railway system as our primary means of transportation." She opened a small hidden panel and skimmed her fingers over a series of buttons. "If something happens and your life is threatened in any way, this is your best and only escape route. The passcode is *chocolate*."

"Funny," Aspen said as the rock wall in front of them slid aside.

"Needed to be something you'd remember in a pinch."

They both came out of the closet together, the irony of the moment not lost on Aspen. As the closet light blinked out and the door slid shut behind them, a narrow rock tunnel was instantly illuminated by a long row of torches set high in the wall.

"I've stationed three trolleys here," Tora went on. "Each trolley seats six, so all seventeen of you can leave together if there's an evacuation."

"Has that ever happened before?" Aspen asked.

"No." Tora climbed inside the green trolley first in line. "The government hasn't found us yet, but it's good to be prepared."

Aspen seated herself beside Tora. "Is there anything you haven't thought of?"

"I hope not," Tora admitted. "A lot of people are counting on the fact that I've prepared for every contingency."

Aspen saw the immense weight of responsibility on Tora's shoulders. The doctor's bossy bravado was just that—bravado. This woman was focused, organized, and efficient. Tora obviously knew how to get things done and would move heaven and earth to help her people. It struck Aspen like a falling brick from a tall building that Tora was someone she could count on. She thought back to what Mouse had told her in the tunnel. "I heard about your father. I'm sorry."

Caught off guard, Tora's poker face softened. "Thanks." She switched on the trolley's headlights, put it in gear, and drove forward. "That happened two years ago. He was a good man. You would have liked him."

Aspen grew curious and suddenly found herself wanting to know more about Tora. "Did you grow up here?"

"Pretty much. We had a house in Wellesley, but we stayed here mostly. My father homeschooled me, so we spent a lot of time working on this place together. He was a doctor—a neurosurgeon. One of the best in the world. Ironically enough, that's what ended up getting him killed." She slowed the trolley as they rounded a sharp bend in the tunnel.

"A patient requested an emergency consultation for a rare form of brain cancer," she went on. "Every neurosurgeon he'd seen informed him it was inoperable—everyone except my father. He was the only one who would even attempt resection. The day before the surgery, my father received word that this patient led an anti-Shroud movement known for inciting violence against our people. The Shroud community implored him to take this man's life while he was on the table, but my father wouldn't do it. He said he'd made an oath as a doctor to save lives, not end them. He went ahead with the surgery and successfully resected the tumor to save his patient's life. When the man woke up from anesthesia, he told my father to get his affairs in order. He thought my father was too successful and making too much money for a Shroud. He offered a large sum of money to any human for my father's prompt execution."

Aspen knew most crimes against Shrouds went by the wayside. Crimes against humans always took priority.

"My father called and asked me to meet him at our favorite diner down the street from the hospital. We both assumed meeting in public was safe. We were making plans to go into hiding when a masked gunman stormed through the front door. Fifteen people died that day. My father was one of them."

"I remember that," Aspen said. "BPD never caught the guy. From what I heard, the trail went cold." She knew the only reason they'd launched an investigation after the attack was because two of the fifteen victims were human.

"You never found him because one of my people found him first."

Aspen was silent as she processed this new information. "After your father saved the life of this patient, the patient turned around and put a price on his head?"

Tora nodded.

"Hell of a way to say thank-you." Aspen sighed. She glanced at Tora's hand on the steering wheel. "How'd you avoid getting the mark?"

"My father had adoption papers drawn up before I was born and a very credible story to go with them. The government never questioned it."

"What about your mother? You haven't mentioned her. Where is she?"

"She died during childbirth, which is why you need to see how Shrouds come into the world. Giving birth is a very vulnerable time for a Shroud." Tora eased the trolley to a stop and turned to Aspen. "This is where we get out."

Something told her she wasn't ready for this. Determined to see it through, she braced herself and followed Tora's lead.

Tora entered the passcode on a side panel with lightning-quick fingers, and the rock wall slid aside. The tunnel lights blinked out as they stepped into a medical supply closet. "Stay close. By now, everyone has heard about you and will want to shake your hand. We don't have time for that right now, so just keep walking."

"Copy that," Aspen said, less than happy with her new celebrity status.

They exited the supply closet and came out into what appeared to be a hospital corridor. There were no rock walls, floors, or ceilings here. Pastel blue walls, gray linoleum, and a white ceiling made Aspen feel like she'd stepped back into the world she just came from. Everything looked modern, clean, and sterile—just like a real hospital on the surface.

She and Tora marched past a nurses' station. Making no attempt to conceal their curiosity, everyone stopped and stared at Aspen as she passed. She felt their eyes follow her down the corridor. Not wanting to encourage their approach, she refrained from making eye contact and kept her eyes dead ahead.

Tora led her to a room with a sign on the door that read *Mother in Labor—Proceed with Caution.* Aspen swallowed hard. *Caution* was in bold red letters. This couldn't be good.

"Whatever happens, just know you're safe," Tora said in a reassuring voice Aspen would bet she reserved for her patients. "I promise, we won't let her hurt you."

Aspen didn't have time to ask the questions that raced through her mind all at once. Before she knew it, they were inside a private birthing room.

Save for one small night-light in the far corner, the room was dark. There was a thunderstorm soundtrack playing from the speakers overhead. Aspen waited until her eyes adjusted to take in her surroundings.

The room was quite spacious. In place of the traditional birthing bed that usually accommodated a human birth, pillows and blankets were bunched up on the floor in one corner. She felt something underneath her sneakers and looked down. Hay? It covered the floor from wall to wall. *This should be interesting.*

Chapter Twelve

Aspen could hardly believe her eyes. A huge thousand-pound Cape buffalo with massive horns was standing in the center of the room. She had only seen the Cape buffalo on TV—usually as it was being chased down and hunted for food by a lion. The irony of the moment was almost comical.

Making no motion to approach, Tora called out from where she stood. "Sophie, it's Tora. How are you feeling?"

At the sound of Tora's voice, the buffalo instantly shifted into a very pregnant woman. She was wearing a hospital johnny. "Tora, I'm scared."

"This is your first time," Tora said, walking to her. "It's normal to be scared, Sophie. We're all here to help you through this."

Now that her eyes were fully adjusted to the darkness, Aspen saw two men and two women standing against the walls around the room in silent support.

Sophie clutched her stomach and held on to Tora as a contraction took hold of her body.

"Stay with me, Sophie. It's just a contraction. Breathe."

Sophie mimicked Tora's quick, forced breaths until the contraction passed. "Is that her?" she asked, out of breath.

Tora nodded with a glance at Aspen.

"It's an honor to have her here, but do you really think it's safe?"

"Let me worry about that." Tora guided Sophie to the pillows and blankets. "All you need to focus on right now is having this beautiful baby." A woman in scrubs joined Tora, and they both lowered Sophie to the floor.

"I'm trying really hard to stay in control."

"You're doing great."

"Contractions are now a minute apart," the woman in scrubs announced.

Tora held Sophie's hand between hers. "As soon as the next contraction starts, it's time to start pushing."

Sophie let out a wordless grunt, leaned forward, and pushed.

Without warning, she shifted into the buffalo once again, her massive horns swinging dangerously close to Tora's head.

"No!" Tora shouted, standing. "You must shift back now, Sophie!"

Sophie was back in human form in the blink of an eye, still pushing.

"Can't hold on," she told Tora. "I'm sorry."

Tora grabbed her assistant by the arm, yanked her to her feet, and shoved her out of the way as an angry buffalo appeared before them once again. The buffalo swung her head from side to side, trying to gore everything in her path with dangerously sharp horns as she bucked furiously around the room.

Everyone dodged the out-of-control animal, including Aspen. This was not at all what she had expected. Completely at a loss as to how to help, all she could do was watch. She hoped Tora knew what she was doing.

"Jake!" Tora shouted from across the room.

Aspen watched as a man shifted into an Irish wolfhound and began antagonizing the buffalo with loud, threatening barks. The buffalo immediately swung around, set her sights on the dog, and charged. The dog leaped out of the way at the last minute as the buffalo thrust her horns into the wall.

A woman stepped away from the wall, shifted into an orangutan, and bravely jumped onto the buffalo's back. Feeling the intruder, the buffalo bucked furiously. With long, strong arms, the orangutan hung on for dear life. The buffalo finally tore her horns free from the wall with a thunderous scrape that reverberated through the floor beneath Aspen's feet.

Tora tossed something to the orangutan, who swiftly caught the object and slid it over the pointy tip of one of the buffalo's horns. They repeated the process until both horns were effectively padded and stripped of their lethality. Barely dodging the buffalo's rear hooves as they pummeled the air, Tora motioned to the second man still awaiting his turn at the wall.

Taking his cue, he instantly shifted into a gorilla. The gorilla galloped forward, grabbed one of the buffalo's horns in his immense hand, and jerked the beast to a stop. He then reached around to take hold of the second horn, pulled the buffalo's head to the floor, and held it there with unfathomable strength.

Unable to buck with her head held down, the buffalo could only snort and paw at the floor in protest. The orangutan climbed down from the buffalo's back and joined the gorilla to help him maintain control of the head.

After several minutes, the buffalo's rapid breathing slowed. Tora cautiously approached, laid a hand against the buffalo's neck, and spoke soothingly in her ear.

Aspen watched in amazement as a pair of small hooves were pushed from the buffalo cow on the heels of a big contraction. A black nose appeared, followed by the head and shoulders of…a baby deer? The Irish wolfhound shifted back into a man, picked up a blanket from the floor, and caught the fawn as it was expelled from the cow with one final contraction.

He set the fawn on the floor, cleared her nostrils, and wiped her face with a towel. Aspen smiled as the fawn's chest expanded with her first intake of breath. She lifted a wobbly head and let out a little bleat, calling for Mom.

Tora nodded at the gorilla and orangutan team near the buffalo's head. They slowly released their grip until they were sure she was calm. Responding to the call of her newborn fawn, the buffalo turned, spotted her baby, and promptly began grooming and nuzzling her.

Tora knelt beside the duo and checked the fawn from nose to tail. "Congratulations, Sophie. You have a healthy baby girl."

Sophie snorted in reply.

"Remember what we talked about. The two of you will remain like this for several hours before you're able to shift back into human form. You can stay in this room, and we'll provide you with everything you need. One of my nurses will check on you every hour."

Sophie stopped grooming the fawn to look over at Aspen.

"I think she wants you to bless her baby," Tora said, waving Aspen over. "Myriads would traditionally bless a newborn just after birth. It was rumored to give them special abilities."

Aspen stepped over to join them. She knelt in front of the fawn while Mom watched closely, her large head and horns over Aspen's shoulder, her steaming breath on Aspen's neck. She was about to ask Tora what she should do when instinct suddenly took over.

As if balancing on stilts, the fawn gathered long, gangly legs and struggled to a precarious stand. Aspen peered deeply into the fawn's huge brown eyes, so innocent and pure. She sensed this fawn was special—much like Skye but in a different way. Her hands rose to cup the fawn's cheeks. She let out a long breath. Shimmering particles of blue light danced in the air around them, circling more rapidly and expanding in number as she continued to exhale.

Transfixed by Aspen's gaze, the fawn remained perfectly still. The shimmering particles spun faster, their blue light made brighter by the increase in motion, until a sphere of blue light had completely enveloped them. She felt warm, safe, and protected, and she knew the fawn felt the same. The blue sphere started pulsating with their hearts, which were now synchronized in rhythm and beating as one. The particles of light gradually deviated from their spherical path and disappeared, one by one, as both she and the fawn slowly inhaled them.

Aspen finally realized what was happening. She was making this fawn a Myriad, like her.

At that moment, she sensed the vault of information locked away deep inside herself. She was just beginning to access the vault in bits and pieces, confident more would be revealed when the time was right. She now understood what Skye had meant by following her instincts when she brought Oscar back from death.

Finished, she released the fawn and stood.

The buffalo cow cautiously approached. As if asking permission to see her baby, she gently brushed her head against Aspen's shoulder.

"Your daughter's a Myriad now," Aspen whispered, stepping aside. "Keep her safe."

The cow nodded and then sniffed the fawn all over before allowing it to suckle for the first time.

A heavy silence filled the room. Watching that sacred moment between mother and baby, Aspen felt a powerful calling to do more. She looked around, confused. The blessing was finished. What else was there to do?

Tora cleared her throat. "Let's give them some privacy," she announced. She led Aspen out of the birthing room, down the corridor, and into an empty conference room.

Inside was a long mahogany table and numerous swivel chairs on wheels. Aspen had the sudden urge to challenge the nurses to a chair derby down the hospital corridors. Since chocolate wasn't readily available, that would be a great way to break the tension. She frowned, wondering how she could convince Tora to let her do it.

"How are you feeling?"

Aspen shrugged. She couldn't shake the feeling that she was supposed to do more. "I'm okay. A little weirded out, but okay." She narrowed her eyes, suddenly suspicious of Tora's incentive for taking her to the birth. "Did you want me to go with you because you knew that was going to happen?"

Tora leaned against the table. "I was reading from an ancient Shroud text when you came into the library this morning. It described the Myriad Birth Blessing in detail, providing a very similar account to what just happened. Each Myriad imparts a different gift to the newborn recipient. It's never known ahead of time what gift the newborn will receive. The ancient texts also revealed that the gift most needed will be provided. I didn't fully comprehend that part until now. At this point in time, what our people need most are Myriads like you. The mere existence of one Myriad makes winning this war against humans possible. And now there are two." She smiled. "Our odds just got even better."

Taken aback, Aspen said nothing and just stared. This was the first genuine smile she'd seen from the doctor since they'd met. Reaching even her amber-gold eyes, it made them sparkle and dance. Her smile was beautiful, filled with warmth, honesty...hope.

"What's wrong?" Tora asked, looking suddenly concerned.

"You smiled."

"Do I have something in my teeth?"

Aspen shook her head, sad to see the smile falter. "No."

"Then what?"

She stepped over, leaned against the table beside Tora, and playfully bumped shoulders. "You're starting to like me."

"No offense, but that's just not possible."

"I'm very likeable, so it is possible. I'm growing on you. I can tell."

"I certainly don't want to give you the wrong impression, Aspen. From now on, I won't make the mistake of smiling when you're around."

"I'm pretty funny, so that'll be difficult."

Tora frowned. "I'll manage."

It didn't escape Aspen's attention that Tora hadn't moved away. Their shoulders were still touching. She felt the doctor's guard coming down. One baby toe was now inside Tora's impenetrable fortress. "So. What now, Coach?"

Tora checked her watch. "Let's head back to—"

A woman in scrubs burst through the conference room door. Her nametag identified her as the charge nurse. "We have seven more expectant moms out here," she said, out of breath. "They're all asking to have labor induced so their babies can be blessed." She turned her eyes to Aspen. "Sorry, word travels at warp speed around here."

Tora sighed and regarded Aspen for a long moment. "Actually, it's not a bad idea. They're all my patients and due any day now.

Shroud births are typically fast. If we piggybacked induction one at a time, you could potentially go from one blessing to the next. What do you think?"

Aspen considered the idea, intrigued by the possibility of bringing new Myriads into the world. This would explain why she'd felt the urge to do more after blessing the fawn. She dug into the vault deep inside and was amazed to discover she already felt a connection to these unborn Shrouds. It was almost as if they had sensed her presence months ago from afar and were now excited to finally meet her.

For a moment, she struggled with questioning her own sanity. But she shrugged it off, deciding to take Oscar's earlier advice and just go with the flow. She trusted Tora would do everything in her power to ensure the newborns were delivered safely. "Sure, why not?" she said finally.

Tora turned to the charge nurse. "We'll need all the off-duty nurses and doctors to report in."

"And chocolate," Aspen added. "Lots of chocolate."

"Ten-four. Nurses, doctors, and chocolate," the nurse replied with a grin. "I'll make it happen." She turned and ducked out in a hurry.

Tora yawned and rubbed her temples. "This will be a long day for both of us."

"When was the last time you slept?" Aspen realized then that Tora probably hadn't slept at all last night. How could she? She was too busy prepping an entire wardrobe for her and Skye, and doing whatever else sanctuary leaders do in the middle of the night when faced with planning for every contingency.

"I don't remember," Tora admitted. "I'll sleep after these babies are born." She turned to Aspen. "Sorry I didn't let you sleep in a little longer this morning."

"An apology?" Aspen set the back of her hand against Tora's forehead to check for a fever. "That's another sign."

"Of what?"

"Your fondness for me."

Tora swatted Aspen's hand away, stood, and stretched. "Chalk it up to delirium from lack of sleep. No more smiles or apologies from this moment forward."

"We'll see about that."

"Yes, we will," Tora said, a ghost of a smile tugging at the corners of her mouth. She caught herself and looked away. "Be sure to let me know if there comes a point when these blessings get to be too much for you. Since I don't understand how a blessing works physiologically, there's no way for me to predict how much of a toll this will take on your body."

Aspen intuitively knew she'd be fine. Tired maybe, but none the worse for wear. "The chocolate should help. Just hope there's enough."

Tora walked out of the conference room and headed to the nurses' station. As soon as she was out of Aspen's sight, she let her smile break free. There was no denying Aspen was funny. What Tora had seen as a liability just twelve hours ago might turn out to be Aspen's greatest asset. The cruelty with which humans operated was bound to reach Aspen, one way or another. A sense of humor would help her cope with the inevitable losses along the way.

Tora tried to remember the last time she'd smiled, laughed, or played. Admittedly, it had been a while. She'd been so busy with her duties here and her job at the hospital that she'd forgotten how to be in the moment and have fun. She hadn't even noticed anything was missing from her life...until Aspen showed up.

Suddenly unable to catch her breath, she ducked into an empty room, shut the door, and leaned against it. Was she starting to feel a connection with Aspen? Worse, was she feeling the first stirrings of *attraction*? She squeezed her eyes shut and willed whatever she was feeling to stop. There wasn't room in her life for self-indulgence of any kind. Too much was at stake. Feelings would only distract her from her responsibilities and compromise her judgment, which could lead to careless mistakes. Her people would be the ones paying the price for those mistakes.

She opened her eyes, stood up straight, and took a deep breath. It boiled down to a simple case of mind over matter. Impervious to the effects of Aspen's wit and charm, she would fortify her walls and keep them in place for the good of her people.

Chapter Thirteen

Munching on a king-size Butterfinger, Aspen waited alone in the conference room while the nurses, Tora, and three other doctors tended to the expectant moms. Restless, she peeked out into the deserted corridor and looked back longingly at the swivel chair behind her. Unable to fight the urge any longer, she took a seat and sped backward down the corridor as a freckled, auburn-haired boy was rounding the corner. She spun around, reached out, and caught him, pulling him safely into her lap as she braked with her feet. "You okay?"

He climbed down and turned to face her. "You're the Myriad!"

"Aspen."

"I'm Jacob. I'm nine. My dad's at the surface, so my mom had to bring me here. She's having a baby today."

"Congratulations. You'll be a big brother soon."

"We don't know if it's a boy or a girl yet. Mom wanted it to be a surprise. Hey, I heard you were a panther. That's cool. We don't have any panthers here." He held out his hand. "Can I see your eyes?"

Aspen smiled, realizing her privacy was now a thing of the past. "Sure." She barely registered the fluffy red fox standing before her as Jacob's small hand grasped hers. Without warning, the vault door deep inside swung wide open.

Something was terribly wrong. There were seven newborns getting ready to come into the world, but only six would make it. The seventh—Jacob's baby sister—was going to die.

For reasons unknown to Aspen, it was critical that all of the newborns survive. Of that she was sure.

But the infant was in distress. Aspen felt her telepathically reaching out for help. That's when she realized these newborns were already a part of her. She was aware of them, and they of her. Like a bolt of lightning, the realization knocked the breath out of her. It left her trembling, dizzy, and sweating.

She released the boy's hand, willing herself to put the panic aside and focus. She knew exactly what she needed to do. "Where's your mom?"

Jacob pointed to a room around the corner. "Room three."

Aspen sprinted down the corridor and stepped inside the medical supply closet. She moved the panel aside and entered *chocolate*. The wall slid open, revealing the same green trolley she and Tora had used to get here. She climbed inside as the tunnel torches lit up. Relieved to find a keyless ignition switch, she put the trolley in drive and headed toward chamber one.

The infant reached out again with a telepathic cry for help. It was a strange sensation, like an SOS call that dialed straight into Aspen's brain, making the adrenaline course through her body. "Don't worry, honey. I hear you. I'm bringing someone who can help," she said aloud as she raced through the tunnels at top speed. All she could think about was getting to Skye.

The internal vault spewed forth words, images, and flashes of future events faster than her mind could comprehend. This newborn would be the smallest of the group, but she would have the biggest heart. Her parents had already chosen her name—Hope. The other newborns needed her. She would be quiet and wise beyond her years, her inherent goodness a beacon from which the others would draw strength. She would be the foundation for this group. Without her, Aspen knew they would not be complete.

She braked to a stop, hopped out, and started searching for the hidden panel. The rock wall was seamless. Everything looked uniform and so well camouflaged that it took her precious minutes to locate the damn thing. She punched in the code, stepped inside her bedroom closet, and threw open the door, coming to an abrupt stop. There, perched on the edge of her unmade bed, was Skye.

Barefoot and sleepy-eyed, Skye was wearing red-and-white-striped pajamas that made her look like a human-sized candy cane. Her short white hair was pointing in all different directions. She rubbed her eyes and smiled. "So, you're finally out of the closet?"

"Been there, done that. How'd you get in here?"

"Passcode was easy. You should've come up with something harder."

"You can thank Tora for that." Aspen set her hands on her hips, trying to think of a way to explain all this. "Listen, I know this is going to sound crazy—"

"I already know." Skye stepped toward the closet. "The baby woke me up and told me you were coming. She's really scared. We should go to her," she said, already searching inside the closet for the hidden door.

Aspen stood there, stunned.

"Like, now." Skye leaned out, grabbed the back of her shirt, and pulled her inside.

They exited from the closet and climbed into the trolley. Aspen put the trolley in drive and floored it. "Has that ever happened to you before?"

"Do you mean, has an unborn baby ever woken me up from a deep sleep and communicated with me?" She looked over at Aspen like she was crazy.

"When you put it like that, I'm guessing no."

"This baby is really special," Skye said, suddenly serious. "The world needs her."

Aspen couldn't help but think Skye was really special, too.

"What if I can't do it again?" Skye asked. "What if bringing Oscar back was just a one-time thing?" She brought both hands to the sides of her face. "Oh. My. God. What if I'm like a battery that needs time to recharge?"

Aspen eased slightly off the gas as they rounded a sharp curve. "We can run ourselves in circles with the what-ifs if we think about this stuff too much. I find it helps if I don't think and just—"

"Follow your instincts," Skye finished for her, rubbing the phoenix pendant around her neck between thumb and forefinger.

The tunnel lights flickered. Aspen felt the infant growing weaker. She was dying.

"Hurry, Aspen. I can't hear her anymore."

With a sense of dread greater than any she had known before, she pushed the gas pedal all the way to the floor and accelerated through the tunnels as fast as the trolley would allow.

❖

Aspen held the closet door ajar as Skye rushed into the hospital corridor. "The baby's in room—"

"I know," Skye said, pushing past her to room three.

By the time Aspen got there, Skye was already lifting the dead baby from the hospital bassinet. Her skin had a bluish tinge. She looked like a very petite and beautiful doll. Supporting her head as she carried her to the bed, Skye carefully laid the infant beside her motionless mother.

Aspen's heart broke as she realized both mother and baby had died. The mother's blue johnny was saturated with blood. It had turned the white sheets on the bed a dark crimson. A crash cart stood nearby. Blood-soaked towels, spare IV tubing, discarded syringe caps, and oxygen masks littered the floor, bed, and hospital bassinet—evidence that lifesaving measures had been taken. Two nurses paused in their efforts to collect the equipment, their eyes on Skye.

Aspen looked over at Tora. She was standing to the side of the bed with tears on her cheeks and defibrillator paddles in each hand. Smears of blood covered the front of Tora's blue hospital scrubs. Aspen stepped over, withdrew the paddles from her hands, and replaced them on the crash cart. "It's okay," she whispered. She took Tora's hand and held it.

Skye's arms shifted into the huge white wings of an owl. Head bowed, she draped her wings around mother and child as her feathers emitted a radiant light. Aspen watched in wonder as the light slowly spread through the rest of Skye's body until she resembled a human glow stick.

No one in the room moved as seconds stretched into long minutes. Aspen was trying to remember if it had taken this long with Oscar. Was something wrong? Were they too late? She closed her eyes and reached out to the baby in her mind. *You're supposed to be here with us, Hope. It's time to come back.*

She felt the familiar pull of the baby on her consciousness— like an infant affectionately tugging on a parent's finger. Aspen opened her eyes. A translucent ball of white light had formed around Skye, enveloping the bed with mother and child. She felt irresistibly drawn to the light. Something told her to step inside, so she did.

Images of Hope's future spread through her mind like fire. Her first word…her first steps…the first time she shifted into her primary animal—a white tiger with golden eyes, her black stripes prominent against a snow-white coat. Hope's innate wisdom and desire to do good were as much a part of her as her physical characteristics. She was powerful beyond measure and would teach the others how to harness their powers, as well. Hope would grow and mature quickly as a Myriad, always with Skye at her side. The two would be inseparable.

Skye's wing brushed against Aspen's shoulder, interrupting the steady stream of information. A comforting warmth instantly coursed through her body. On the heels of Hope's future came bits and pieces of Skye's past: her parents singing happy birthday with a Sesame Street cake…sitting atop her dad's shoulders as they walked along the beach…riding her bike without training wheels for the first time…letting go of her mother's hand to climb on the bus for the first day of school…her parents cheering from the sidelines as she scored the winning goal in soccer.

Aspen braced herself. She knew what was coming next. The images were like a faucet she could turn off at will, but she owed it to Skye to keep going.

She watched as Skye's parents were gunned down inside their home, felt Skye take flight for the first time, ripe with despair over her parents' murder. She saw the faces of human cops who failed her by refusing to investigate, the homeless guy getting a solid kick to the groin with the same red high-tops he was trying to steal. She felt cold on the streets as Skye was getting ready to sleep...saw the dismissive shrugs of passing humans who knew she was homeless but didn't want to stop and help a Shroud. Lastly, she glanced over her shoulder as Skye was getting ready to jump and saw herself on top of the building, Snickers in hand...watched the syrup dripping from her own chin across the table at IHOP...felt the comfort of the pendant between Skye's fingers...felt the comfort of a hug from Oscar when Skye showed up at his door in tears.

Through it all, the thing that struck Aspen the most was how Skye had managed to hold on to her humanity, kindness, compassion, and inherent goodness. Skye and Hope were truly made for each other. They'd make an unstoppable team.

The baby kicked her legs on the bed and let out a soft whimper. Her skin was now a healthy shade of pink. Aspen sensed it was time to do the blessing. She knelt beside the bed, held Hope's tiny hands, and exhaled. The same particles of blue light appeared in her breath. Except this time, the particles instantly multiplied and encircled them in a fury of activity with an audible *whoosh*. The air felt electrified. Loose strands of Aspen's hair waved wildly in the resultant wind and tickled her neck.

The sense of power she felt in that moment was immense and intoxicating, but she knew it wasn't hers to keep. So she let it go. She opened her mind, body, and spirit to let Hope take everything she required for her journey. Aspen trusted this young soul would take only what was needed. She closed her eyes and waited patiently as Hope sifted through her being, gently and respectfully gathering her arsenal for the long road ahead.

She felt the blessing drawing to a close. The wind dissipated, and the blue light faded. Finished, she heard the faint echo of Hope's voice in her mind. *Thank you, Aspen.*

Aspen stood and stepped aside as Tora wrapped the infant in a blanket and lifted her from the bed. "You did it," Tora said, looking at Skye. "You saved her."

"But I didn't save her mom." Crying, Skye reached out and took the dead mother's hand to caress it gently. "I tried so hard, but she wouldn't come back. She said this baby belongs with us. She named her Hope." She released the mother's hand and looked to Aspen. "She and Hope said good-bye to each other. I saw everything. It was beautiful."

Aspen didn't know what to say. It was all so overwhelming. Where were a candy bar and a clever quip when you needed them? "You did great, kiddo." She took Skye in her arms and gave her a long hug.

"I think someone wants to meet you," Tora said behind them. Aspen turned and saw the baby had broken free from the blanket burrito. She was reaching her arms out to Skye.

Skye wiped her tears and reached back as Tora handed over the wriggling infant. She settled at once in Skye's arms. "Hi, Hope. It's nice to finally meet you." She glanced up at Tora. "She's so small."

"Six pounds, five ounces," Tora said.

One of the nurses wheeled the bassinet over and gave Tora a nod. "I'll take her to the nursery." An electrifying *zap* rang through the air as she leaned in to take the baby from Skye. "Whoa," the nurse said, drawing back.

"What's wrong?" Tora asked.

"I got zapped. Felt like an electric shock."

Tora didn't hesitate as she stepped forward and lifted the baby from Skye's arms. Setting her in the bassinet, she pulled the blanket aside, did a cursory exam, and placed a diaper on the tiny bum like a pro. "Here," she said, handing her to the nurse. Another zap singed the air as the nurse made contact with the baby. "Ouch! That one hurt!"

"Maybe she's part electric eel," Aspen said jokingly.

Nobody laughed.

She stepped in. "Give her to me." The baby reached up, and Aspen gathered her in her arms. Hope smelled heavenly. She had never held a baby so small and new. Life was truly miraculous. "Maybe she doesn't like you."

The nurse crossed her arms. "All babies like me."

"It's not that," Skye said. "I think she only wants us—the three of us. And Oscar, too."

"What makes you think that?" Tora asked.

"I don't know." Skye shrugged. "It's just a gut feeling."

Tora stared at the baby in disbelief. "But she's never even met Oscar."

"She knows Aspen trusts him," Skye said. "So she trusts him, too."

"But she's just a baby," the nurse said. "How could she possibly know all that?"

Aspen looked down at the adorable bundle in her arms and felt a sudden urge to have a baby of her own someday. "She's not just a baby. She's a Myriad. And she's very special."

Tora turned to the nurse. "Make sure you tell everyone not to touch this baby. Her father's returning from the surface tomorrow. Aspen and Skye are in charge of her care until I finish with the other deliveries."

Skye tenderly tucked a loose corner of the blanket under Hope's tiny chin. "When Hope and her mom were saying good-bye, her mom told me Hope's dad died last night, but no one here knows that yet. Hope and her brother, Jacob, they're orphans now. Her mom showed me a picture of Jacob with a family who had another son his age. The other boy had a scar under his eye."

"Oh my God. That's Dillan." Tora covered her mouth with both hands. "He's Jacob's best friend."

"Hope's mom said she wants Jacob to be with Dillan and his parents."

"They're Jacob's godparents," Tora said. "Hope and Jacob's father…he's dead?" She stared at Skye. "Are you sure?"

Skye nodded. "The SEA found him and killed him last night."

Tora turned to Aspen. "Caring for a baby is a full-time job. How will we find time for your training?"

"I'll take care of her," Skye volunteered. "She wants to be with me the most. I can feel it."

Tora frowned. "A brand new baby is more work than you could ever imagine. Two *adult* parents struggle to meet all the demands of a newborn. I could never ask you to do that, Skye. You're only thirteen."

"You don't have to ask me. I want to do it."

Tora hesitated.

"I'll take really good care of her. I promise," Skye pleaded.

"You're hired." Aspen kissed the baby on the forehead before placing her in Skye's capable arms.

"Hold on," Tora cautioned. "We can't just hand over a newborn baby to a thirteen-year-old girl. In case you've forgotten, this baby also happens to be one of only three Myriads in existence right now."

Aspen locked eyes with Skye. "There's no one I'd trust more with Hope. They're supposed to be together." She turned to Tora. "Trust me on this."

The lion doctor shook her head, unconvinced.

"Is there a room in chamber one big enough for me, Hope, and Oscar? Maybe we can all stay together while the two of you train." Skye looked down at the baby. "I think that would make her feel safe."

Aspen raised a hopeful eyebrow in Tora's direction. "Oscar loves babies," she added to sweeten the deal. "Hope will have him wrapped around her chubby little finger in no time."

"Fine." Tora sighed. "There's an adjoining room in chamber one with ample space for the three of you. I'll make arrangements to have everything the baby needs brought over."

Skye smiled as the baby reached up to touch her face. "Hear that, Hope? We can stay together."

Tora watched the two of them with a smile of her own. "I know you and Oscar will take good care of her," she said, setting a hand on Skye's shoulder. "I'll have someone drive you back to—"

"I'll drive them." Aspen didn't trust anyone else. She wasn't taking no for an answer.

Apparently sensing her conviction on the matter, Tora accepted the terms without protest. "Hurry back," she said, checking her watch. "There are still six other pending arrivals waiting to be blessed."

CHAPTER FOURTEEN

Aspen led Skye into the hospital corridor. They were retracing their steps to the medical supply closet when Skye halted and looked ahead. "What's up?" she asked, following Skye's gaze.

"I feel Jacob nearby."

"Hope's brother?"

Skye nodded.

At that very moment, Jacob came skipping around the corner and stopped short. His eyes grew wide when he saw the baby in Skye's arms.

Aspen's heart broke for the boy. She didn't think it was her place to tell him about his mother, about both of his parents. But how could she possibly leave Jacob behind without telling him and ride off into the sunset with his newborn baby sister?

He stepped forward and peered down at the blanketed bundle in Skye's arms.

Aspen swallowed the lump in her throat. "Jacob, meet Hope."

"I have a baby sister?" he asked with a grin. Before she thought to warn him against physical contact, he reached out to caress his sister's cheek.

Hope grasped his pinkie finger. Her baby blue eyes took on a beautiful golden hue. A soft light spilled from her small hands, setting Jacob's arm aglow before spreading through the rest of his body.

Aspen watched as Jacob closed his eyes and silently began to cry. After several minutes, he opened them and met Aspen's gaze. "It's okay. Hope just took me to see my mom and dad…one more time," he said with a quivering chin. "I got to say good-bye to them. I'll be staying with Dillan and his folks now." Jacob paused, and Aspen could see he was trying his hardest to be brave. "My mom said it has to be this way for the good of our people."

"I'm so sorry, Jacob." Aspen didn't know what else to say as the boy kissed his sister on the cheek and turned to walk back the way he had come.

Tora moved on to the next delivery, her heart still heavy from losing Hope's mother. Harmony had entrusted Tora with her life, and she had failed her, plain and simple. She'd hemorrhaged immediately after giving birth, just like countless Shrouds before her. Despite exhaustive research, Tora still hadn't found a way to stop this from happening.

With great effort, she set the loss aside. She'd return to Harmony's body later to hold her hand and mourn, just like she'd done with every Shroud patient she'd lost over the years. Now wasn't the time to indulge in her own grief. She had six other babies to deliver and six other moms to keep a close eye on.

Every Shroud she'd ever met possessed an intuitive understanding of the greater good within the Shroud community. Even though they knew their chances of survival were fifty-fifty at best, every female Shroud who was capable of reproducing eagerly jumped at the chance to bring new life into the world.

All Shrouds felt the immense weight of responsibility to do their part to increase the Shroud population. At the rate humans were killing them off, extinction of their species was inevitable. All Shrouds were aware of the need for a Myriad. Their only hope for survival as a species was to bring a new Myriad into the world by giving birth to one.

Shrouds were selfless creatures. Tora couldn't say the same for humans. Deep down, she loathed humans—a prejudice she was keenly aware of that she constantly fought to keep under control. All of the humans she knew were self-centered, narrow-minded, ego-driven, and consumed with finding the quickest and easiest route to self-gratification. Humans could learn a thing or two from Shrouds. She had always believed the world would be a much better place if humans were more like Shrouds.

Her thoughts returned to Aspen as she prepped for an all-day marathon of deliveries. She froze as the memory of Aspen reaching over to hold her hand returned. Still reeling from Harmony's death, Tora hadn't resisted. At all. She should have pulled away, made it known in no uncertain terms that she was off limits.

She shook her head, chastising herself. Hadn't she just vowed to maintain a professional distance from Aspen for the good of her people? She searched for reasons to explain her sudden lack of self-control. Self-discipline had never been a problem in the past. Once she made up her mind to do something, she did it. No exceptions. Unwavering focus and the determination to see tasks through to completion had always come easy to her. Why should this be any different?

She did a quick internal check. Physical and mental exhaustion. That explained it. Her resolve to keep Aspen at arm's length was compromised by lack of sleep. After this was over and all the babies were safely delivered, she would make it a point to get some rest. With sufficient sleep, she'd be back to herself and better equipped to resist any temptations that came her way. In fact, she'd probably find Aspen just as irritating as when they'd first met.

Back in chamber one, Aspen lifted Hope from Skye's arms and made her way to the kitchen where everyone had gathered for breakfast. All fifteen Shrouds were seated around a mammoth bench table with enough food to feed a small army—which was kind of what they were, Aspen reminded herself.

Oscar was at the head of the table with Miller on his right—he was literally and figuratively Oscar's right-hand man. Beckett,

Johnston, and the other five pack members were seated in a row after Miller. To Oscar's left sat Helga, Mrs. B, Liam, Hank, Tony, and Pierre. Everyone was engaged in conversation. No one seemed to notice as she and Skye approached. Aspen looked around and smiled to herself. It felt good to see everyone gathered around the table like family.

Her stomach growled at the tantalizing aromas. Chocolate chip pancakes, cinnamon buns, bagels, hash browns, scrambled eggs, oatmeal, fresh fruit. She practically drooled when she spotted the crepes near the edge of the table. Their close proximity made it difficult to focus.

"Can I have everyone's attention?" she said as the conversation ebbed to an awkward silence. Forks paused in midair. All eyes shifted to her. She leaned over and whispered to Pierre, "Are those your famous chocolate-strawberry crepes?"

Pierre nodded with a wink and a half smile that made his handlebar moustache tilt to one side.

"Focus, Aspen," Skye whispered beside her.

She straightened and cleared her throat. "Everyone, I'd like to introduce you to our newest Myriad, Hope."

Murmurs of excitement coursed through the room like adrenaline. Oscar shot up from the table at the other end and made a beeline for Hope. He was drawn to the baby like a magnet. She'd seen it happen countless times throughout her life. Without fail, Oscar would drop whatever he was doing just to have the chance to *look* at a baby. If he was lucky enough to catch a toothless smile or a coo, he'd be all sunshine and rainbows for a week.

Hope wriggled in her arms as Oscar approached. "Another Myriad," he said in wonder, peering down with the goofy grin he reserved for anything cute. "She's gorgeous. Who does she belong to?"

"Me," Aspen replied.

"Very funny."

"Not kidding."

"I thought we had this talk already. No boys." He frowned. "You pinkie swore."

"That hasn't changed—"

"Then how'd this happen? I didn't even know you were pregnant."

"I wasn't."

Oscar looked from Aspen to Skye. His eyes grew wide.

Skye took a step back. "Don't look at me. I don't like boys, either."

Aspen made a mental note to ask Skye about that later. "Hope's mom and dad are both dead," she said sadly.

"Oh." Oscar let out his breath. "For a minute there, I was ready to make another hasty departure with a heart attack."

"Glad you didn't." Aspen transferred the baby to Oscar. "She needs you."

He accepted the tiny Myriad, supporting her head like a pro. Hope looked even smaller and more vulnerable in Oscar's muscular arms.

Hank came up alongside them and slapped Oscar on the back. "Sounds like congratulations are in order. Welcome to the family, little one." He reached out for Hope's hand and jumped back in surprise as the sound of a live wire sizzled in the air. "Ouch," he yelled, massaging his hand in earnest.

"Thanks for the reminder, Hank." She turned to Oscar. "I should also mention she won't let anyone but you, me, Skye, and Tora near her."

"You could've led with that," Hank said, still rubbing his hand.

"I still have six other newborns to bless. They're due any time now." Aspen glanced at her watch. "I need to head back."

Twelve hours and six blessings later, Aspen and Tora shuffled out of the closet like two old ladies. They collapsed on Aspen's bed, side by side.

Aspen lay there, exhausted and unable to move. Six additional Myriads were born healthy—all girls. Unfortunately, four out of eight moms hadn't made it. Even though Tora had explained that the Shroud maternal mortality rate was high, Aspen could hardly believe it. In today's day and age, those odds were staggering. But she reminded herself that these were Shroud mothers, not human.

"Do I still have feet?" Tora asked.

Lifting her upper body with Herculean effort, Aspen balanced on her elbows and glanced down. "I think that's what they're called," she said, delirious from exhaustion. "Those are the things at the end of your legs?"

"Yeah. Those. I can't feel them anymore. Good to know they're still attached."

Aspen sank back down to the bed and kicked her sneakers to the floor. "So you *do* have a sense of humor."

"I wasn't being funny. When you're a Shroud and you're this tired, sometimes body parts can shift on their own."

Suddenly feeling wide awake, Aspen imagined herself in human form with furry black paws in place of both feet. "How often has that happened to you?" she asked, not knowing if she wanted to hear the answer.

"Never." Tora grinned as their eyes met. "I'm kidding."

"And the sense of humor finally pokes its shriveled-up self out of the dark hole it's been hiding in."

"I had you there for a minute, didn't I?"

"Not a full minute. A few microseconds, maybe."

Tora sighed. "We should practice melding."

"You want to do the naked thing? Now?" Too tired to lift her arm and check her watch, she glanced at the clock on the nightstand. "It's ten fifteen at night. We're both totally wiped."

Tora sat up and removed her sneakers, setting them neatly on the floor beside the bed. "Believe me, there's nothing I want more than sleep right now. But these are ideal conditions for melding. Chances of successfully shapeshifting during a melding session increase substantially when you're this tired." She yawned. "Physical and mental exhaustion push you closer to your animal instincts."

"My animal instincts are pushing me toward eight hours of hibernation."

Clad in blue scrubs, Tora stood from the bed and loosened the knot at her waist. "It won't be as bad as you think. Once you shapeshift for the first time, you'll forget all about these melding sessions." She slid her pants down long legs.

"Sessions? As in"—Aspen stood and unbuttoned her jeans—"more than one?"

Tora nodded, slipping out of her shirt. "We'll continue these sessions nightly until you feel confident in your shapeshifting abilities."

Before Aspen knew it, Tora was facing her in nothing but a sports bra and underwear. With a deep breath, she told herself it wouldn't be weird. She wanted desperately to shapeshift. This was nothing more than a quick stop on the road to getting there. *Just ignore the weirdness of getting naked with this beautiful doctor. Focus on learning how to shift.*

Tora reached over and grabbed a hunter-green throw from the end of the bed. Unfolding it, she shook it out flat to cover the floor. "Once we remove the last of our clothing, you'll lie down first. I'll lie on top of you. We'll take several deep breaths together, and you'll mirror my breathing. When our hearts start beating in sync, you'll hold on to my body as tight as you can while I shapeshift. I'll try to slow it down as much as possible to let you feel my body as it's changing. We'll repeat this process several times. Any questions before we start?"

Tora's gaze was forthright and strong. No games. No hidden agenda. Not even a hint of self-consciousness. Impressed with the leader standing before her, Aspen hesitated. Getting naked with another woman had never been an issue. But as soon as she removed her shirt, Tora would see the scars on her stomach from her suicide attempt eighteen years ago. Whenever someone asked about them, Aspen always handled it with a made-up story about emergency surgery for something or other. All the women she'd dated over the years had taken her at her word. No one ever pushed for the details, and she'd never once felt guilty for lying to them. But today with Tora felt different. Aspen was surprised to realize she didn't want to lie to her.

"Something's wrong. What is it?" Tora asked, looking suddenly concerned.

"I have scars." Aspen met her gaze. "You'll see them when I undress. I always lie about how I got them." She pulled her shirt and sports bra over her head.

Tora glanced down to look at Aspen's stomach before resuming eye contact. "What happened?"

"When I was twelve, I tried to kill myself."

Tora sighed, looking concerned. "Things had to have been pretty awful for a twelve-year-old to do that to herself."

"They were. But Oscar saved me. That's how we met."

"And that's how Skye met you. She was going to jump from the building to commit suicide, wasn't she?"

Aspen nodded. Separated by just a few feet, she locked eyes with Tora. They held gazes for long seconds.

"Are we sharing a moment?" Aspen set her hands on her hips. "I'm only asking because standing here half-naked makes sharing this moment with you a little awkward."

"Oh, right." Tora looked down at herself. "Best to be mutually naked when a moment is shared." Quickly shedding her undergarments, she folded them, set them neatly on the bed, and turned to face Aspen. "There. Better?"

"Much. But I'm not going to say you're beautiful because that would just make this weirder than it already is." Aspen slipped out of her underwear and tossed it on the floor.

"And I won't say it back to you because I'm not in the habit of complimenting somebody I don't like." Tora knelt on the blanket and patted the floor. "Come on."

CHAPTER FIFTEEN

As Aspen eased her body down to the blanket, Tora instructed her to close her eyes and imagine what it would feel like to be inside the body of a panther. "We're going to do some guided imagery," she said, her voice like silk. "Your human body is just a mask. Beneath that mask lies a panther. Your black fur coat is sleek, shiny, and soft to the touch. You're a top predator. With that comes strength, cunning, and confidence. Your teeth and claws are formidable weapons. Your sense of hearing is extraordinary, picking up the slightest rustle in the trees above or a whispered conversation on the ground hundreds of yards away. Even in darkness, your eyes hone in on the tiniest detail because your eyesight has evolved to match your nighttime predatory instincts. This is who you are—who you were born to be. You're a panther."

Tora had moved into position directly above her. Aspen kept her eyes closed. She could feel the heat from Tora's body, now just inches from her own.

Tora whispered in her ear, "Breathe with me, Aspen. Listen to my breaths, and stay with them."

Aspen blocked out all other thoughts as she listened to Tora's steady breathing. Goose bumps traveled the length of her body when she felt their hearts begin to synchronize in rhythm. As Tora lowered herself and their bodies connected, Aspen had a vision that shook her to the core.

She and Tora were in a birthing room. This time, however, Tora was the patient. Round and pregnant, she was in active labor and pushing with all her might. Aspen was at Tora's bedside, holding her hand. Showing an unfathomable level of self-control, Tora remained in human form the entire time.

Aspen looked down at their intertwined hands and saw they were both wearing wedding bands. She suddenly realized they were married. Tora was giving birth to their first child—a girl. They had already chosen Dawn as her name. Born a Myriad, there was no need for Aspen to do a blessing. Like her beautiful mother, their daughter's primary animal would be a lioness.

The doctor placed the infant in Aspen's arms as he cut the umbilical cord. Her exhilaration in that moment was soon replaced with dread as the machines attached to Tora began sounding their alarms. A nurse stepped over, shouldering Aspen aside. "She's losing blood. We need to transfuse her. Tora? Stay with us."

And just like that, the love of her life was gone. Aspen was left to raise their daughter alone.

"Keep your eyes closed." The sound of Tora's voice jolted her from the vision. "Hold on tight."

Aspen felt Tora's body growing longer, heavier, and bulkier. Tora's feminine curves shifted into muscular shoulders. Their hearts still beating in rhythm, she was aware that Tora's head and jaw were taking on a more predatory shape. Despite the fact that her eyes were still closed, she watched as Tora's cells morphed within her body, seamlessly coordinating their structure into those of a lioness.

She was so tuned in to Tora that she pushed aside the sound of buzzing in her own ears. A nuisance at first, she was able to ignore it and focus on Tora. But the buzzing soon grew in volume, pulsing through her body like a thousand bees. Before she had time to think about it, her own body began to change.

Aspen felt powerless to stop it. It was like rolling downhill in a car without brakes. Part of her was afraid. Realizing she wasn't the one in the driver's seat of her own body, she felt truly out of control for the first time in her life. Once the initial panic subsided, she was surprised to discover that a part of her longed to surrender completely. So she did.

As her body finished shifting, she rolled over, sprang to her feet, and faced Tora. She felt powerful, fierce, deadly. She flashed back to carrying her weapon in full police uniform for the first time on the streets. That feeling of empowerment paled in comparison to what she was experiencing now. But she wasn't as comfortable in this form as she thought she'd be. Felt like she was wearing shoes that were just a little too big.

Tora immediately shifted back to human form. "Well done!" she said with a grin. "I didn't expect you to shift on the first try. Returning to human form is a lot easier. I'll walk you through it, but you should take a look at yourself first." She opened the closet to reveal a full-length mirror on the inside of the door.

Aspen stepped closer to the mirror, exhilarated as each of her paws made contact with the floor. Expecting the reflection of a panther, what she saw in the mirror startled her. There, staring back at her, was a large and ferocious-looking lioness. Confused, she looked up at Tora in question.

"You're probably wondering why you shifted into a lioness instead of a panther. I don't know the answer to that yet—I'll have to look it up in the library—but I suspect it's because you're a Myriad. As a Myriad, you can take the shape of any animal. I'm guessing you assumed mine because you were focused on me. You were probably just following my lead." She knelt beside Aspen. "But you do make a beautiful lioness," she added, studying her. "Your eyes are set farther apart than mine, your fur is a darker shade of blond, and you're a little longer and taller than me." She lifted one of Aspen's paws to examine it more closely. "Your paws are also slightly larger and more squared-off than mine. Like humans, no two Shrouds are identical when they shift." She let Aspen's paw fall back to the floor and returned her gaze to the mirror. "Ready to shift back?"

With one last look at herself as a lioness, Aspen nodded.

"It's easiest to shift when you're in motion. Just walk forward, take a deep breath, and remember what it feels like to walk on your feet in your human body. The rest of your body will follow suit." Tora stood. "Go ahead. Give it a try."

Aspen did as Tora instructed and realized immediately that something had gone awry. Instead of shifting back to human form, she now had wings. She turned around to look at herself in the mirror and caught her own reflection as a snow-white owl.

Tora came up alongside her. They both stared at her image in the mirror. "Amazing. Were you trying to shift into an owl?"

Aspen shook her head and extended a wing to examine it. Strangely enough, her instincts were telling her to stay on the ground. She *still* hated heights, even in this form.

"Well, you also make a convincing and very beautiful owl," Tora said, standing. "Try shifting back to human form. Remember what I told you?"

Turning, Aspen ambled away awkwardly on owl feet. This form was even less comfortable than a lioness. She focused and immediately felt her body begin to change. She knew she was a wolf before she even looked in the mirror—a wolf as black as the darkest shadow, just like Oscar. Bewildered, she turned to face Tora.

Once again, Tora knelt beside her as they both studied her image in the mirror. "Were you trying for a wolf?" she asked.

Aspen shook her head, a little concerned.

"It seems you're shifting into the animals you've seen in the order you've seen them: a lioness, an owl, and now a wolf. Maybe this is typical shifting behavior for a Myriad," Tora suggested. "I read everything I could find on you in the library this morning. Since Myriads haven't existed for over a century, the information we have is pretty outdated. There are bound to be surprises along the way. I'm sure this is the first of many, but don't be discouraged." She stood. "Keep going. You're doing great."

Aspen shifted into a tiger, grizzly bear, and cheetah. On the heels of one animal came another. Her body had its own agenda, seemingly beyond her control. Each time she saw the reflection of yet another animal, she grew more concerned at the thought of not being able to return to her human body.

A gorilla, snow leopard, and rhinoceros followed. She felt her body going for the elephant next. Through sheer force of will, she braked it to a screeching stop because she knew the bedroom ceiling wasn't tall enough to accommodate such a large animal. A little disoriented by the raw power and massive size of an elephant, she felt herself shrinking into a tiny brown field mouse.

"Show-off," Tora said, peering down at her like a giant. "All that's left now is—"

Aspen felt herself growing in size and caught sight in the mirror of a large brown Cape buffalo with menacing horns.

"The buffalo," Tora finished.

She wasn't done yet. Her body rapidly assumed the shapes of an Irish wolfhound, an orangutan, and then a gorilla.

"Forgot about them," Tora said. "Well, I think that about covers it."

But there was one more Tora didn't know about. The chance encounter with Jacob in the hospital corridor accounted for the red fox she found herself now facing in the mirror. Feeling dizzy, Aspen wondered if she would manifest the primary animals of the newborns she had blessed but was relieved to feel the familiarity of her human body once again.

"Welcome back," Tora said. "How do you feel?"

"Like I could sleep for a week," she admitted, thankful to be walking on human feet. She sat on the edge of the bed and glanced down at her body. She was so tired she'd almost forgotten she was naked. "What about my panther?" she asked, too tired to grab the throw off the floor to cover herself. At least they were both naked.

"Did you try to shift into your panther?"

"I really didn't try for anything. It all sort of just…happened." She yawned. "Can I put some clothes on and go to bed now?"

"Not until you shift into your panther." Tora put her hands on her hips and locked her gaze on Aspen. "This is important, Aspen."

If she wasn't so damn tired, this moment would be comical— Tora standing there, hands on hips, stark naked. But she couldn't even muster enough energy to laugh. "Fine. Tell me what to do," she said, standing from the bed.

"Just do what I do. But instead of a lioness, envision yourself as who you really are inside: a black panther. Embrace your instincts, Aspen. Embrace who you are. *Feel* the details." Then, without another word, Tora dove headfirst toward the bed, effortlessly shifting into lioness form.

Aspen watched, mesmerized. It was a breathtaking display of grace, beauty, and magic. Tora landed on the bed with all four paws and turned to face her. Flicking her tail in agitation, she flattened her ears, snarled with menacingly sharp teeth, and swiped a paw—hard—at Aspen. She glanced down at her shoulder to find a trail of blood where Tora's claws had sliced her.

She brought a hand to her shoulder and held it to stanch the bleeding. "What the hell, Tora? That hurt!"

Tora leaped from the bed and stalked around her in a circle like a lioness toying with its prey before the kill, her amber-gold gaze perfectly mimicking a hungry and very dangerous predator.

Aspen imagined herself as a panther, but she remained in human form as Tora continued to circle her. "I'm trying to shift. It's not working."

The rock floor under her bare feet vibrated as Tora growled deeply. Another lightning-quick strike to Aspen's thigh drew more blood.

"Stop, Tora. This isn't funny anymore." Without taking her eyes from the lioness, she brought a hand to her thigh and felt the blood oozing between her fingers.

The lioness didn't back down. She appeared to be in true predatory mode. Had Tora's primal instincts taken over? "Tora?" She searched the lioness's eyes but saw nothing of Tora in them. "I said, *stop*."

The lioness reared up, set massive paws on Aspen's chest, and knocked her to the floor in the blink of an eye. Aspen soon found herself trapped beneath the lioness's muscular girth. She felt four-inch canines begin to puncture her delicate human skin as powerful jaws clamped around her throat.

Her instincts suddenly kicked in. She wasn't born to be prey. She, too, was a powerful predator. She felt her body changing so swiftly that she didn't have time to think about what it was changing into and was relieved to see that her hands had shifted into furry black paws with formidable-looking claws.

At once bursting with power and strength, she kicked at the lioness and flipped her onto her back. Before Aspen knew what had happened, she had the lioness pinned to the floor by the throat. The lioness froze, so she stopped just short of sinking her canines into the lioness's tender flesh. She gradually eased up and finally released her grip when the lioness made no move to challenge her. It was clear who won this battle.

The lioness righted herself and rose slowly on all fours. They circled one another warily in the center of the room. Aspen growled in warning, her head and tail held high. The lioness finally lowered hers in submission.

Aspen caught a glimpse of herself in the mirror. Her fur was shiny and sleek, her muscular physique clearly defined, but her eyes were the most startling. A piercing yellow against her black-as-night fur, they had an ethereal quality. This was the body that was truly hers. It surprised her to realize this panther body felt even more comfortable than her human body. Not too big, not too small. The perfect fit.

Tora came up alongside her, and they both gazed in the mirror. They were of equal height and build. The yin and yang of their coloring once again struck Aspen. Remembering the lacerations to her shoulder and thigh—courtesy of the lioness beside her—she gave Tora's cheek a long lick with her sandpaper tongue.

Tora shifted back to human form, a look of disgust on her face. She wiped her cheek with the back of one hand. "You *licked* me."

Aspen followed suit, shifting back into her human self with little effort. Shapeshifting was a lot more fun than she'd imagined. She doubted it would ever grow old. She glanced down at her body. The lacerations on her shoulder and thigh were still there. They hurt like hell. "Payback's a bitch. But for the record, I'd rather be licked than mutilated by those insanely sharp razor blades you call claws."

"You're a Shroud. You'll heal fast. Besides, that was for your own good. I had to do something to get you to shift into your panther."

"And I gave you *that* as a small token of my appreciation," Aspen said, pointing to Tora's cheek. "Since I'm the dominant female, I get to lick whoever I want."

"It's *whom*ever. And no, you are *not* the dominant female. I let you win that wrestling match."

"Did not."

"Did too."

Aspen gave her a playful bump on the shoulder. "Whatever you say." She stood and used the last of her energy to walk to the bed. "Can we get some sleep now?"

"As much as I enjoyed the show, we could both use a good night's rest."

For a moment, Aspen wasn't sure if Tora was flirting. Was that comment about her body or the endless stream of animals? It wasn't worth contemplating in her current state of mind because her judgment was undoubtedly impaired by sheer exhaustion. Unable to peel herself from the bed's soft mattress, she watched as Tora went to a duffel bag in the corner, unzipped it, and threw on blue-and-white-striped pajama bottoms and a white V-neck T-shirt. Aspen wanted to get dressed, too. But she didn't have the energy to move even a single pinkie toe.

Glancing over her shoulder at a still-naked Aspen, Tora slid open a dresser drawer. "Boxers or sweats?"

"Boxers."

"T-shirt or tank top."

"Tank."

Clothes in hand, Tora slid the drawer shut and joined her. "Here," she said, sliding the shirt over Aspen's head without hesitation. Aspen pushed her arms through as Tora knelt to place the boxers around her ankles.

She could barely stand as Tora pulled the boxers up for her. Longing to throw out a clever quip, she came up empty. She had never felt this tired before in her life.

Tora eased her back down to the bed and pulled the covers around her. "I'm staying with you here tonight. You've been through a lot today, and I want to make sure you're okay." She went to the closet, took out a sleeping bag, and unrolled it on the floor beside the bed.

"We can share the bed," Aspen protested.

"I'll be fine on the floor." Tora clicked off the lamp on the bedside table and climbed inside the sleeping bag. A night-light switched on automatically in the corner.

As exhausted as she was, Aspen would never be able to fall asleep knowing Tora was on the floor. The doctor needed a good night's sleep as much as she did. "A lot happened today," she admitted. "I'd feel better if you were up here beside me."

"Fine." Tora gathered the sleeping bag, walked around to the other side of the bed, and set it on top of the covers. "But we are *not* spooning." She climbed inside, and they were both quiet.

Aspen considered sharing the vision she'd had earlier but decided against it. Things were just starting to feel easy between them. Sharing something like that would only make things weird. Besides, she couldn't say with any certainly that it was even a vision of the future. Maybe what she saw was the result of an overtired mind after a long day of blessings.

Fading fast, she reached over and found Tora's hand. Tora responded to her touch as their fingers slowly entwined. Funny how much had changed between them in the last twenty-four hours. She nodded off, the feel of Tora's soft, warm skin reassuring against her own.

CHAPTER SIXTEEN

Tora watched Aspen as she slept, their hands still touching. Each time she tried to loosen her grip and pry her hand away, Aspen would tighten hers and inch closer. After the fifth attempt—with Aspen steadily invading her side of the bed, making an all-out snuggle imminent—Tora finally gave up. Sighing in defeat, she tightened her hand around Aspen's. That one simple gesture seemed to do the trick. Aspen finally settled in place, and the persistent inching ceased.

Was holding hands really a big deal? Tora decided it wasn't that bad in the big scheme of things, not if it provided Aspen with the comfort she so obviously needed right now. There were worse offenses. Like kissing. Kissing was most definitely off-limits. She assured herself their relationship would never get that far.

Above all else, Aspen needed Tora to be her mentor. She was committed to training Aspen to the very best of her ability. As a Myriad who knew little about the ways of their people, Aspen would have to devote herself entirely to learning and making up for lost time.

Tora had feared Aspen's first attempt to shift would be catastrophic, but her shapeshifting was spot-on. The features of each animal were exquisite, not carbon copies of the animals she'd seen. Aspen had woven her own colors and details into each animal like a gifted artist. First-time shifting was usually sloppy, unimpressive, even comical at times. Fledgling Shrouds needed time, practice, and experience to perfect the details of their primary animal. Aspen, however, had nailed each one her first time out of the gate. Was this typical for Myriads, or was Aspen just particularly adept at shifting? Tora had no way of knowing. She wished she could find more information on Myriads to better prepare them both. But they'd have to make do with what little they had for now.

Her mind was finally starting to quiet when she remembered the scars on Aspen's stomach. Aspen had chosen to tell her the truth about how they got there. That type of honesty took courage. Not privy to the details of Aspen's life in foster care, Tora could only imagine how bad it must've been to decide that living on the streets would be better. Skye's story bore an uncanny resemblance to Aspen's, which, she now realized, accounted for their instant connection.

With everything that had happened in the last twenty-four hours, Skye's suicide attempt had taken a back seat. Tora would make a point of checking in with the girl tomorrow. She was glad Skye had someone she could trust, someone who'd gone through what she did.

She studied Aspen's thick dark eyebrows and silky black hair. She'd always wondered what it would be like to wake up and not have to battle with her curls every morning. Confident Aspen was sleeping deeply, she reached over with her free hand and swept Aspen's hair aside. High cheekbones, full lips, and a refined nose rested on a broad moon-shaped face. Even in sleep, Aspen's beauty was spellbinding.

She took a deep breath, bracing herself for whatever lay ahead. Despite her efforts to the contrary, her feelings for this Myriad were deepening.

Timothy Decker looked up from his early morning breakfast as Finkleman rapped lightly on the Oval Office door and stepped inside. "General Vickers is on the line, sir."

Tim had personally appointed Vickers as head of the SEA. It was a well-known fact that Vickers was an extremist in his views on

Shrouds and a ruthless sonofabitch when it came to managing their numbers. All in all, the perfect man for the job.

He set his fork down, took a swig of orange juice, and pressed a button to take the call. With the intel from Finkleman, he'd reached out to Vickers, asking him to oversee the annihilation of the sanctuary and everything in it.

"Morning, Mr. President."

"What do you have for me, General?"

"We're still getting a layout of the underground nest, sir."

He didn't care about operational logistics. He just wanted it gone. "Have you come up with a plan to destroy it?"

"That's what I called to talk to you about, sir. The infestation appears to be extensive. Extreme pest control measures are needed."

Tim leaned back in his chair. He liked where this was heading. "What do you have in mind?"

"So far as we can tell, the nest has its own air supply and ventilation system. This is the perfect opportunity to test Z-23 in the field, sir."

"The nerve agent?"

"Affirmative."

The things Tim valued most about himself were his decisive nature and his unflinching ability to take action when others around him hesitated. "Do it," he said. He ended the call with a press of a button, anxious to get back to his meal.

Aspen sat up in bed and glanced at the time on the bedside clock: 5:41 a.m. Tora was there beside her. Even in sleep, she looked radiant. One hand was tucked under her cheek, the other wrapped snugly around the sleeping bag. Her golden locks spilled across the pillow and reached out enticingly. Aspen found herself wondering what it would be like to run her fingers through Tora's hair.

Tora stirred, opened her eyes, and looked up. "How long have you been awake?"

Aspen watched the digital clock as it changed to 5:42 a.m. "Thirty seconds longer than you."

Tora sat up and stretched. Her curls were pointing in every possible direction.

"Your curls…" she said, trying hard not to smile. "There are more of them. And they look very angry."

With substantial effort, Tora wrestled her hair into a makeshift bun before returning her gaze. "There," she said, patting her head and checking for stragglers. "Better?"

Aspen nodded.

"How are you feeling this morning?"

Aspen did a quick internal checkup. She felt well-rested. Strong. *Famished*. But what she was craving surprised her. She wanted oatmeal, scrambled eggs, and a toasted sesame bagel with cream cheese in the worst way. "Hungry," she said finally. "But not for chocolate. I think I want…normal food?" She checked her own forehead for fever. "Something must be wrong."

"Remember what I said yesterday?" Tora turned on the bed to face her. "I suspected your sugar cravings had something to do with the vaccine you were given to thwart your shapeshifting abilities. Your cravings are bound to change now that you're letting your body do what comes naturally."

Aspen frowned, unsure of how she felt about this change. She'd been eating that way for so long she couldn't imagine anything different.

Tora pressed two fingers against the inside of Aspen's wrist and checked her watch, counting heartbeats. After a minute, she looked up. "Sixty beats. Perfect resting heart rate." She climbed out of bed and went to the duffel bag in the corner. Toothbrush and workout clothes in hand, she headed to the bathroom. "Up for a quick run?"

"As long as there's an all-you-can-eat breakfast buffet afterward." Aspen stood from the bed and stretched, careful not to reopen the wounds on her shoulder and thigh. Surprisingly, she felt no pain and glanced down to realize her wounds were nearly healed.

She was already dressed by the time Tora emerged from the bathroom. They made their way to the indoor track and set out for a leisurely five-mile run. With an unspoken truce, they ran together this time instead of against one another.

"Why'd you decide to be a cop?" Tora asked.

"Oscar," Aspen said honestly. "He used to come home and tell me all about his days on the streets as a beat cop. I figured out pretty quickly that's what I wanted to do. He worked the day shift, so we ate dinner together every night. I'd just sit there listening to everything he saw—all the different people and situations he encountered and how he handled them. He'd reflect on the mistakes he made, how he could've handled things differently, and what he could do better the next time around. Pretty soon, he was running me through all sorts of scenarios, asking me how I'd handle them if I were a cop. Some families play board games. We played cop scenarios." Aspen laughed, remembering how she couldn't get enough of it. It was still their favorite game to play over Sunday brunch at IHOP. They awarded each other extra points for creativity and had been keeping a running tally for seventeen years. Oscar was currently up by three points. Since there was an endless supply of what-ifs in the policing world, they never ran out of subject matter. "My training started long before I entered the police academy," she went on. "Back then, Oscar was my hero. Still is. I would've done anything to be like him."

"He sounds like a good man," Tora said with a smile.

"What about you?" she asked, wondering if what she'd just shared made Tora think about her dad. "What made you want to be a doctor?"

"The obvious answer would be my father because he was a doctor. But in reality, he had very little to do with it. He tutored me, encouraged me, and supported my choices along the way, but being a doctor—a world-renowned surgeon, as fate would have it—was never his passion."

Aspen couldn't imagine doing something she didn't feel passionate about. She believed everyone had a calling. It was up to each person to figure out what that calling was. Like her, some figured it out early in life. She'd met more than a few who never figured it out at all, and she always found that incredibly sad.

"It was actually my mom who set me on the path to becoming a doctor."

Aspen was confused. "I thought you said she died during childbirth."

"She did. Identifying why Shroud mothers are dying during childbirth and how to prevent it is what inspired me to go into medicine."

A lofty and admirable goal. "Have you figured out why they're dying?"

"Shroud bodies release an anticoagulant enzyme during childbirth. In certain Shrouds, this enzyme is produced in excess, which leads to massive postpartum hemorrhaging."

Aspen knew little to nothing about medicine. "Can't you just give them some kind of—I don't know—clotting medication?"

"A colleague of mine tried that already. Administering an antifibrinolytic before, during, or immediately after childbirth triggers the body to shapeshift and renders the patient permanently unable to shift back into human form."

An anti-*what*? Aspen shook her head, deciding she didn't need to know the details. "But isn't that better than dying?"

"Not for a Shroud."

Aspen thought about how challenging it would be to remain in animal form for the rest of her life. "What about your dad?" she asked, changing the subject so she wouldn't be tempted to share the details of her vision. "If he wasn't passionate about medicine, why'd he become a doctor?"

"His passion was building this sanctuary. He predicted this day would come—the day humans would decide they didn't want us around anymore. He figured our people would need a safe haven sooner or later." Tora laughed. "I'm pretty sure the only reason he became a doctor was to make lots of money. Almost every penny he made went into building this sanctuary. Getting this place up and running was his sole mission in life. He was in the process of recruiting an elite group of Shrouds to invest in building sanctuaries in other parts of the world when he was killed."

As much as Aspen admired his dedication to helping Shrouds, there had to be a more efficient way to address the problem. Turning the tables on the SEA and wiping *them* off the face of the earth might be a good place to start.

"The investors bailed as soon as they learned of his death. They were convinced he was killed because the government caught wind of the sanctuary. It took me over a year to convince them my father was murdered simply because he was a Shroud. When they saw the sanctuary here was unharmed, they began to revisit the idea of investing in others." Tora shook her head. "But it's been a long road with them. They're moving at a snail's pace because they're afraid for their lives."

Those same Shrouds were probably wishing they'd listened and invested a lot sooner—if they were still alive. Aspen shuddered to imagine what was going on at the surface.

There was a long silence between them as they ran. She imagined they were both thinking about the Shrouds who were being massacred at this very moment.

Tora slowed to a walk and set her hands on her hips, breathing hard. "Being tucked away down here while our people are being slaughtered"—she shook her head—"it's a lot harder than I thought."

Aspen reached out to set a reassuring hand on Tora's arm and was instantly rewarded with a vision. Something was trapped beneath Tora's skin. A transmitter. When Tora was darted, a microscopic transmitter had been injected into her body, allowing the government to track her.

Aspen got a quick glimpse into SEA headquarters. Top officials had gathered and were now calculating the dimensions of this underground facility. The faces sitting around the table were cold and detached. It was clear to her they thought of Shrouds as nothing more than cockroaches that needed to be exterminated, immediately and without remorse. They were trying to determine the best and most efficient way to eradicate *the nest*. She shuddered at the term.

She took a deep breath and pulled her hand away. Time to alert the others. The SEA knew they were here.

Chapter Seventeen

Aspen and Tora took turns showering and then headed to the kitchen for breakfast. Oscar and Skye were sitting together at the table, engaged in a heated debate about pacifiers.

"She doesn't need a binky," Oscar insisted.

"But she likes the binky. It makes her feel calm."

He shook his head. "It'll warp her teeth and keep her from talking."

"I had a binky when I was a baby, and I can talk just fine."

"What if they're made from something toxic?" he asked.

"They're made from medical-grade silicone." Skye held up the packaging. "Says right here on the box."

As Aspen got closer, she saw Hope nestled against Oscar's chest in one of those baby carriers. Like a backpack worn in reverse, two straps fit snugly over his broad shoulders with a pouch in front for precious cargo. Hope's head was up, her eyes wide open. She appeared to be listening to their conversation. The pacifier in question bobbled up and down as she sucked away contentedly.

Aspen reached out to smooth the infant's white-blond hair, which seemed to have quadrupled in quantity since yesterday. She also looked much larger than Aspen remembered.

Tora came up alongside them and gasped. "What have you been feeding her?" she asked, her keen doctor's eye noticing the increase in size right away.

"Just the formula your nurses brought over." Oscar stood, unhooked the pouch, and carefully withdrew the infant. "She's growing faster than a normal baby," he said, handing her over to Tora for inspection.

"She's almost doubled in size." Tora sat in Oscar's chair and set the baby in her lap. "And she's holding her head up on her own. I've never seen head control like this in an infant so young." Tora locked eyes with Aspen. "She weighed just six pounds, five ounces yesterday. Infants typically *lose* weight in the first few days after birth. I can't say for sure without a scale, but I'm guessing she's at least twelve pounds today. Developmentally, she's more like a three-month-old than a newborn."

Hope reached her chubby arms out to Aspen, silently asking to be picked up. She obliged and turned to Oscar. "Wake the others. We need to have a meeting."

Oscar hurried off to round up the other Shrouds. With Hope in her arms, Aspen paced the kitchen, deep in thought. Her vision was unsettling, to say the least. She wasn't looking forward to delivering this news.

"Everyone's awake," Oscar announced as he stepped back into the kitchen. "They're on their way." He stationed himself at the coffeemaker, ready to take orders with a variety of flavored coffees from which to choose. Tora was busily stacking assorted bagels on a huge platter while Skye worked the toaster as their unlikely group filed into the kitchen and took their places in the food line.

Aspen watched the process in wonder. Everyone was silent as the assembly line unfolded. They all worked together seamlessly. Would they work this well together if their lives were on the line in a battle against the SEA? She sure hoped so.

Within minutes, everyone was seated at the table, passing around containers of cream cheese and commenting on Hope's overnight growth. Oscar, Tora, and Skye sat nearby. They left the seat at the head of the table for her.

Excited chatter abated as she approached with a giant mug of cinnamon-bun flavored coffee. Oscar had left it on the counter for her. The mug read: *I Like Big Cups and I Cannot Lie.* She stood at the head of the table and took a sip, trying to figure out how to break the news without inciting panic. "The SEA knows we're here. They're coming for us."

Everyone froze and stared at her.

"That's the bad news." Aspen took another sip and calmly set the mug on the table. "The good news is they're still trying to figure out how to destroy this place."

"Your definition of good news is seriously warped," Liam said, his blue hair drooping lazily over one eye.

"Yeah. What he said." Hank returned his bagel to the plate without taking a bite and looked at her like she'd lost her mind.

"Let's hear her out." Mrs. B adjusted her glasses. "I know that look. She has a plan up her sleeve."

"Is immediate evacuation and running for our lives included somewhere in that plan?" Tony asked, already on his second bagel.

"It can be, if that's what you want," she said without explaining further.

"Our chances on the surface might be better," Tony went on, talking around a mouthful of food. "If you haven't noticed, we're kind of trapped down here."

"Not kind of," Hank corrected him. "We are."

"What's option B?" Beckett took a bite of his bagel with strawberry cream cheese and came away with a pink-tipped moustache.

Aspen bit into her own bagel and chewed in thought. "We evacuate everyone in chamber two and get them someplace safe as soon as possible."

"Where?" Hank pressed. "No place is safe."

Tora interjected, "There's an underground network of humans offering refuge to our people. Michael and the others are making the arrangements right now."

"What about us?" Liam asked, looking more than a little worried.

"The rest of us stay." Aspen popped the last bagel bite into her mouth nonchalantly.

Olga scooted closer to Oscar. "And do what exactly?"

"We wait."

"For a slow and painful death at the hands of the SEA?" Hank asked, removing his ball cap to scratch the top of his head.

"We stay here as long as possible and wait for the newborns to mature. I have a feeling they'll be strong enough to help us by the time the soldiers arrive."

They all looked at the infant inside Oscar's pouch with skepticism.

Derby, the quietest member of Oscar's pack, spoke up. His sparkling blue eyes and big dimples made him a hot commodity with the ladies, who were all out of luck because Aspen knew he batted for the other team. "But they're just babies," he said, voicing what everyone else at the table was probably thinking. "We should be the ones protecting them."

"She's stronger than she looks." Oscar stood and nodded across the table at Skye.

Skye took a few steps back as Oscar unclipped the pouch and held the baby aloft. "Go ahead, Hope. Show them what you can do," he said, tossing her in the air.

In a flash of skilled and magical shapeshifting, a white dove burst forth in place of the baby. Flapping small but powerful wings, she circled their table at great speed before perching gracefully on Oscar's shoulder. It took a moment for Aspen to realize there was now a translucent bubble around them. It was barely discernible but definitely there.

She reached out to run her fingers over the smooth surface. It was unlike anything she had ever touched before—warm and dry but cool and moist all at once. A steady vibration made her fingertips tingle.

She watched as Skye withdrew several serrated knives from the wooden block on the counter and chucked them, hard, against the bubble's outer surface. One after another, the knives bounced off and skidded violently across the kitchen floor, slamming against the rock wall on the opposite side of the room.

"From what we can tell, it's impenetrable," Oscar explained. "But keep watching. It gets better."

Skye spoke from the other side, "Hope, can you put a shield around this?" She held up a spoon. "And me, too," she added.

In the blink of an eye, Hope dove from Oscar's shoulder, circled both Skye and the spoon, and promptly returned to her perch. Oscar reached up as she hopped onto his finger. Safely in his hands, she shifted into the beautiful blue-eyed, blond-haired baby once again.

Aspen watched, intrigued, as Skye handed the spoon to Oscar and then passed through the bubble to join them inside.

"There are seven others like her?" Hank asked in disbelief.

"Yes." Aspen shifted her gaze from the baby to Hank. "But I believe she's the most powerful."

Tony leaned back and crossed his arms. "Even if the newborns help us, what's the point of staying here?"

Aspen nodded. "I get it. You've all been taught to run from humans pretty much since the day you were born—always looking over your shoulder, keeping one eye open, ready to bolt at the first sign of danger. Those instincts have kept each of you alive until now. But for the first time in over a century, Myriads are back. This changes everything. We have options now. We can afford to think outside the box." She looked over at Tora, who returned her gaze with a mixture of confidence and curiosity.

"Tora's father spent his life dreaming about this place," she went on. "He worked hard and sacrificed everything to build this sanctuary. He thought the day would come when humans would wage war on our people, and he wanted to do something to protect us. I never had the chance to meet him—he was murdered by a human two years ago—but I'm pretty sure he'd want us to start fighting back now that we have Myriads on our side. And I'd bet anything he'd want us to take our stand here, in the sanctuary he built for *us*. This place, his dream—it's worth protecting. The SEA has their headquarters." Aspen intended to find out where. "This will be ours. Who's in?"

With tears in her eyes, Tora was the first to stand.

Skye stood from her chair and slipped her hand inside Tora's. "Bet our headquarters are way cooler than theirs."

Pierre was next. He graciously bowed to Aspen. "Count me in as well, my friend."

"This is a no-brainer," Mrs. B said, also standing. "I've been dying to stick my rhino horn up the government's ass."

"Hope I'm there to see that." Laughing, Tony got to his feet and set a hand on Mrs. B's shoulder. "It's time I put my teeth and claws to good use."

Hank stood beside Tony and removed his ball cap. "Can't let you guys have all the fun without me."

"You got room for a cheetah?" Liam tucked his blue hair behind one ear and stood. "Speed is kinda my thing."

Beckett stood, playfully bumping shoulders with his son. "This old wolf can't run as fast as a cheetah, but I've got me a mean bite."

Johnston stood beside Beckett. "Happy to donate my bite pressure to the cause."

Having already met his word quota for the day, Derby stood and simply nodded.

The other five wolf pack members followed suit—Rivera, Barnes, Delacruz, Kennedy, and Malenko. Like Oscar, all of them were cops. They'd been like Aspen's uncles growing up, always dropping by for a meal or a ball game on TV.

Miller stood and stared long and hard at everyone around the table. As Oscar's second-in-command, Aspen knew he was the serious one, always the slowest to smile and the last to laugh. He was also the soul of the pack. "I think I speak for all my pack members when I say it would be an honor to fight alongside each of you."

Olga stood beside Miller. "I will fight for all of you like family." She winked at Aspen.

Oscar was the last to stand. He puffed his chest out proudly. His usual air of authority was somewhat compromised by the baby strapped to his chest in a fashionably patterned pink-and-green pouch. "A new pack is born today. We run together, fight together, lay our lives down for each other, and leave no one behind. Our loyalty to the pack knows no bounds." He made a point of looking into each Shroud's eyes. "From this moment on, we're family."

"Works for me. But do we have to call ourselves a pack?" Still hungry, Aspen took a seat and emptied half the tub smothering her second bagel in strawberry cream cheese.

"Hey, leave some for me," Skye said, plucking the knife from Aspen's hand. "How about a flock? That has a nice ring to it."

"Or a pride," Tora said, joining in the fun. "That makes us sound fierce."

"I rather like herd," Mrs. B chimed in.

"We need a politically correct term that's inclusive of all species," Beckett pointed out.

Liam sat beside his dad. "Let's just give ourselves a kick-ass superhero name."

Skye glanced up from her bagel. "Like The Avengers?"

"Exactly. But something original." Liam swept the blue hair from his eyes. "How about The Ferals?"

"Has potential."

"Simple and to the point."

"Makes us sound like wild animals."

"Shall we put it to a vote?" Oscar raised his hand. "All in favor of The Ferals?"

Hope's head popped up from the pouch on Oscar's chest as she defiantly spat out her binky with an audible *pop*. Her angelic baby face did not look happy.

"Our youngest member has cast the first vote," Oscar said, catching the binky before it hit the floor.

Hope's eyes took on a golden hue as she gazed up at him.

"Alpha Genesis," Oscar announced with a shrug. "Just came to me. Those in favor?'"

Everyone grew quiet as they met one another's gaze around the table. One by one, they all raised a hand.

"It's official," Oscar said, grinning. "Welcome, everyone...to Alpha Genesis."

"Can we have T-shirts made with little logos?" Hank asked.

"I've never been in a superhero group before," Mrs. B admitted. "Wait. Does my knitting group count?"

Aspen finished her bagel and sipped her coffee, watching everyone as the banter continued. She was acutely aware they had all just made an oath to one another. Family, for better or worse.

Until now, it had always been just her and Oscar. Their family had grown overnight. Something told her these Shrouds were destined all along to be here with her and the newborns.

It was clear in her vision that the SEA's arrival was imminent. All they needed was more time—time for the newborns to grow, time for her to finish her training and gain a better understanding of her own abilities. She shuddered to imagine what would happen if SEA soldiers found them before they were ready. The Shrouds sitting around this table already meant so much to her. There was no way in hell she was going to let anything happen to them.

CHAPTER EIGHTEEN

They all finished breakfast and moved their meeting to the main room of chamber one. The early morning chill in the underground tunnels made Aspen shiver. She ignited the gas fire pit as everyone took a seat on the massive circular sofa and burrowed into the plethora of throw pillows.

Tora returned a few minutes later with maps of the sanctuary in hand. She passed them out and then pressed a button on the side of the fire pit. A hidden panel in the rock floor opened as a huge screen rose up and towered above them.

Aspen stood in the center of the group, hands on hips. "Now that we have our own headquarters, the first thing we'll do is get to know every inch of this place like our lives depend on it. Tora's going to familiarize us with the layout of the tunnels and chambers. We'll need to commit all of this to memory as quickly as possible." She made a point of looking over at Oscar. "I know it's been, like, *eons* since some of you were in school. Just do your best to keep up with the rest of us."

Oscar rolled his eyes.

Aspen turned the group over to Tora and took a seat beside Skye.

Tora pointed a remote at the screen and brought up livestreams from various points within the sanctuary. "There are five chambers," she explained. "Each one is roughly the size of two football fields. All are connected through a series of tunnels with limited entry and exit points. We'll review the layout here, and then Michael will take you on a tour."

On cue, Michael stepped forward and nodded at the group.

"What about the other residents?" Hank asked.

"All residents are being evacuated and relocated as we speak," Tora said in the clipped, no-nonsense tone Aspen had come to expect when there was business at hand. "A handful of nurses, two doctors, the newborns, and their parents are the only exceptions."

"And me," Michael added as he smiled through his lumberjack beard. "I'm staying, too."

Aspen thought back to the impressive security measures for this chamber—no keyhole, doorknob, or keypad on the other side of the door. For all she knew, Michael was their sole means of entry. She'd have to ask Tora about that later. "Are you staying because you have to or because you want to?"

The group was silent as they watched him.

"Both," he said finally, tugging at his beard as he appeared to give the question serious thought. "I gave old Doc Madigan my word I'd stick around and help out here if anything ever happened to him." He looked up from the floor and shrugged broad shoulders. "If I die protecting what he built, I'm okay with that."

Well, Michael obviously understood the stakes. Aspen gave him a quick once-over and promptly decided to follow her instincts with this particular Shroud. She trusted Michael. Built like an NFL linebacker, he could easily intimidate those around him with his size and deep voice. Yet he moved with the grace and humility of a truly gentle man. She sensed he was not only aware of his imposing stature but felt obliged to compensate for it.

Oscar called out from his place on the sofa, "Is your loyalty to the sanctuary?"

Head bowed, Michael met Oscar's gaze. "This sanctuary is supposed to be a refuge. Doc had plans to build them all over the world so Shrouds like us could be safe. We can defend this place. We *should* defend this place. By taking our stand here against humans, we show our people there's hope. We let them know it's time to fight back. My loyalty is to our people. All Shrouds. Everywhere. They're worth dying for."

Aspen couldn't have said it better herself. Members of the group nodded and murmured in agreement as Oscar stood and extended his hand to Michael. "Welcome to Alpha Genesis."

"To what?" Michael asked, reaching over to shake Oscar's hand.

"Alpha Genesis," Oscar repeated.

"That's what we named ourselves," Skye said, grinning. "We're a superhero group."

"With a mission to kick the SEA's ass from here to kingdom come." Mrs. B pushed her glasses up with one finger and gave Michael a serious staring down.

"Consider yourself an official member," Beckett said proudly.

"We're having T-shirts made," Hank chimed in. "We'll get you an extra-extra-small," he added as everyone laughed. Even Michael chuckled at his own expense.

Derby and Miller scooted aside to make a space for Michael on the sofa.

Everyone unfolded their maps and followed along as Tora reviewed each section of the sanctuary. Efficient as ever, her presentation was concise and to the point. Even her posture was ramrod straight. Aspen shook her head and smiled to herself. Tora needed to loosen up a little, have some fun. Times like these were *exactly* when goofing off was most needed.

Oscar studied the map in his lap intently. "The only way to get to the other chambers is to come through this one first?"

"Correct," Tora replied.

"Is Michael the only key?" Oscar asked the question before Aspen had the chance. As usual, they were on the same page.

Tora started to shake her head but stopped. "Actually, he is our only key right now. We had a second Shroud who was small enough to fit through that hole, but he's being evacuated with the others."

Aspen knew where Oscar's thoughts were heading next. "Shouldn't we have a backup?" he asked.

Tora looked over at Aspen. They hadn't told anyone about last night's shapeshifting lesson. "Aspen will be our backup."

"You did it?" Skye sat up, bursting with excitement beside her. "You shifted?"

"Into a mouse?" Oscar asked, frowning.

Tora came to her defense before Aspen could respond. "In her first session, she was able to shift into each of your primary animals."

"Wow!" Skye reached out to give her a congratulatory hug. "That's amazing!"

Aspen smiled, aware all eyes were on her. "They all just sort of came out on their own," she admitted.

"True. But each animal was exquisite," Tora countered.

"And the panther?" Caught up in the excitement, Oscar scooted to the edge of his seat. "Did you shift into your panther?"

She nodded.

"Atta girl," Oscar cheered. He smacked his leg and beamed with pride.

Liam peered at Aspen through long blue bangs. "I remember my grandpa telling me a story about a Myriad who shifted into his primary when he lost control. Like the Hulk." He glanced at Beckett. "Remember that story, Dad?"

Beckett nodded, leaning forward. "My great-grandfather, Amos, was best friends with a Myriad. His name was Felix. He and my great-grandpa were like brothers. My dad passed on all the stories that Papa Amos told him. There's one in particular about how Felix could shift into any animal at will, except his own. He was a lion like you, Tora. Hard as he tried, though, he could never shift into one.

"Amos and Felix were walking home from a poker game at a friend's house one night when they saw a father beating his little boy through an apartment window. They banged on the door and demanded he stop. But he ignored them, kept right on beating his boy. That's when Felix just lost it. He shifted right there in the hallway. It was the first time Amos ever saw him as a lion."

"First and only," Liam added. "Humans caught up with Felix soon after and killed him."

"But not before he saved the boy," Beckett said, smiling as he reminisced. "That boy later became my grandfather. Great-grandpa Amos adopted Henry and raised him as his own."

"The boy was a Shroud?" Tora asked, clearly surprised as she sat on the edge of the fire pit.

Beckett shook his head. "He was a three-year-old *human* boy. His mother had died and he had no other family. When Great-grandpa Amos confronted the father, he offered to take the boy off his hands."

Oscar scowled. "Offered or threatened?"

"Probably a little of both," Beckett admitted.

"Your grandfather was human?" Tora asked, taken aback. "But you're a Shroud. I saw it myself. You're a wolf."

Beckett's grin widened. "Damn right, I am."

Aspen looked around at the group. Everyone was on the edge of their seats, silent as they waited for him to explain. She'd never heard of such a thing happening.

"Henry was raised by Great-grandpa Amos and Great-granny Edith—both Shrouds. They had five biological kids who were all Shrouds, of course. Grandpa Henry was human, but he was raised as a Shroud. He obviously never shifted, but he was a Shroud in every other sense. Later in life, he even married a Shroud. She gave birth to my dad and three uncles. Then my dad had me, and I had Liam." He reached over to tousle Liam's blue hair. "There you have it. My family lineage."

Everyone stared at him. From the looks on their faces, Aspen could tell they were all just as surprised as she was.

Humans and Shrouds could bear children together? Maybe that was the answer to everything. Mixing human DNA with Shroud DNA would make it impossible for the government to distinguish between the two. Aspen wondered if that was what those in power had been afraid of all along: corrupting the human gene pool. The motivation behind the president's all-out extermination rampage was finally beginning to take focus.

"That's why they're trying to get rid of us," Aspen said.

"Because Great-grandpa Amos raised a human?" Frowning, Beckett looked at her like she was an idiot. "Shroud discrimination started long before that."

"Exactly," she said, standing in front of the group. "That's what they're afraid of—Shrouds corrupting the human gene pool. Think about it. They don't care about who we are, how we feel, how many kids we have, how successful we are, or how much we contribute to society." She glanced at Tora. "Just look at your dad. He was the epitome of success and brilliance. Hell, he was the only neurosurgeon with the skills to save that ass wipe of a human who ordered his hit." She shook her head. "All they care about is keeping the human gene pool free from Shroud influence."

Mrs. B looked up, her face a mix of disappointment and rage. "Pure and untainted."

"Like Nazi Germany," Skye said sadly.

"Yep." Hank removed his ball cap and held it against his chest, his eyes haunted. "And we all know how that turned out."

"But humans from this country were the good guys back then." Tony rolled his shoulders.

Derby broke his characteristic silence. "Until they weren't."

"This isn't just limited to the US. Nations have banded together all around the world with one goal in mind."

"To wipe us out of existence," Skye said, her eyes filling with tears.

Humans were everywhere. From her experience, they outnumbered Shrouds by at least two to one. Why was that, she wondered? Her mind flashed to Hope's mother, Sophie, who died during childbirth. She turned to Tora. "Are Shroud mothers required to report a pregnancy?"

Tora nodded. "They're mandated by law to do each prenatal checkup with a designated human doctor."

All of a sudden, everything made sense. "That's how they're controlling our numbers."

Tora's eyes widened. "They're administering something to trigger the postpartum hemorrhaging."

She'd been thinking about this all wrong. If they took out the SEA's top officials, more would just be sent to take their place. If they took out SEA headquarters, might take a little longer, but it would be rebuilt eventually.

"Taking out SEA headquarters here in the US *should* be part of our plan," she said. "But it's only a short-term solution."

Oscar nodded. "They'll just rebuild and send new people." He met her gaze, and she could see he was following her line of thought.

Miller shook his head. "If you're going to say our new mission is to rally Shrouds from around the world to fight those in power, that could take years. Possibly decades."

Aspen instinctively knew time wasn't a factor in the fight to save her people. This war couldn't be won overnight. "Our mission will have three distinct parts: the short-term plan, the long-term plan, and the hope-I'm-still-alive-to-see-it plan."

Oscar looked up. "Conspiring with Shrouds from around the world to overthrow governments obviously falls under that last plan. The short-term plan is to find and destroy SEA headquarters." He frowned. "What's the long-term plan?"

"Tell all Shrouds to start seeking out and forming alliances with humans." She nodded at Beckett. "We need to follow in the footsteps of Grandpa Henry."

Oscar's frown deepened. "You want us to start knocking boots with humans?"

Aspen sighed. "No one uses that term anymore, Pop."

"Right, sorry. Don't mind me. I'm ancient."

Tora locked eyes with her. "You want us to mix up the gene pool so governments all over the world can't discern human from Shroud. It would be like splitting hairs."

"Exactly. Since that's what they're most afraid of, let's do everything we can to mix things up at, like, warp speed."

Skye looked up, her expression one of confusion and worry. "But we were always taught to be wary of humans. Keep them at arm's length and try to act as human as possible around them."

"And those teachings had merit. But if Shrouds ever hope to share a peaceful existence with humans, we'll need to change the way we relate to them. Let them see us for who we are. Our people are beautifully different from humans. There's no shame in that."

"She's right." Oscar sighed. "It'll take some re-education within the Shroud community, but this is something we probably should have started doing long ago."

"This comes with substantial risk to our people," Tora countered. "Especially now. By exposing ourselves as Shrouds, we face certain death." She shook her head. "Not to mention the fact that most humans can't be trusted. How are we going to sell an idea to Shrouds that *we* don't even believe in?"

The room grew quiet. Everyone's questioning gaze landed on Aspen. This was, understandably, a sore spot for Shrouds. Humans' centuries-long discrimination against Shrouds had turned into an extermination campaign overnight. Trusting humans right now was an unfathomable concept.

Chapter Nineteen

Aspen sat on the edge of the stone fire pit, the fire's blazing warmth at her back as she addressed the group. "I've been living in the human world—believing I was one—my entire life. So I speak from experience when I say there are lots of humans out there who make piss-poor choices in life. They lie, steal, do drugs, cheat on their spouses, drink themselves into oblivion, beat each other up, and even commit murder. As a cop, I've definitely seen more than my share of their dark side. But I also know there are people out there who make much healthier choices in life. There are humans on the surface right now that I would lay down my life for, and I know—beyond a shadow of a doubt—they would do the same for me."

"Would they change their minds if they found out you were a Shroud?" Skye asked.

Aspen set her elbows on her knees and hung her head as she considered the question. "Some of them, maybe," she said honestly, meeting Skye's green gaze. "But a lot of them wouldn't care. If the shit hit the fan, those are the people I know I could trust."

Skye's eyebrows knitted together in doubt. "But how do you know who to trust and who not to?"

"Takes time, kiddo. Getting to know humans and building relationships takes time, patience, and practice. And good instincts," she added with a wink.

"It's the practice part that has me worried," Tony said. "Baseball practice is one thing. Striking out won't get you a bullet in the head."

Aspen looked around at the group, taking inventory as her gaze bounced from one face to the next. The shared trauma of losing friends, family, and loved ones was stitched into every expression as they waited for her to respond. Even Oscar was leaning back on the sofa, his face ambivalent. The bottom line here was trust. She was asking them to trust humans and go against long-held beliefs that had become the very foundation of their survival.

She stood, slid her hands in her pockets. "All of you work with humans on the surface. Skye, you don't work with humans, but you've gone to school with them since kindergarten. Let's face it... they outnumber us by, like, a lot. Why limit ourselves to socializing with only our own kind? Those in power are trying to keep their gene pool clean, but aren't we doing the exact same thing?"

"They're *actively* killing us off to keep their gene pool clean," Tora pointed out. "We're in hiding. Our clean gene pool is simply a by-product of fear. Big difference in our core motivation."

Aspen stood her ground. "But the results are the same. And sometimes in life, results are all that matter." She let that hang in the air for a minute before she went on. "There are lots of good people out there. I like to think the truly good people outnumber the bad—not an easy perspective to keep in my line of work, believe me. There are humans on the surface who are kind, caring, and want to do the right thing. Once they understand who and what we are, I have no doubt they'd want to help us, protect us, even learn from us. We're cheating our people from the benefits of knowing humans. We're also cheating humankind of the things *we* have to offer."

"Like what?" Liam asked. "What could we possibly teach humans?"

"Teamwork, for one. I'm still new to being a Shroud, but I've never seen strangers work together as seamlessly as all of you."

Pierre shifted on the sofa. "Humans won't care about that."

"See, that's where I think you're wrong," she said. "I think most humans are extraordinarily selfish—"

"Our point exactly," Tony quipped.

"Humans think being selfish will meet their needs and make them happy," she went on. "But many of them aren't happy—they're downright miserable. Deep down, they long to be part of something bigger than themselves. That's where we come in. The ways of the Shrouds will inevitably rub off on humans."

Hank spoke up, "And their ways will inevitably rub off on us. I can't speak for everyone here, but I'm not too eager for that to happen."

The room was quiet as Aspen considered everyone's perspective. She really had no right to suggest such a dangerous plan. The loss of her parents probably paled in comparison to the repeated traumas and discrimination these Shrouds had experienced throughout their lives. For the first time since being introduced to this world, she felt like an outsider. How would she lead her people in a war against humans if they couldn't accept and trust her *human* instincts?

Oscar cleared his throat. "Love. When you strip everything else away, it's the most basic of all instincts—to both human and Shroud."

Aspen nodded.

"You're asking us to love humans?" Hank looked back and forth between Aspen and Oscar. "Even though they're trying to scrub us off this planet?"

"Not all humans are trying to kill us," Oscar said.

"You're missing the point." Hank leaned forward. "Our government is run by humans."

"Our government doesn't represent all of humanity."

"Don't they?" Hank removed his ball cap and hung it over one knee. "How do we know every last human on this planet doesn't share the president's contempt for us?"

"Because I can't even fathom that. If that was the case, Shrouds should just give up now. I don't know about you, but I wouldn't want to live in a world where we were despised by every last human in existence." Oscar looked around, meeting everyone's gaze. "Come on. Aspen's right. We've been around humans. We know they're not all bad. Some of them can be trusted."

"Yeah, but which ones?" Mrs. B asked.

"Only you can answer that." He sighed. "We all just need to do what we do best."

"Trust our instincts," Skye finished for him.

Hank replaced his ball cap with the brim facing backward. "And just how do you propose we convince other Shrouds to love thy fellow human?"

"That's easy. We tell them the truth." Oscar gazed up at Aspen proudly. "Orders came directly from the new Myriad in charge."

Aspen followed at the back of the line as Michael led their group to the rec room. He waved his keycard in front of a small sensor in the rock wall to unveil a hidden keypad. "The new passcode is *chocolate*," he said, punching in the code.

Everyone turned to stare at Aspen.

"Why's everyone looking at me?"

"Because we all know you have a problem," Hank said.

"Not anymore. I had two bagels for breakfast," she announced proudly.

Tony snickered. "And I'd bet my pension you washed it down with six chocolate doughnuts."

"No doughnuts. Just the bagels," she said, indignant.

Miller shook his head. "Once an addict, always an addict."

"Seriously. Tora said I'd start craving different foods as soon as I shifted. She was right."

Skye put a hand on her shoulder. "It's okay, Aspen. Even Myriads have their weaknesses."

"But that's what she said." She looked at Tora, who was standing beside her. "Go on. Tell them."

"About the three candy bars you ate *before* the bagel?" Tora asked with a barely discernible wink.

Turning away and shaking their heads, they all filed through the doorway and into the tunnels.

"Very funny. She's joking!" Aspen called out as she stepped over the threshold and onto the tunnel's solid rock floor. "Not the best time for your sense of humor to make its debut," she whispered. "It's the perfect time," Tora whispered back.

Torches overhead came alive with a *whoosh*, instantly illuminating the four trolleys in front of them. Aspen did the math: Eighteen in their group, plus Michael. Each trolley seated six.

"That one's ours," Tora said, grabbing Aspen by the elbow and leading her to the last trolley in line.

"I'm not going anywhere with you until you tell them I'm a reformed chocolate addict."

"It's been less than a day. I'd hardly call that reformed."

"But I've never gone this long without chocolate. That kind of thing at least deserves—"

"A gold star." Tora nodded. "I'll grab one from the teacher's desk and put it on your forehead later." She stepped inside the trolley and sat in the driver's seat as the other three trolleys sped away.

"I was going to say a hug." Aspen stood in place and did her best to look offended.

"We're preparing to wage war on the SEA, and you're asking for—"

"A hug," Aspen finished. "That's right."

"I'm not a hugger. Now get in." Tora pressed the ignition switch and glanced over.

Aspen made no motion to join her. She crossed her arms and met Tora's gaze.

"One hug." Tora sighed impatiently. "Then can we go?"

"Of course."

Tora climbed out of the trolley, stepped over, and gave Aspen the most pathetic hug she'd ever received in her life. To avoid bodily contact, Tora was hugging her like a second grader might hug someone with cooties. Adding to the torture, Tora finished it off with a few quick pats. "There," she said, drawing back. "Happy?"

"No." Aspen grimaced. "On a scale of one to ten, that totally sucked."

"Like I said, I'm not a hugger. Can we go now?"

"Was your dad a good hugger?"

"Aspen"—Tora threw her hands up in frustration—"I have no idea."

"How can you not know where your own dad rated on the hug scale?"

"Because we never hugged. He was more a pat-on-the-head type of father when I was a kid. Can we go now?"

She suddenly felt sad for Tora. "I don't know how you've made it this far without learning how to hug. It's like going through life not knowing how to read."

"I beg to differ." Tora crossed her arms. "And I've gotten along just fine, thank you."

"Hugs are like hot cocoa during a snowstorm. They make you feel like, no matter what's going on outside, everything will be okay. Haven't you ever gotten one of those?" She'd gotten more than her share of those kinds of hugs from Oscar, and she knew her life was made much richer because of it.

"I'm sure I have at some point. I don't remem—"

"Then the answer is no, you haven't. Those are the hugs you never forget." She stepped closer to Tora and opened her arms. "May I?"

"If I let you hug me, then can we go?"

Aspen nodded. She swiftly closed the gap between them, wrapped her arms around Tora, and pulled her in for a full-body hug.

Tora immediately stiffened. It was like hugging a telephone pole. "It's your turn to wrap your arms around me and hug me back," Aspen whispered. She felt Tora's arms at her back, applying tentative pressure. "Tighter," she urged.

"This is silly," Tora said as she tightened her embrace.

"A little tighter."

"There are other things I could be doing with my time right now, Aspen. My to-do list is about a mile long."

"Now…relax a little, breathe, and hug me like you mean it."

"How long is this going to take?"

"Shh. No talking. That's what's so great about hugs. They convey everything you want to say without the need for words. Like what I'm saying right now, for instance, is thank you.

"For what?" Tora asked, sounding surprised.

"For helping us. Training me. Caring about our people as much as you do," she answered. "And for taking your guard down and sharing this moment with me." They stood there, hugging in silence, their shared body heat keeping the cold, damp air from the tunnels at bay. She smiled as she felt Tora's walls slowly crumbling.

Satisfied Tora had received the full benefit of an authentic hug—not one of those knockoff hugs that people often tried to get away with—she loosened her grasp and pulled back, surprised to see the tears in Tora's eyes. She frowned. "Hugs are not supposed to make you cry."

"There's something in my contact lens."

"You wear contacts?"

"No. But can't we just go with that for now?" Tora climbed back inside the trolley.

"Fine. But I hope you're a better kisser than a hugger," Aspen said, settling in alongside her.

Tora looked over. "I beg your pardon?"

"Kissing is a lot harder to teach. Not saying I'm not willing. Just saying I hope you have a natural aptitude for that particular skill."

"I don't even know what to say to that, Aspen. This topic of conversation is totally inappropriate—"

"You don't have to say anything." She shrugged. "I'll find out for myself sooner or later."

"I certainly don't want to mislead you. I am not looking for any kind of involvement with you beyond…"

"Beyond what?"

"Friends."

"Past that already. We slept together last night, remember?"

Tora turned in her seat to face Aspen. "We slept in the same bed as *friends*," she said firmly.

"But we held hands, and you liked it." She grinned. "I won't mention the naked thing because that was part of the training, so it doesn't count."

Shaking her head, Tora hit the ignition switch.

"Can I drive?" She had to raise her voice to be heard above the engine.

"No. I'm taking you on a tour."

"I'm a hands-on learner. If you make me sit here while you drive, I won't retain anything. I'll be too distracted by your beauty," Aspen admitted. "And then I'll start fantasizing about our first kiss. Is that what you want?"

"You really are impossible."

Aspen could tell Tora was trying hard not to smile as they traded seats.

CHAPTER TWENTY

Tora took a deep breath as they sped through the railway system. Aspen was making it virtually impossible to stay focused. She didn't have time for these antics. Neither of them did.

She found herself thinking about Aspen's hug. No one had ever hugged her like that before. She'd felt safe, connected, and cared about. There was something else, too. Hugging Aspen had made her feel vulnerable in a way she wasn't accustomed. For some reason, it had brought back all the pain of losing her father.

She'd ended her last relationship with a hospital colleague shortly after her father passed away. Neither of them had been emotionally invested. They'd only been dating a few months, if you'd even call it dating. More like friends with benefits. Now that she thought about it, there was never really a friendship to speak of. Their arrangement had simply provided a convenient means to sex. She was much too busy at that time in her life to want or allow for anything deeper.

Hard to believe two years had passed since she was intimate with someone. Had it really been that long? She'd been too busy to notice. So many Shrouds had been murdered in the last few years. It was simply too risky to form attachments. Chances were good they'd end up dead before long.

Her decision to keep everyone at arm's length wasn't a conscious one, she realized, but it *was* practical. She had a sanctuary to run and big shoes to fill in her father's absence. Putting up walls and staying focused on productivity for the good of her people made sense two years ago. It made even more sense now because more was at stake.

Aspen was working feverishly to get inside those walls. And succeeding, Tora admitted. If they took this any further, their feelings would only serve as a distraction for both of them. Too much was on the line to allow this to continue. She had to put a stop to…whatever this was. Now.

"We're coming up on chamber two. Park behind the other trolleys."

"Copy that." Aspen slowed the trolley to a stop and cut the engine.

"I'm not gay," she blurted. "I only said that so you wouldn't feel self-conscious during our melding session."

Aspen just stared at her.

"I'm sorry," she said honestly.

Long seconds ticked by as they held one another's gaze. The connection between them was palpable. Tora looked away.

"Why were you crying when we hugged?"

The question caught her off-guard. "What does that have to do with anything?"

"Just tell me why."

"It's none of your business."

"And telling you I tried to kill myself when I was a kid was none of your business. I chose to share that with you because I trusted you enough to tell you the truth."

Aspen was right. Sharing that had taken courage. Tora hadn't considered the trust factor until now. Part of her yearned to explore their connection. Momentarily conflicted, her resolve to keep Aspen at arm's length faltered.

"I think you're starting to have feelings for me, and that scares you," Aspen went on. "You've kept yourself out of everyone's reach for a long time—maybe your whole life, I don't know. I think you're hiding…like a mouse. But you're a lion, Tora."

Tora's back went up. "What the hell is that supposed to mean?"

"You're hiding behind your responsibilities here at the sanctuary. If this place spontaneously combusted, I'm sure you'd find something else to hide behind. You take life *way* too seriously—"

"And you think everything's a joke!" she shouted, her temper slipping from her grasp. "You're impulsive, inexperienced, impetuous. If someone doesn't rein you in—namely, me—you'll likely get us all killed!"

Still side by side in the trolley, they locked eyes. She was fuming. How dare Aspen accuse her of being a coward?

"I don't hide, Tora, no matter what. When you're ready to stop hiding, come find me." She looked over Tora's shoulder and cleared her throat. "I'd prefer to make a dramatic exit here, but you're blocking my way. Climbing over you, all angry and indignant, would just be comical and defeat the point entirely."

Tora threw open the trolley door and stepped out. Aspen couldn't even make it through an argument without cracking a joke.

"And another thing," Aspen said, climbing out from the trolley. "Insulting me with words I don't know the meaning of is just plain dumb."

Tora crossed her arms and raised an eyebrow.

"What the hell does *impetuous* mean anyway?"

Tora sighed. "Go join the others. I need to check on the newborns."

"If you ask me nicely, I'll do it."

"Do what?" she asked absently. Tora brought her fingers to her temple. A headache was galloping around the track, headed straight for her at top speed.

"Join the others." Aspen sighed. "It's called asking politely. Here, allow me to demonstrate." She hopped to the opposite side of where she'd been standing and pretended to address herself as Tora. "Aspen, can you please join the others so I can go do some important doctor stuff?"

Without a word, Tora climbed back inside the trolley, put the trolley in gear, and sped away. What she needed right now was physical distance from Aspen.

She took a deep breath as the overhead torches ignited, illuminating the tunnels before her. These tunnels were more familiar to her than the hallways in her house on the surface. She felt relief wash over her as she was alone once again.

Time to regroup, get herself squared away. At this point, perhaps it was best to let someone else take over Aspen's training. But who? She mentally reviewed the list of available candidates and sighed. There was no one else.

Maybe Aspen had a point. Was she using her responsibilities as an excuse to make herself inaccessible to everyone around her?

She braked to a stop at the hospital's entrance and squeezed her eyes shut against the headache that was now an all-out migraine. The pain was almost unbearable.

The sound of fluttering wings echoed through the tunnels. Tora felt a slight draft against the side of her body as a small white bird landed on the seat beside her. A dove. For a moment, she wondered if it was Hope, but this presence felt annoyingly familiar. She closed her eyes and leaned back against the headrest, the light from the overhead torches like branding irons on her brain.

Aspen's voice interrupted the stillness. "You have a migraine."

So the Myriad had taught herself how to fly. She was a quick study. With a little luck, their training sessions together would be brief. "No, I don't."

"Yes, you do."

"How could you possibly know that?"

"Call it one of my newly emerging talents as a Myriad. I can sense you're in a lot of pain."

"I'm not in the mood to talk right now, Aspen."

"Would you prefer we sit here in an uncomfortable silence while I watch you suffer?"

"Whatever you're doing—*however* you're causing this—you can stop now. You've made your point."

"I'm not the one causing it…exactly."

"What the hell does that mean, *exactly*?" Tora felt her temper flare up again, which made her heart beat faster and the throbbing worse.

"Your migraine—I think it's being caused by the anger you're feeling toward me."

That theory was beyond ridiculous. She kept her eyes closed and brought both hands to her temples. "Are you saying I'm the one causing this?"

"Yep."

"I can't see your face right now—because if I open my eyes, my eyeballs will leap from my skull to escape the pain in my head—but I'm definitely sensing a self-satisfied smirk."

"I prefer smug-yet-playful smile."

"How do I make this stop?" Tora didn't know how much more agony she could withstand.

"Two choices. Either you put some distance between us, or you talk about what's upsetting you."

"Option A." Tora squinted through her eyelashes, tapped the ignition switch, and put the trolley in drive.

"I neglected to mention how far."

She hesitated. "How far?"

"Tahiti should do it."

Tora put the trolley in park and cut the engine, feeling suddenly nauseous from the pain. At this point, she was willing to do just about anything to make it go away.

"Guess that leaves option B," Aspen said. "I've been told on more than one occasion that I'm a really good listener."

She swore she could hear Aspen grinning.

"Unless there's someone else you'd like to talk to."

Tora couldn't think of a single Shroud. She confided in no one.

"Exactly what I thought. You're a loner. You keep everything close to the chest. Am I right?"

"That's what a good leader does."

"Good leaders strive to find balance between meeting their responsibilities and taking care of themselves. They realize they can't possibly do everything alone. Good leaders have an inner circle of people they trust—a support system, if you will. Do you have that?"

Tora shook her head, instantly regretting it as the pain ratcheted up another notch.

"Why not?"

"I work best alone."

"Not buying it. Try again."

Tora tried to think through the pain. "I *prefer* to work alone."

"Why?" Aspen pressed.

"Because most Shrouds can't stay alive long enough for me to count on them." She felt the truth of her words like a punch to the stomach.

"And that makes you feel…?"

"Scared," Tora admitted. "I'm afraid of depending on someone only to lose them." The pain in her head instantly diminished as soon as the words were out of her mouth. She opened her eyes and sat up.

"Welcome back," Aspen said, studying her. "How do you feel?"

"Better, but the headache is still there." She met Aspen's gaze. "Why isn't it gone?"

Aspen shrugged. "Maybe it means you're still holding on to something."

Tora already regretted what she'd shared so far. "Like what?"

"Like, oh, I don't know, your feelings for me?"

"I already told you, I'm not gay." Tora brought both hands to her head as the migraine returned with a vengeance. This headache was like Pinocchio's nose. "Are you doing this, Aspen?"

"I swear on my life, I am *not* giving you that headache."

Felt like it was escalating from a migraine to a brain aneurysm. Dammit. "Okay, okay. That's a lie. And yes, I do have feelings for you." Just like that—*poof*—the pain was totally gone.

"See?" Aspen reached over to take her hand. "Was that so bad?"

Tora pulled away. "I said I have feelings for you. I didn't say I wanted to act on them."

Aspen nodded. "Baby steps. I can roll with that."

"Trust me," she said through clenched teeth. "There's *nothing* to roll with."

"Whatever you say."

"I'm serious."

"Okay." Aspen raised both hands in surrender.

"Can we go inside please, so I can check on the newborns?"

"As long as you keep your anger in check."

"That won't be an issue, as long as you keep your talking to a minimum."

"I've been told I have a very soothing voice."

Tora couldn't argue with that. There was a calming, hypnotic quality to Aspen's voice that she found extremely appealing. "I hadn't noticed." And just like that, the headache was back. Her hands moved to her temples once again.

"Another lie?" Aspen asked. "This is fun."

Tora rubbed her temples furiously. "If I find out you're responsible for this—"

"I promise you"—Aspen laughed—"I'm not."

"Glad you find this funny."

"What I find funny is you're a living, walking lie detector, detecting your own lies."

Tora laughed in spite of herself.

"Here's what we've established so far: you're gay, you like me, and you think my voice is sexy. Anything else you'd like to add?"

Tora hesitated, reluctant to admit that Aspen was right. "That'll do for now." Once again, the pain in her head subsided. She was tempted to deny the sexy part, but it just wasn't worth the risk.

Aspen followed Tora into the hospital to check on the newborns. After the recent evacuation of all nonessential personnel, the hospital looked deserted. Save for the sound of a TV in a nearby waiting room, the place was eerily quiet and still.

She felt the newborns' excitement at seeing her. Their connection and awareness of one another was growing. One by one, she was able to sense each of the distinct personalities.

There was one in particular who'd already caught her attention—the rogue Myriad of the bunch. Independent, sassy, and fearless, Raven was a born troublemaker. Aspen liked her already.

But there was a dark side to Raven that she'd have to keep her eye on. Raven and Hope would lock horns on more than one occasion for control of the group. Hope, Aspen knew, would always prevail. But Raven would grow resentful and restless over time. Aspen knew it was her job to keep the peace between the two and mentor Raven as best she could. She had her work cut out for her with that one.

It was appropriate that Raven's primary animal was a black raven—brazen, loud, and, at times, taunting. That was Raven to a tee.

She put a hand on Tora's arm to stop her as they headed toward Raven's room. "The newborns need to be together."

"I wasn't planning on separating them," Tora said. "They're all staying here."

"That's not what I meant." She looked down at the floor and tried to focus as an urgent message welled up from that mysterious vault deep inside. "The newborns need to be in the same room. All of them. Together."

"Oh." Tora bit her lip in thought. "I don't think we have a room in the hospital large enough to accommodate eight newborns and their parents."

"Their parents can't stay here. It's too dangerous. They should be evacuated immediately."

"But they're babies." Tora's face grew somber. "Who will take care of them?"

"They have us. And they'll be able to take care of themselves before long. The window for evacuation is closing. This needs to be done now."

"You're sure about this?" Tora asked, looking doubtful.

"Positive."

"Can I at least check in on them first?"

Aspen shook her head. "Not enough time."

She watched as Tora instantly shifted gears, her expression of uncertainty morphing into razor-sharp resolve. "I'll bring their parents to the surface myself," she said, already jogging down the corridor.

Within minutes, parents were bidding tearful farewells to their children in the hospital corridor. Aspen shook her head in amazement. They were leaving the sanctuary with nothing but the clothes on their backs and entrusting her with the lives of their infants—their very own flesh and blood. She couldn't begin to imagine how difficult this was for them. Yet another example of how different Shrouds were from humans. No human she knew would ever leave their newborn behind.

These Shroud parents obviously understood the importance of the greater good. With the very future of their species hanging in the balance, they were willing to make this personal sacrifice. But she could see how agonizing it was for them.

Tora turned to her. "Take the newborns to chamber one. I'll meet you there as soon as I get back."

"Copy that."

"One problem," Tora whispered. "I need the four trolleys outside to transport everyone to the surface at once. The other trolleys are scattered all over the sanctuary. How will you relocate the newborns?"

"We'll manage."

Tora looked doubtful. Aspen could tell she was trying to puzzle out a solution.

"Will you please stop trying to micromanage everything? Just let it go." She slipped her hand around Tora's. This time, Tora didn't pull away. "Put your trust in someone else for a change."

"That someone being a reformed chocolate addict who likes to hold hands?" Tora smiled and gave Aspen's hand a gentle squeeze.

Parents with tearstained cheeks stepped in line behind Tora and disappeared into the tunnels.

CHAPTER TWENTY-ONE

Trolley-less, Aspen decided to shift into a dove. She was hoping these newborns possessed the same ability to shift that Hope had demonstrated earlier in the kitchen.

Her optimism paid off. After a handful of test runs, all seven Myriads shifted with her and flew through the tunnels in formation behind her. Even though she'd discovered her own aptitude for flying, she still very much preferred the feel of solid ground beneath her feet.

The trick to retaining her clothes, she'd discovered, was to remember what she was wearing before she shifted. Then, all she had to do was envision her body inside the same clothes as she shifted back.

Aspen led them through the maze of tunnels and returned to human form, landing just outside the hidden entrance to chamber one. She watched as each Myriad glided in and effortlessly shifted back into their primary animal: a polar bear cub, a mountain lion cub, a coyote pup, a black bear cub, a fawn, a cheetah cub, and a fuzzy black chick that would mature into a raven. The only one missing was the white tiger cub. Aspen knew Hope was in safe hands and still on a tour of the sanctuary with Oscar and Skye.

The seven newborns followed her into chamber one through the hidden door in her closet. Each baby climbed onto her bed and lay down. Snuggled in like littermates, they all peered up at her. She pulled up a chair beside the bed and kept watch as they lowered their heads, closed their eyes, and dozed off.

Satisfied they were sleeping peacefully, she ventured into the hallway and quickly turned back. It was *freezing* out there. She grabbed a heavier sweatshirt from a dresser drawer, unzipped the one she was wearing, and slipped the new sweatshirt over her head. After rifling through a few more drawers, she found a pair of gloves and some Spider-Man earmuffs. Perfect. She was a huge Spider-Man fan. How Tora had managed to find these in an adult size was beyond her. She pulled the gloves on and proudly nestled the earmuffs over her ears. Instantly warmer, she made her way to the main room of chamber one.

For the first time since they'd parted ways, she wondered if Tora would make it back safely. A lightning bolt of fear shot straight through her. What if SEA soldiers were already waiting at the surface, ready to ambush Tora and the Shroud evacuees? Tora was fierce—no doubt about that—but she was no match against an army of trained soldiers.

Suddenly torn between checking on Tora and staying with the newborns, Aspen felt her heart pick up speed. That's when she knew her feelings for Tora ran deeper than she'd even realized. She shook her head, wondering if she'd completely lost her mind. It wasn't like her to be obsessing about a woman she hardly knew.

After delivering everyone safely to the surface, Tora decided to check in with Edna at the cabin and bring her back to chamber one. Edna could ride out the battle there and return to the cabin later, if it was ever safe to do so.

She parked the trolley and jogged through the labyrinth of tunnels until she reached the cabin's basement. Entering the passcode to unlock the hidden panel, she cautiously stepped through the doorway. The basement was cast in perfect darkness. Without even a pinprick of light, her nocturnal vision was useless. But she knew her way around this place by heart.

In the early stages of construction—before there were lights— she and her father used to trek through the maze of tunnels on foot, side by side in total darkness, quizzing one another and committing every square inch to memory. The simple act of walking hand in hand with her father for hours on end—those were the memories she wouldn't trade for the world.

She ascended the stairs, turned the doorknob, and froze. Her instincts told her something wasn't right.

❖

Warm at last, Aspen stared into the fire. Oscar stepped out from the hallway and walked over to join her on the circular sofa. "Nice earmuffs," he said, eyeing them with envy. He was a Spider-Man fan, too. He reached out and rubbed his hands together vigorously in front of the fire. The baby carrier around his chest was empty.

"Where's Hope?" she asked, feeling suddenly anxious.

"I added her to the pile of fluffy cuteness on your bed as I was passing through."

She smiled. "They are pretty cute, aren't they?"

Oscar nodded but said nothing more.

Something was bothering him. "What's up?"

"I can't shake the feeling that Hope doesn't need me anymore. She's with the other Myriads now." He frowned. "I'll miss taking care of the little bugger."

There was a thoughtful silence between them. Aspen could tell he was struggling to keep his composure. "Some Spidey earmuffs might lift my spirits," he said sadly.

Now it was her turn to frown. She reluctantly took them off and handed them over.

Oscar clamped the earmuffs over his ears and shot up from the sofa with a look of pure satisfaction.

Something told her she'd been played.

"By the way," he said, grinning happily, "Helga and I have decided—if we make it out of this mess alive—the first thing we're going to do is find a baby to adopt."

Aspen couldn't be happier for them. Oscar would finally get his chance to have his own baby and not have to keep borrowing everyone else's. She held out her hand. "Now that you're not all pathetic and depressed, I'd like my earmuffs back, please."

He slid them off and handed them over with a sigh.

The rest of Alpha Genesis trickled in and gathered around the fire.

Skye sat on the sofa beside Aspen. "I'd like to stay with Hope until she wakes up." She looked from Oscar to Aspen. "That's where I'll be if you need me."

"Copy that," they said in unison.

Heading off to tunnel one, the girl halted in her tracks. She turned and pierced Aspen with her signature bright green gaze.

Aspen hurried over. "What's up, kiddo?"

"Cool earmuffs."

"Thanks."

Skye hesitated. "Can you ask Pierre to make me one of those chocolate-strawberry things?"

"A crepe? Sure. But just one?" she asked with a wink.

"Well, maybe more than one." Skye whispered, "I'm really hungry. And cold, too," she added, looking at her expectantly.

Aspen watched as Skye made her way down tunnel one. She waved good-bye to her beloved earmuffs. First the Skittles, then the lava cake, and now Spidey. She shook her head. When would the madness end?

Tora cracked the basement door open and listened at the threshold. Since the age of ten, she'd always been greeted by Edna's singsong humming upon ascending these stairs. Even when Edna was reading in her armchair, she hummed along to a song only she could hear.

Edna wasn't humming today.

Now on full alert, Tora shifted into her lioness and pushed the door open the rest of the way. She heard a man's voice as she crept down the long hallway.

"Make this easy on yourself, and tell us how to get inside the damn nest."

"Young man, I don't know what you're talking about," came Edna's befuddled reply. "I'm just an old woman. I live here alone."

"You may look like an old woman, but we both know what you *really* are. You're an abomination!" he spat.

Tora rounded the corner as he struck Edna's face with the butt of his gun. The sickening sound of a shattering cheekbone filled the small room. She barely registered the other four soldiers standing nearby as she reared up and sank her teeth and claws into his face and neck.

Edna took that opportunity to shift into the massive African elephant Tora knew her to be. But the cabin was much too small to accommodate such a huge animal.

Tora was already leaping through a window for the safety of the outdoors before the soldiers knew what hit them. Chunks from the cabin's roof and walls crashed to the floor as Tora's paws landed on the snow-covered ground.

She looked up to find hundreds of SEA soldiers waiting outside. Armed with fully automatic weapons, they were poised and ready to kill. There were so many of them. Even with Edna's size and strength, Tora knew confronting this army was a suicide mission.

With debris from the cabin still raining down around them, Edna stepped past her and gently ran her trunk along the side of Tora's face, as if to say good-bye.

The elephant trumpeted loudly, swayed her mammoth head from side to side, and charged at the soldiers. She managed to pulverize the first line of defense and skewer the second with her tusks before the onslaught of gunfire halted her in her tracks.

Unable to leave her faithful sentry, Tora could only watch as the giant finally collapsed and drew her last breath. The soldiers continued their assault long after her death, oblivious to the fact that they had just murdered the kindest and most gentle soul Tora had ever known.

❖

Aspen's breath caught in her throat as she watched Tora exit the bedroom and walk toward her. She was thankful to set eyes on the beautiful doctor once again, but she could tell something was wrong.

"Edna's dead," Tora said, trembling.

Aspen set a hand on her back and led her farther down the hallway. "SEA?" she whispered.

Tora nodded.

"What about everyone else? The parents, hospital staff…are they—"

"Fine. Everyone got out safely. Our vehicles are located five miles from the entry point at the cabin. No sign of soldiers there." Tora took a breath. "I went by to check on Edna. I wanted to make sure she was okay and give her a heads-up that the SEA was coming. My plan was to bring her down here with us, but the soldiers were already there." Her eyes welled up as she met Aspen's gaze. "Dammit, Aspen. I should have gotten her sooner."

She took Tora into her arms for a long hug. Aspen thought about the frail-looking old woman who'd shuffled out in her pink bathrobe and fuzzy slippers to greet her with a hug when she first arrived. Now *there* was a Shroud who knew her way around a hug. Her heart broke for Edna.

Tora didn't pull away from the embrace. She allowed Aspen to comfort her. Baby steps, Aspen reminded herself. She was proud of Tora for taking them.

"We need to tell the others," Tora said, drawing back to dry her cheeks. "Looks like this battle with the SEA is closer than we thought."

Aspen nodded in agreement. There was no time to waste. They needed to formulate a definitive plan.

She glanced at her watch: 7:33 p.m. Felt like the day had sped past at warp speed. Her stomach growled. She and Tora had skipped lunch. She was pretty sure everyone had. It was quite possibly the first time in her life she hadn't thought about food for the better part of a day. "Let's gather the crew and have another meeting over dinner."

"I'll meet you in the kitchen," Tora said. "I'd like to check on Skye first."

"Just saw her. She already put in her dinner request and hijacked some really cool earmuffs."

"She's my patient, Aspen. I need to make sure she's doing okay."

Aspen lowered her head, ashamed of herself. With everything that had happened over the last few days, Skye's suicide attempt had been pushed to the back burner. She hadn't even taken Skye aside to ask how she was doing—like, *really* doing. How could she have let the kid down like that?

Tora set a hand on her arm, apparently sensing the internal browbeating session. "That's not your job. It's mine," she said firmly. "Your job is to lead us. I'll take care of Skye."

Aspen stepped closer, studying Tora's face and lips. Her senses as a Shroud were now heightened. She could hear Tora's breathing and heart rate increase. "Just promise me one thing."

"What?"

"None of that robo-doctor stuff."

Tora met her gaze.

"Skye doesn't respond to that. Just be real with her." Tora's eyes were mesmerizing. A very pale brown, there were small golden flecks in them that made them sparkle.

"Now look who's trying to micromanage."

"Touché."

"Is the kissing lesson about to start?" Tora licked her lips seductively and studied Aspen's with the bold confidence of a lioness.

"I hadn't penciled that in to my schedule yet—"

Tora shoved her against the tunnel wall and slipped her tongue inside Aspen's mouth with a ferocity that surprised her. Nothing tentative about this kiss. Tora dove right in for the kill, sparing them both the torture of an awkward getting-to-know-you kiss. The feel of Tora inside her mouth made her forget everything else. They were suddenly two predators vying for dominance…with a kiss.

Tora pulled back, breathless.

Hands down, that was the most passionate kiss Aspen had ever had the pleasure of sharing with someone. It left her mind and body reeling, feeling things she'd never, *ever* felt before.

"You haven't been intimate with anyone as a Shroud, have you?" Tora asked, narrowing her eyes.

Barely able to catch her breath and focus, all Aspen could manage was a shake of her head.

"You're in for a big surprise." Tora threw her a devilish grin as she sauntered off down the hallway to check on Skye.

Totally unfair. Tora deserved to be benched with a yellow card after pulling such a reckless stunt. How was she supposed to get her head back in the game after a kiss like *that*?

CHAPTER TWENTY-TWO

Tora savored the look on Aspen's face as she made her way through tunnel one. In an uncharacteristic change of heart, she'd decided to throw caution aside and move their friendship to the next level. She shook her head, chastising herself. Who was she kidding? She hadn't *decided* anything. She was drawn to the Myriad, like a moth to a flame. She couldn't stop herself. Their connection was fierce...raw...primitive. Resisting that type of attraction was simply beyond her control.

She'd read about this in her youth—in one of the ancient Shroud texts her father had kept in his collection—but she hadn't given it any real thought since then. Myriads hadn't been around, so it had never been worth her time to contemplate. Until now.

The text had claimed there was a certain process a Myriad would initiate when choosing a mate. Myriads were known to be particularly adept at finding their soul mate. Tora had never believed in soul mates. She believed Shrouds fell in and out of love at will, just like humans. Love, to her, was like a revolving door. You were either falling in love—pushing the door forward from the outside while trying desperately to get inside; in love—trapped inside the enclosed space between the entrance and exit but too blinded by the thrill of being there to realize the door had stopped moving; or falling out of love—the door would resume its forward motion as you were granted sweet release from quarters that, over time, grew to feel unbearably confining.

Tora had never been in love. Not once. She had finally come to believe that kind of nonsense just wasn't for her.

Ironically enough, when referencing the Myriad's hunt for a soul mate, the ancient text had likened the Myriad to a lion—one that had fatally maimed its prey before allowing it to escape. The prey would then run off, believing it had escaped with its life. All the lion had to do at that point was follow the scent of blood until the prey succumbed to its injuries.

Something told her she was the prey in this scenario. *Damn.*

Aspen looked up and frowned as Tora waltzed into the kitchen wearing her Spider-Man earmuffs. Those earmuffs sure got around. Maybe they were like a boomerang and would eventually return to their rightful owner.

All hands were on deck helping with meal prep. They had decided on salad, garlic bread, and rigatoni topped with Oscar's top-secret marinara that was tangy, sweet, and spicy all in one bite. She had never tasted another that could even come close to rivaling the deliciousness of his sauce. All in all, Oscar was an incredible cook. She'd already decided he would launch his own restaurant after he retired. She just hadn't told him yet.

Aspen watched Tora from the corner of her eye as she quickly intuited where she was needed. Efficient as ever, Tora went straight to the industrial-sized oven as the timer marched down to zero. She grabbed a red oven mitt from the counter and was already withdrawing the last of four baking sheets when the timer sounded its alarm. The aroma of fresh-baked garlic bread filled the kitchen.

Tora was someone Aspen knew she could count on. She was strong, smart, independent, hardworking, opinionated, and damn sexy—Aspen's equal in every way. Minus the sexy part. Tora definitely had one up on her there. *That kiss.* She just couldn't get it out of her mind.

Oscar sidled up beside her. "Are we feeding mutant Shrouds with itty bitty mouths?"

"Huh?"

He glanced at the stack of veggies on her cutting board and raised an eyebrow. She'd unwittingly chopped every single piece into teeny tiny slivers. "Easier to digest this way," she lied.

He shook his head and sighed. "Have you kissed her yet?"

"I am *not* talking to you about this, Pop. We've been down this road. Remember?" Anytime she made even the tiniest reference to being intimate with someone, Oscar would get this look that made her think he could go into cardiac arrest at any moment. She remembered the months he'd wasted trying to convince her to become a nun instead of a cop, despite the fact that neither of them was a practicing Catholic.

"Good, because I really don't want to hear about it. All I'm saying is, if you haven't kissed her yet, you should probably do it soon."

"I didn't know there was an expiration date on that sort of thing." She grabbed a green pepper from the pile. "And for your information, *she* kissed *me*. Pretty forcefully, I might add. She threw me against the wall and—"

"TMI." Oscar winced.

"My bad. Sorry, Pop."

He plucked a knife from the chopping block, grabbed a pepper, and began slicing alongside her like a professional hibachi chef.

She stared at his hands, mesmerized by the speed with which he chopped. How come he wasn't missing any fingers? "You trying to make me look bad here, Pop?"

"There are certain things you need to know"—he lowered his voice to a whisper—"when it comes to choosing a Shroud mate. Things I've never prepared you for."

"Who said anything about choosing a mate?" she whispered back. "All we did was kiss."

"But you're a Shroud now. Everything will be...different," he said vaguely. "We should sit down after dinner and talk."

"Is this, like, *the talk*?" she teased. "I can't watch you go through that again, Pop. I don't think your heart could take it a second time around."

"I'll be okay." He nervously cleared his throat. Some sweat was already beading on his upper lip. "Is it hot in here?"

"You're too valuable, Pop. We need you for this fight. I can't afford to lose any of my soldiers before the battle even starts." She spotted Helga across the kitchen and smiled at her. "Why don't you pass this one off to Helga?"

"Really?" he said, his face suddenly filling with hope. "You'd be willing to let Helga talk to you about this?"

"Why not?" She shrugged. "She did a pretty good job the first time around." Oscar had made numerous attempts to talk to Aspen about sex when she was a teenager. It always ended in disaster. She remembered the time he fainted in the kitchen and smacked his head so hard against the table on the way down that he knocked himself unconscious. Another time, he choked on an apple, and she was forced to do the Heimlich. There was also the time he wrecked his patrol car after he'd decided that talking about *it* over the phone might be easier than a face-to-face conversation. She could go on and on. Out of genuine concern for Oscar's safety, Aspen had been the one to suggest turning the job over to Helga. She'd been seeing her for weekly therapy sessions anyway, so it was no big deal. Helga had handled it like a pro.

"Super." Oscar slapped her on the back. "I owe you one, kiddo."

She threw a glance at Tora. "Get me my earmuffs back, and we'll call it even."

Alpha Genesis gathered around the table for dinner. The only one missing was Skye. Aspen had no idea how long the newborns would sleep, but she was secretly relieved Skye had been sidelined. What she was about to propose to the group would be dangerous. She didn't want Skye involved at all.

She took a sizeable helping from the pasta bowl and passed it to Oscar. When Tora handed her the garlic bread without taking any, Aspen hesitated, momentarily conflicted between her love for garlic bread and her desire to kiss Tora again. After much deliberation, she passed the platter to Oscar without taking a piece. He raised an eyebrow in question but said nothing. She'd be damned if she was the only one with garlic breath later.

"Who made the salad?" Hank had already removed his ball cap before taking a seat at the table. His thick graying hair was a prizewinning example of hat head.

Oscar wasted no time in pointing his finger at Aspen, so she kicked him under the table.

Hank leaned so close to his salad bowl that his nose was practically touching it. "The vegetables are *microscopic*. I need a magnifying glass to see them." He looked over at Aspen. "Did you think you were feeding a family of mice?" he asked, casting a glance at Michael. "No offense."

"None taken," Michael said with a wave of his hand.

Tora updated the group on her recent trip to the surface to evacuate the parents and remaining hospital staff. She also told them about Edna.

Everyone set their forks down and lowered their heads. They shared a moment of silence in Edna's honor.

"How could they kill a helpless little old lady?" Liam asked, looking up.

"Edna was little and old, but she was hardly helpless. In fact, she was our largest and most powerful Shroud here at the sanctuary." Tora had tears in her eyes. "She did everything she could to stop them. She managed to crush more than a few soldiers on her way out and even impaled a few with her tusks."

"Way to go, Edna!" Beckett cheered, clapping and whistling loudly. Everyone else joined in with gusto. A long round of applause ensued for their fallen comrade.

Tora looked around at everyone. Aspen could tell she was touched by their support.

Wineglass in hand, Miller stood from the table. "To Edna."

Everyone stood and raised a glass.

"Welcome to Alpha Genesis, Edna," Oscar said as they all clinked glasses.

They took their seats with forlorn expressions and began eating in earnest.

Beckett was the first to break the silence. "So, the SEA is here already?"

"Dad, we knew they were coming sooner or later," Liam said. "No big surprise there."

Beckett sighed. "Guess I was hoping we'd have more time to prepare."

"What if they found that hidden door in the cabin's basement?" Tony asked, already going for seconds. "Couldn't they be in the tunnels by now?"

Tora shook her head. "We have security cameras with motion detectors at each entry point. Any unauthorized activity would've triggered a silent alarm. I would have been notified immediately on this." She held up her watch. "Whenever someone enters the sanctuary, I must manually disarm the system, camera by camera, as they make their way through the tunnels on foot."

"Are you the only one with access to the system?" Oscar asked.

Tora nodded at Michael near the end of the table. "We both have one."

Michael pushed up his sleeve to reveal a watch identical to Tora's.

Aspen wasn't familiar at all with the ins and outs of the security system in place down here. Learning how everything worked would be time-consuming. Right now, her efforts were needed elsewhere. Tora clearly trusted Michael, and so did she. She hadn't known him long, but instincts told her he was solid. "The good news is this place is built like a fortress, so that'll buy us some time," she said. "But it would be foolish to believe the sanctuary's impenetrable. Soldiers *will* breach the perimeter. That's what we need to prepare for."

Oscar turned to Tora. "I'm sure your security system is more than adequate, but I'd feel better if we posted some actual Shroud bodies in the tunnels."

"Good idea, Pop." Aspen had been thinking the same.

"We don't want to spread ourselves too far or too thin," he went on. "At the very least, we should implement a rotating post outside both entrances to chamber one." He set eyes on the eight members of his wolf pack. "Four-hour shifts," he announced, centering his attention on Derby and Rivera. "My men and I will assume that responsibility."

Without a word, Derby and Rivera stood from the table, carried their empty plates to the sink, and headed off to their respective posts.

Mrs. B raised her hand. "How long until the newborns are ready to help us win this fight?"

Mrs. B's optimism put a smile on Aspen's face. Some things never changed. That same optimism got Aspen through high school. When she was convinced she'd flunk the science final that would bar her graduation, Mrs. B bought her a cap and gown and gave them to her the day before her test. "Hopefully soon," she replied with a reassuring smile.

"What about you?" Tony set his fork down and pierced her with the same challenging gaze she remembered from her days at the academy. "Myriads come equipped with certain abilities, right? Do you have any superpowers that would give us an edge against the SEA?"

She shook her head. "Nothing yet," she said, not quite ready to share the details of her visions.

There was a collective pause around the table as they all regarded her.

"Does anyone know where SEA headquarters are located?" She was itching to find out.

Gazes darted around the table as, one by one, they all shook their heads and shrugged. No one seemed to know. Not even Oscar.

Tora finally answered in her no-nonsense tone, "Their headquarters are in Vermont."

"Correct me if I'm wrong, but aren't *we* in Vermont?" Hank asked, scratching his head.

Tora nodded. "They're about an hour away."

Aspen couldn't believe it. "Your father built this sanctuary right under their noses?"

"They weren't the SEA back then, but my father believed they were plenty dangerous. I advised him against building here, but he said this location made the most sense so he could—"

"Keep an eye on them," Aspen and Oscar finished in unison. She locked eyes with Oscar. Putting the sanctuary here was a brilliant idea. The SEA would never suspect any Shroud would be brazen enough to hide on their home turf.

"And you never thought to mention this fact before now?" Hank asked, incredulous. "For instance, *before* all of us got our asses in the car and drove here?"

"I didn't want to scare anyone. I wanted all of you to feel safe here."

"Kind of impossible to feel safe with the SEA right on top of us." Hank gazed up at the rock ceiling. "Now it feels like they're walking on our grave."

Chapter Twenty-three

Aspen realized being neighbors with the SEA had some downsides, sure. Like, they probably wouldn't be knocking on the door to welcome them to the neighborhood with brownies anytime soon. There was also the so-minor-it-was-barely-worth-mentioning issue of the SEA having *all* their resources—weapons, soldiers, vehicles—at their disposal in such close proximity. They'd barely have to spend any money on gas getting here.

Aspen stood, diverting the attention from Tora. "Actually, this works in our favor. They know where we are now, but that's fine. They're not familiar with the layout of this place like Tora is. You saw the maps," she said, gesturing at everyone around the table. "You know how extensive this place is—miles of tunnels, hidden entry and exit points, secret passageways. We can use all of that to our advantage."

"You want us to play hide-and-seek with the enemy?" Liam grinned. "That actually sounds like fun."

She turned to Tora. "Can you control the lights in the tunnels?"

Tora nodded, looking over at Michael. "Between the two of us, we can coordinate that."

"When soldiers breach the tunnels," she said, thinking aloud now, "we can assume they'll be on foot."

"Armed with weapons and night vision goggles," Oscar added.

She hadn't thought about the night vision goggles, but he was probably right. "Our first objective is to strip them of their NVGs. Our second is to disarm them."

"And then kill them. Right?" Tony asked, clearly enthused about that last part.

"No." Aspen shook her head, adamant. "Only go for the kill if it's absolutely necessary—if there's no other viable option."

"You're joking." Tony shoved his plate aside, stood, and pounded his fist on the table. "They're coming here to *murder* us— every last one of us—and you're asking us to disarm them and send them on their merry way?"

She'd never seen Tony lose his temper. It surprised her that he even had one. She clarified her position, her gaze unwavering. "I'm not asking," she said. "That's an order."

Oscar stood from the table. "Stand down, Tony."

She watched as Tony set his hands on his hips. "You've got to be kidding me!" he shouted. "You expect us to blindly follow her orders when she clearly doesn't know what the hell she's talking about?"

"Stand down. Now." Oscar's voice rose to a level Aspen had never heard before.

She sensed Tony was on the verge of losing control. There was an ominous sensation in the air that made her skin tingle. Out of the corner of her eye, she saw Oscar shift into a wolf. A split second later, Tony shifted into a tiger. He locked golden predatory eyes on Aspen. Before she realized what was happening, the entire wolf pack had shifted and moved to her side. They growled and bared their teeth menacingly in Tony's direction, standing guard like her own personal security detail.

Tony turned away and paced the length of the kitchen for several minutes as the wolves eyed him. He was truly magnificent in this form. She had no doubt Tony could be dangerous in battle, but instinct told her it was never his intention to inflict harm—at least not on her. SEA soldiers were a different story. At the moment, however, he was just blowing off steam—the equivalent to slamming a door and storming out during an argument to take a walk around the neighborhood. Except Tony couldn't do that here because they were all locked inside.

Were her Shroud instincts telling her this, she wondered? Were they just now developing, or had they been there all along without her knowledge? She watched as Tony effortlessly shifted back to human form. Oscar and his pack did the same.

"I can't go down this road with you, Aspen," Tony said from across the room. "Letting their soldiers go free is like signing another Shroud's death warrant. They'll just turn around and murder someone else." He walked over to her and extended a hand in apology. "But I never should have lost my cool like that." He shook her hand. "I'm sorry."

"Families argue. It happens." She shrugged it off. "From now on, we settle all internal disputes with the time-honored tradition of thumb wrestling."

With his head hanging, Tony returned to his seat. Oscar also resumed his place at the table, nodding at his pack to do the same.

She sighed, steeling herself against the inevitable onslaught of resistance. "It's time someone steps up to be the bigger person here. That someone will never be our government." She paused for effect. "So that leaves us. Shrouds. We need to lead by example and show those soldiers we're not the monsters the government is saying we are."

"Way to go, Tony," Hank joked. "Your furry tiger ass just proved we *are* the monsters they're saying we are."

The tension finally broken, everyone laughed.

Tony shook his head, clearly disappointed in himself. "My apologies to everyone here. It won't happen again. Like Aspen said"—he held up both thumbs—"thumb wrestling from now on."

Still standing at the head of the table, Aspen kept her focus as she met each Shroud's gaze. "By making it obvious that we're sparing the soldiers their lives, we'll transform the way they think about us, even if it's just one soldier at a time. It'll be slow at first, but a strategy like this is bound to gain momentum. Word in the ranks will spread. Soldiers will start questioning the SEA's mission of total annihilation. Sooner or later, the SEA will have a mutiny on their hands. Defectors will start looking to join us. *That's* how we'll win this war—chipping away at the SEA, making alliances with humans, mixing up the gene pool, and—"

"Destroying their headquarters?" Hank asked, looking hopeful. "Please tell me at least we still have that." He clapped Tony on the shoulder. "Poor Tony here needs to blow *something* up."

Satisfied she gave the pitch her all, Aspen sat down. "As long as we evacuate their facilities first, then yes, that can still be part of the plan."

Hank stood and started gathering empty dinner plates. "Can we leave just one person inside the place when it blows? Like, one really bad guy?"

Oscar regarded Aspen, a new respect in his eyes. "That's actually a stellar plan."

"Right?" Hank agreed, carrying their plates to the sink. "We can tie the bad guy to a chair or, even better, duct tape him to the wall. I've always wanted to do that."

"Fill us in on the rest of your plan." Oscar leaned back in his chair. "There's more."

He knew her all too well. "Some of us will stay behind to defend the sanctuary, and some of us will pay a visit to SEA headquarters. We'll hit them back by taking one of theirs."

"You want us to abduct someone from the SEA?" Beckett asked, looking doubtful.

"Not just anyone. I want the number one guy." She turned to Tora. "Do you have any intel on who that might—"

"Gaylord Cobbledick."

"Holy hell." Hank returned to the table to gather more plates. "Capturing the poor bastard and putting him out of his misery would be an act of mercy."

"He's the man in charge." Tora met her gaze. "He's the one who ordered the hit on my father."

The room fell silent. Aspen realized this battle with the SEA had just come full circle. A window of opportunity was opening for them: steal the SEA's top guy, get as much information as they could from him, and get justice for Tora's father—the man who'd dedicated his life to building this place for them. From the looks on everyone's faces, they were all thinking the same.

"Tell us everything you know," Oscar said, handing his plate to Hank. "We'll find a hole in their security and get this bastard."

Hank shook his head. "While we're at it, we should consider adding his parents' names to the list. What kind of parents would give their kid a name like *that*?"

"I've been trying to get to Gaylord for two years," Tora admitted. "It's virtually impossible."

Aspen looked over at Tora. "You're not running a solo operation anymore," she said, as much for Tora's benefit as for the group. "Now you're part of a team. We'll get him together."

"I am *not* comfortable with this plan," Tora whispered as she and Aspen made their way to the library. "Any number of things could go wrong. Every likely scenario ends with your death."

"Your pep talk really needs work."

They were on their way to the library to look up bird species native to Vermont. With a little luck, maybe she could shift into a convincing sparrow and get a bird's eye view of SEA headquarters. She'd return to give Alpha Genesis a full report, and they'd go from there.

Aspen wasn't crazy about the idea of flying, but she was the only Shroud who had a shot at pulling this off without being noticed. Not only was Skye's white owl too conspicuous, but allowing her to participate in such a dangerous mission was simply off the table.

Approaching the library ahead of Tora, she entered the passcode and watched as the doors slid open. They stepped inside. The Tiffany lamps beside each armchair clicked on automatically, casting an ambient glow in all four corners of the room. This was, by far, her favorite room in the sanctuary. With books from floor to ceiling, this place felt magical. She envisioned curling up in one of the armchairs with a throw blanket and a good mystery for a leisurely afternoon of reading. If they were successful in their endeavor to protect this sanctuary—and each other—maybe, just maybe, she'd be able to do that someday.

"It makes no sense that you should be the one to lead this mission," Tora went on. "You just learned how to shapeshift, you hardly know anything about the SEA, and—"

"Are lions native to Vermont?" Aspen turned in circles, wondering where in the hell she should begin her search.

"No, but—"

"What about cheetahs, rhinos, or tigers?"

"Of course not."

"So that leaves Skye and the wolf pack. I'm sure you and I can both agree that Skye is too young and too valuable to send anywhere right now."

"Agreed."

"Which leaves the wolves—"

"Who are all more than capable of executing this mission," Tora said.

"And you don't think the SEA will take notice of a wolf skulking around their property, spying on them?" Aspen frowned. "Come on, Tora. We both know the wolves would be spotted in no time and probably shot on sight."

Tora opened her mouth to say something but wisely thought better of it.

Aspen winked at her. "For the record, though, I think it's cute."

"What's cute?"

"That you're already invested enough in our relationship to start worrying about me." They were surrounded by thousands upon thousands of books. Finding one little book on birds could take all night. Where was Google when you needed it? Tora had already explained providing internet access in the sanctuary would've given the government a way to trace their location. It was obviously a moot point now because the SEA knew exactly where they were. "I have an off-the-wall question." She'd always wondered about this but had never been brave enough to ask Oscar.

Tora stared at her, waiting.

"Do Shrouds ever…eat people?"

"God, no." Tora wrinkled her nose in disgust. "How could you even think that?"

"How could I not?" She hoped she hadn't offended Tora beyond repair. "That's what animals do in the wild."

Tora strode across the room and pushed the rolling ladder a few rows down. "Aspen, we're more than just animals." She climbed up, reached out, and plucked a single book from the top shelf with barely a sideways glance. "All Shrouds are vegetarians," she said, climbing back down. "I assumed you already knew that, seeing as you're one, too."

It was true. Aspen had been a vegetarian for as long as she could remember. When she'd moved in with Oscar as a teenager and discovered he was also a vegetarian, she thought it an odd coincidence but never connected the dots.

Tora returned and handed her the book. "Shrouds have a natural aversion to meat."

Aspen looked down. It was a field guide to the birds of New Hampshire and Vermont. "How'd you do that?"

"Do what?"

"You found this book without even looking for it. There must be thousands of books on these shelves—"

"We have four hundred and sixty-five thousand items: books, maps, manuscripts, drawings, historical Shroud documents." Tora smiled proudly. "We have something to suit even the pickiest Shroud reader."

"And you remember the location of every single book?" Impossible.

Tora shrugged. "Most Shrouds have good recall."

This went way beyond good recall. It was a superpower—another clear advantage Shrouds had over humans. "I could've used some of that in high school," she said sadly.

"You're just a late bloomer," Tora assured her. "Give it time. It'll come."

There was obviously a lot Aspen still needed to learn. What other tidbits had she missed out on over the course of her life? Playing catch-up might take longer than she'd initially thought.

Tora led her to an armchair in one corner and sat on the adjacent ottoman. "Go ahead and ask."

"Ask what?"

"Whatever questions are floating around in your mind right now. I promise not to take offense. Go ahead. You can ask me anything."

Perfect. She hadn't had a chance to talk to Helga yet. "How do Shrouds have sex?"

"Except that," Tora said.

"But you just said I could ask you anything."

"I meant anything except that."

"Is it really that hard to explain?"

Tora sighed. "It would be a lot easier just to show you."

Aspen raised an eyebrow. If there was any more fitting moment in history to raise an eyebrow, she couldn't think of one.

"It was a figure of speech," Tora said. "I didn't mean that literally."

"It's either you or Helga. One of you has to explain the birds and the bees to me."

"Helga?" Tora asked, frowning.

Aspen nodded.

"That's not a conversation you want to have with the woman who's sleeping with your father."

Aspen hadn't thought of it that way. They were doing *it*? That was a sobering thought. A little sick to her stomach, she squeezed her eyes shut to stave off unwanted images. Now she knew how Oscar felt. Poor guy.

Tora took a deep breath. "When you're a Shroud, the first time you have sex—"

"Make love," she corrected. "When you and I make love. Go on."

"Will you just—will you let me finish, please?" Aspen watched as Tora's cheeks flushed with embarrassment. "Things can get a little...out of control."

"Out of control how?"

"It's not the same for every Shroud, so I don't know how to answer that. Put it this way..." Tora thought for a moment. "You're never closer to your more primitive instincts than the first time you're with someone."

"Is that why they call it *the wild thing*?"

Tora laughed. "I have no idea. From what I remember though, Myriads are a little different from Shrouds, so I'm not sure the same rules apply to you." She shrugged. "I haven't read up on Myriads since I was a kid."

Aspen glanced at her watch. It was closing in on ten o'clock. She felt her eyelids growing heavy. They should get some sleep. It had been a long day for both of them. Everyone needed to be well rested in case the shit hit the fan with the SEA. "Dare I ask, do you have any books on Myriads?" she asked, yawning.

CHAPTER TWENTY-FOUR

It was 2:22 a.m. by the time Aspen finished reading and clicked off the bedside lamp. Tora was already asleep on the bed beside her. They'd taken Skye's bedroom as their new sleeping quarters—adjacent to Aspen's bedroom, where Skye and the newborns were still resting. No longer divided by Tora's insistence on a sleeping bag, Aspen scooted closer to the radiant woman beside her. She lay on her back and propped one arm under her head to gaze at the ceiling, basking in Tora's body heat under the covers.

The high rock ceiling was dotted with tiny pinpricks of light—something Aspen hadn't noticed before now. It looked like she was sleeping underneath the nighttime sky. Tora's touch, no doubt. Probably to stave off feelings of claustrophobia that inevitably came with living underground.

Myriads were fascinating creatures. It was surreal to read about them because, well, she was one. Reading that book gave self-discovery a whole new meaning. She couldn't wait to tell Tora about what she'd learned. Particularly the part about mating for life. Apparently, all Myriads shared the instinct to choose just one partner. Once they set their sights on someone, they excreted a pheromone specifically engineered to attract that person. How all of this could be happening inside of her without her knowledge was beyond her comprehension.

It would take some time to wrap her mind around the rest of what she'd learned about herself. This was a whole new life. Her old life had effectively been vaporized overnight. It was a lot to take in.

She closed her eyes and felt sleep tugging at her consciousness like an insistent toddler. Nodding off, she found herself feeling grateful for Oscar, Tora, Skye, the newborns, and the rest of Alpha Genesis. They were her family now. She knew they were all in this together. And it was her job to make sure everyone came out of this alive.

❖

Tora set her hands on her hips, clearly irritated. Still wet from her shower, her curls clung to the sides of her face and neck. She looked unbelievably sexy in a towel. "So in other words, you're cheating."

"How's that cheating?" Aspen asked, struggling to keep her mind out of the gutter.

"It's just like that potion in Harry Potter—the one that makes you fall hopelessly in love with someone and turns you into an idiot."

Aspen grinned. "I'm really looking forward to the idiot part. Wait a minute." She shook her head, coming to her senses. "*You* read Harry Potter?"

"No wonder I can't control myself when I'm around you."

Aspen felt her grin widen. She had already showered and changed. She finished tying the laces on her sneakers and sat up. "Really?"

"Wipe that grin off your face. This is *not* funny."

She tried, but the grin returned with a vengeance.

"Why do you think I don't drink, smoke, or do drugs?"

"Because you're a control freak?"

"I don't want my judgment impaired. How is what you're doing any different?"

Sharing this with Tora had obviously been a mistake. Too bad she couldn't go back in time and stick her own foot in her mouth. That would be a useful Myriad superpower to have right now. "First of all, I had no idea this was happening. And who knows if it's even true?"

"Oh, so now you want to credit yourself with being naturally irresistible?"

"Second of all, if it is true," Aspen went on, "is it really that big a deal? There's a spark between us that's been there from the beginning. The pheromones are probably just enhancing what was already there."

Tora looked at her like she had completely lost her mind. "You're preparing for a dangerous mission to SEA headquarters, soldiers could breach the sanctuary at any moment, and the newborns are basically helpless next door...and you're asking me if not being able to control myself when I'm around you is a big deal? Of course it's a big deal!" Tora shouted, tossing her hands up in frustration. "I can't focus on anything but *you*. That's a huge liability for everyone here, you and me included."

"On a scale of one to ten, what kind of irresistible are we talking here?" She stood from the bed and set her hands on her hips. "Are we at the level of Helga's chocolate lava cake or more along the lines of, say, Cocoa Puffs?"

"I won't even dignify that with an answer. The point is, we can't let this go on."

Aspen briefly considered putting her pheromones to the test and walking over to kiss Tora. She could smell her soapy freshness from across the room and found herself fantasizing about undoing Tora's towel, carrying her to the bed, and giving her the release she so obviously needed. Instead, she calmly took a breath and, out of respect for Tora, decided to hand the reins over on this one. It was going to take Tora some time to come around and accept that they were meant to be together. Aspen sensed it was of utmost importance to give her that time. "Okay," she sighed. "So what do you propose we do about it?"

"It's simple. You have to stop."

"Stop what?" she asked, confused.

"Stop making those pheromones."

She laughed. "I can't. As a doctor, you should know I don't have control over that. I didn't even know it was happening until I read about it in that book you gave me."

"I know, I know." Tora shook her head. "I'm sorry. I'm not thinking rationally right now."

She took a few steps toward Tora, intent on giving her an innocent and reassuring hug.

Tora put her hand up. "Stop. Right. There."

She did.

"Don't you dare come any closer," Tora said, backing away toward the bathroom. "What I need is physical distance from you."

She shrugged. "Okay."

"Don't come near me," Tora warned, her hand still in the air.

Aspen returned to the bed and promptly sat down. "My derriere is now superglued to this mattress."

"From now on, until this battle is over and everyone's safe, you're not to come within thirty yards of me."

"Like a restraining order?" She was trying her hardest not to laugh.

"Exactly," Tora said in all seriousness.

"How will we get through this mission together?"

"I haven't figured that part out yet." Not taking her eyes off Aspen, Tora backed into the bathroom and slammed the door. "And separate bedrooms from now on," she called out through the door.

"Then the earmuffs are coming with me." Aspen grabbed them off the nightstand.

There was only silence from the other side of the door. Then, "I'd like to propose shared custody."

"Of my earmuffs?"

"You take them today. I'll take them tomorrow," Tora announced through the crack.

She sighed. "Fine. Can I get up now?"

"Yes. Please, go."

Aspen checked her watch: 7:26 a.m. "Breakfast at eight sharp," she reminded Tora on her way past the bathroom. She heard a click on the other side of the door as Tora engaged the lock. "By the way, you're even more beautiful when you're mad."

"And no more flirting!" Tora shouted.

"Thirty yards and no flirting. Copy that," she said, grinning. "I mean it, Aspen. Now go."

❖

Aspen exited the bedroom, happy to be reunited with her earmuffs as she pulled them over her ears. Her old bedroom door slid open as she walked past.

Skye appeared in the doorway, freshly showered and changed. Earlier, Aspen had chosen an outfit for Skye from her room—the room she and Tora were now sharing—and Skye had given her a set of clothes from her old bedroom in exchange. They had agreed to meet in the hallway at seven thirty.

Skye glanced at her watch. "You always this punctual?"

"Try to be."

"I like that. Makes me feel like I can count on you."

"You can." She leaned against the tunnel wall. "Always."

Skye hesitated. "When did you know you were gay?"

Caught off guard by the question, she thought for a moment. "I came out to Oscar when I was fifteen." She thought back, remembering all the girl crushes she'd had growing up. "But I knew I liked girls way before that."

"Did you ever like boys?"

Aspen shook her head.

"Me neither. I was just too scared to tell anyone."

She was glad Skye felt comfortable enough to talk with her about this. "Never be scared to be who you are."

The girl rolled her eyes. "You sound like a Nike commercial."

She took Skye's breakfast order and made her way to the kitchen. Skye was determined to stay by Hope's side until she awoke with the rest of the newborns.

Aspen was on her second cup of coffee when Oscar strolled into the kitchen. He looked like he'd gotten even less sleep than she had. They had agreed to meet earlier than the designated breakfast hour to discuss her mission privately. She had already prepared his coffee. "You look well rested," she said, handing him the steaming mug as he took a seat.

He shook his head and regarded her with a frown. "I'm worried about you, kid."

"I'll be fine, Pop."

He sipped his coffee, leaned back. "I'd feel better if I was going on this mission with you."

"We already agreed they need you down here in case—"

"Soldiers crash the party," he finished, waving a hand in the air. "I know. Still doesn't make me any less worried."

They sat together in silence, buried in their own thoughts. This was sometimes what they did together if a particularly difficult situation presented itself. She'd always found it immensely comforting just to sit in the company of this great man. Oscar was truly her rock in life. Had been from the moment they'd met. She aspired to be that rock for Skye someday.

"If I don't return—"

"Don't talk like that," he growled.

She came at it again in a different way. "I need to know you'll look after Skye if I get an uncontrollable urge to fly south for the winter."

"Of course I will. Goes without saying." He placed a tiny earbud on the table. "This is from Tora. Something about a thirty-yard rule. She said get your breakfast to go and meet her in the tunnels. Oh, and no earmuffs. She said the earbuds won't work with them." Grinning, he held out his hand. "Spidey stays with me."

Standing over the phone, the president dug his knuckles into the Oval Office desk. "What the hell's taking so long, General?"

"Our unit took a hit, Mr. President. There were some casualties."

"Took a hit from what? The Myriad?"

Vickers hesitated briefly on the other end. "An African elephant, sir."

"You're shitting me." Tim Decker shook his head in disbelief. "Those things can turn into elephants?"

"It was news to me, too, sir."

What was next? A dinosaur? A giant centipede? These things needed to be wiped off the planet as fast as humanly possible. As leader of the free world, he knew it was his duty to secure their extinction. "Any sign of the Myriad?"

"No, sir. But we're confident she's in there. We're close to breaching the underground nest. Our boys are gearing up now with Z-23. I assure you, every precaution has been taken to ensure mission success."

Earmuff-less once again, Aspen grabbed a winter coat, scarf, and gloves for her trip to the surface. She had no idea what the weather was like, but it was probably pretty damn cold. She bade Skye and the sleeping newborns farewell, entered the passcode, and stepped into the tunnels.

Miller was keeping watch outside her bedroom door. "On your way to visit our friends?"

She nodded.

"Careful," he warned. "I'd feel better if one of the pack was going with you."

"You and Oscar both worry too much. The pack needs you here. Where's Tora?"

He nodded at the other end of the tunnel.

She squinted into the distance. There, standing beside the first trolley in line, was Tora. She was pointing to her ear.

Aspen withdrew the earbud from her pocket and slid it in place.

"Testing…one, two." Tora's voice came through loud and clear. "Do you copy?"

"You've watched too many spy movies. I can hear you just fine."

"We'll ride in separate trolleys to entry point eleven. I'll lead you there. Obviously, we'll stay in touch with these along the way."

"Obviously." She hoped this arrangement wouldn't last too much longer. She missed being near Tora already. Following Tora's lead, she climbed inside the trolley and started the engine. "Are we there yet?" she joked.

"Entry point eleven is about ten miles out. As far as I can tell, it hasn't been breached." Tora was all business. "Did you pick your bird?"

"Two, actually. The brown booby and the bay-breasted warbler."

There was a brief silence. "Did you pick those for the reasons I'm thinking you did?"

"They reminded me of boobs."

Tora sighed, clearly annoyed.

"Boobs make me happy," she said in her own defense. "I needed happy thoughts for this mission."

"The SEA is headquartered in Chittenden. It's about an hour's drive from here. We'll head north, in separate cars of course."

"Thirty-yard rule," Aspen said aloud, rolling her eyes.

"We'll follow the highway all the way there. It's a pretty straight shot, not far past Rutland. Also worth noting are the electrified fences surrounding their facility."

"Copy that. No perching on the electrified fence." Her stomach did a series of somersaults at the idea of perching anywhere. Highly underappreciated, the ground was a beautiful thing. Every fiber of her being told her the ground was where she was meant to have her feet at all times. But she could do this. She had to. Instinct told her this was the card they needed to play right now. "Anything else I should know?"

"No ledges on the windows, so you'll have to get creative if you want to take a look around. Just don't get too close. Their policy has always been shoot first, ask never. They're pretty unforgiving with local wildlife."

She shook her head. Unbelievable. This all needed to change.

"There's a folder on the seat beside you," Tora went on. "Gaylord's photo is inside. Commit his face to memory so you know who to look for. Entering or exiting the facility, he's hard to miss.

He'll be the only one with bodyguards flanking both sides. He's always impeccably dressed in a suit and bow tie. He wears white gloves and carries a black cane with a golden horse head handle. From above, you'll see he wears a bowler hat with a feather on the side."

"What's a bowler hat?" Aspen wondered aloud.

"It's a black felt hat, rounded at the top with a brim that goes all the way around," Tora explained. "Like a Charlie Chaplin hat."

"He sounds odd."

"I've never met him, but my father shared a few interesting facts."

"Such as?"

"He doesn't need the cane to help him walk but insists on carrying it with him everywhere he goes. He never married, never had children, was born and raised in Boston but doesn't have the accent. My father thought he suffered from an excessive fear of germs because he never touched anything with his bare hands."

Aspen decided odd was too generous. Freakish was more like it. *This* was who the government had put in charge of the SEA?

They drove the next several minutes in silence as she thought about her upcoming mission. She'd retrieve as much intel as possible and return to the sanctuary to plan an attack that would effectively neutralize the SEA. She had no idea if that was even possible or what such an attack strategy would entail. For the time being, she had to do what she did best and fly, quite literally, by the seat of her pants.

CHAPTER TWENTY-FIVE

"Entry point eleven is up ahead," Tora said, interrupting Aspen's thoughts. "It's now ten past eight in the morning. If we're not back by nine o'clock tonight, Oscar will send Miller and Beckett to the surface to track us."

"I'm going alone," Aspen said firmly. After giving it a great deal of thought, she'd already made up her mind.

"That wasn't what we agreed on."

"Makes more sense for me to go and you to stay."

"Is this your passive-aggressive way of objecting to the thirty-yard rule?"

"First of all—and you should know this by now—there's nothing whatsoever that's passive-aggressive about me. I say what I mean, and I mean what I say. Second, as much as I may not like it—which I don't, by the way—I'll respect the thirty-yard rule because it's important to you. You're important to me. So what's important to you is important to me. It's important you understand that," she said, half teasing in an attempt to bring some levity to the situation.

"I can't send you out there alone—"

"You're not. This is *my* decision. You know these tunnels better than anyone. You're indispensable here. With the SEA breathing down our necks, this isn't the time for you to leave. Besides, it'll be easier and less conspicuous if I just shapeshift and fly there instead of driving."

"It's over an hour by car. That's a long way for you to fly. What if you get tired?"

"I'll stop and eat a worm along the way."

"Aspen, I don't like this."

"This is how it has to be. You're needed *here*. And not to sound dramatic, but if nine o'clock rolls around and I'm not back, don't let Oscar send anyone to search for me. If I'm not back by then, it probably means I'm dead. You'll need every last Shroud to stay put and defend this sanctuary. You can come for me later, once the battle is over."

Tora was silent. Since she couldn't see Tora's face, she had no idea what she was thinking or feeling.

"If I don't make it back," she went on, "promise me you won't let Oscar call the shots. You'll need to take command because he won't be able to lead. He'll be obsessed with finding me and will stop at nothing until he does. You can't let that happen. You have to be the one to keep your head in the game." She waited. "Promise me, Tora."

"I don't know if I can do that."

"You've shown me you can. You're logical, rational—"

"Not when it comes to you," Tora said. "I can't think straight when you're around."

"My point exactly. Correct me if I'm wrong, but when I go to the surface, my pheromones come with me. Your logic and reason should return without me around."

"Is that all you think I am? Logical and reasonable?" Tora sounded offended.

There was no winning with this woman. "I think that's all *you* think you are." Aspen knew this wasn't the time to open this particular can of worms, but she couldn't help herself. Tora had extended an invitation for the truth, and she wasn't about to walk away from that. "You're holding on so tightly to who you think you need to be that you've forgotten who you really are. I already know there's so much more to you than logic and reason. I'm not falling in love with a robot. I'm falling in love with *you*, Tora."

There was a long silence. "You're much better at pep talks than me," Tora finally admitted.

"No kidding."

Aspen caught sight of a platform as they drove past. A crimson sign with a golden eleven was framed in the center of the rock wall. "Thought you said we were stopping at entry point eleven."

"I changed my mind. Now that we don't need to access the underground garage, our new destination is entry point twelve. Once we arrive, you and I will part ways. You'll ascend to the surface alone through a series of tunnels and doors. I'll disengage the locks remotely, one at a time. There's a pressurized release valve at the surface for moisture regulation in the tunnels. We'll have to time it perfectly, but I can manually override the release valve to synchronize with you as you shift. When the moisture from the tunnels is expelled, it'll create a white cloud of condensation. This should act as a smoke screen and provide you with some cover when you shift, in case the SEA has the area under surveillance."

"That's my girl." Aspen smiled to herself. "Now all I need is your word that you'll take over command if—"

"You have my word," Tora said, cutting her off. "Once you shift, we won't be able to communicate through the earpiece anymore."

"What about when I get back?" With Mrs. B in mind, she was choosing to think positive.

"All you have to do is shift back to human form, and the earpiece will be there."

"Where?"

"In your nose. Where else?"

"You just made your first joke during a tense moment. I'm definitely a bad influence...and very proud of you."

"I'll keep my earpiece in until you get back. I'll be waiting here at five in case you're early."

"Can we ride back together?" When Tora didn't answer right away, Aspen wondered if she'd pushed too hard.

"Only if you promise me one thing," Tora said finally.

"What's that?"

"Make it back in one piece, and you can have anything you want."

"Anything?"

"*Anything.*"

If that wasn't motivation to stay out of the SEA's crosshairs, she didn't know what was.

❖

Tora talked Aspen through the maze of tunnels and chambers until she reached the final door leading to the surface. She had mixed feelings about this new plan. Part of her saw the logic in staying behind, but another part of her wanted more than anything to be by Aspen's side for the duration of this mission.

If SEA soldiers breached the sanctuary while she and Aspen were away and something happened to Michael, the rest of Alpha Genesis wouldn't stand a chance. She and Michael were the only Shrouds familiar enough with the sanctuary to track an impending attack. By doing so, she hoped they could stay a step ahead of the soldiers and keep them at bay.

Realizing this didn't make her feel any better about sending Aspen into enemy territory all alone. But they'd come this far. No turning back now.

"You still there?" Aspen asked.

"Still here." She took a deep breath to steady herself. "This is the last door. Once it opens, you'll climb twelve metal rungs anchored in the rock wall. There's a red button near the top rung on the right. A circular hatch will slide open when you push that button. The pressure release valve I told you about is located aboveground, beside the hatch. You'll need to shift the second that hatch opens. Wait until the white cloud drifts over the opening, and then fly out as fast as you can."

"Copy that."

"Let me know when you're ready to push the button. I'll trigger the release valve at the same time."

"You know me. I'm good at pushing buttons," Aspen said.

She hesitated, her finger poised over the watch face. One swipe and Aspen would be on her way, possibly never to be seen or heard from again.

"It'll be okay," Aspen assured her. "I'd say I'll do everything humanly possible to make it back, but I'm a Shroud so I can't say that anymore. I considered saying I'll do everything Shroudly possible to make it back, but that just sounded so dumb in my head. Sounds even dumber out loud." She paused. "Is dumber a word?"

"I'm scared to lose you, Aspen."

"Like, really, really scared?"

Tora smiled. "Yes."

"Is now a good time to drop the mother of all bombs?"

"Definitely couldn't be further from a good time."

"When you and I did the naked thing—"

"Are you referring to our melding session?"

"Yeah, that. When you and I did the naked thing, I had a vision."

She shook her head and sighed. "Did this vision involve my boobs?"

"You were in a hospital bed, giving birth to our baby."

Tora was so stunned she didn't know what to say.

"My point is, I don't think I'll be kicking the bucket anytime soon."

"Not to burst your bubble, but—last I saw—you didn't have the proper equipment to get me pregnant."

"That's another thing I learned from the book you gave me," Aspen said. "Apparently, female Myriads have the power to impregnate a same-sex partner. How cool is that?"

"You're making this up."

"It's true. I swear on the earmuffs."

"Finding that book is the first thing I'll do when I get back, so you might as well fess up now or those earmuffs are mine."

"I left the book on the nightstand. Go ahead and look it up."

This was unexpected. Even though she'd never planned on having children, she found herself excited about the prospect of becoming a mother.

"You might want to get cracking on finding a solution to that postpartum hemorrhaging thing. Just sayin'."

"I'll take that under advisement," she said sarcastically. "Is it too late to renege on the offer I made?"

"About giving me whatever I want when I get back?"

"Yes, that."

"Sorry, no backsies. My life is still in peril."

She sighed. "Fine."

"You planning to open this door or what?"

"Be careful, Aspen."

Aspen climbed the metal rungs, counting silently as she went. This was it. Now or never. She imagined the theme from *Rocky* in her mind as she reached up to skim her fingers across the surface of the red button.

"Found it," she whispered.

"On three," Tora said. "One…two…three."

As the hatch opened and daylight claimed the dark space, she shifted into a bay-breasted warbler. She'd studied the tiny bird in agonizing detail the night before. Aspen couldn't see herself in a mirror, but instinct told her she'd pulled it off convincingly enough.

Spreading her wings to get lift, she waited for the white cloud to drift over the opening and then flew up and out at full speed. Airborne, she watched from the sky as the hatch slipped back into place. The surface of the hatch was white, perfectly camouflaged by the snow-covered ground. Was there anything Tora and her father hadn't thought of?

She pumped her wings furiously and flew for the cover of several tall furry pines standing guard nearby. This bird body felt so light and fast. The wintry air was cool and refreshing beneath her wings. She knew the temperature outside was somewhere in the single digits, yet she hardly noticed it at all inside this body. Her downy feathers served as insulation against the cold. Now she understood why down comforters and jackets were so warm.

No sign of the SEA. She considered doing a sweep of the area but decided what little information it would yield wasn't worth the risk. Her mission was clear: get to their headquarters, gather intel, and return as quickly as possible. She just hoped these little wings were round-trip ready.

Hopping from branch to branch until she had a clear view of the landscape below, she positioned herself facing north and spotted the highway in the distance. She'd read that the average speed of a small bird was about twenty-two miles per hour. Tora had said it was a forty-mile trip. If all went well, she should make it to Chittenden in just under two hours.

Hoping her workouts over the years had prepared her for this journey, she took a deep breath and extended her wings. *Here goes nothing.*

With Skye in mind, Tora made a quick pit stop to grab her laptop on her way back to chamber one. She greeted Miller, entered the passcode, and stepped through the opening at the rear of Aspen's bedroom closet.

"That was the quickest mission in Shroud history," Skye said as Tora quietly made her way into the bedroom and shut the closet door. The newborns were still sleeping soundly on the bed. "Where's Aspen?" she asked, standing up from the chair with a look of alarm.

"She decided to go on the mission alone."

"And you let her?" Skye said with an accusatory tone.

"I had to. Her reasoning made sense." Tora shared what she and Aspen had discussed about Tora having to remain at the sanctuary.

Skye chewed her lip nervously. "I don't like her being out there alone."

"Neither do I."

"I could've gone with her. She said I'd be too easy to spot as an owl, but I could fly up high so no one would see me. And when we got to SEA headquarters, I could've just hidden in the trees and kept an eye on things until she was done."

Tora watched as Skye struggled to accept Aspen's decision. It was clear Aspen had already earned this girl's love, loyalty, and respect. A pretty amazing feat, considering everything Skye had been through in her short life. That said a lot about Aspen, but it also said a lot about Skye.

"It's not too late, Tora. Take me to the surface. I'm a fast flyer. I can catch up if we leave now."

"We need you here, honey. You're too special—"

"And Aspen's not?"

"Of course she is."

"You don't even like her." Skye narrowed her eyes. "I bet you couldn't wait to get rid of her."

Tora sighed, studying the scared young woman before her. "Sit down, Skye."

Crossing her arms defiantly, Skye took a seat.

Tora retrieved a chair from the corner and sat beside her. "I do like her." Wondering how much she should share, she remembered Aspen's earlier advice. *None of that robo-doctor stuff. Skye doesn't respond to that. Just be real with her.* She cleared her throat. "I'm in love with Aspen. Sending her on a dangerous mission alone was one of the hardest things I've ever done. I'm just as scared to lose her as you are."

Skye uncrossed her arms, met Tora's gaze, and sat up straighter. "You are?" she asked, clearly surprised.

Tora nodded.

"Does Aspen know that?"

"She does."

"I'm sorry for what I just said. That was really stupid of me."

"It's okay." Tora reached out to squeeze Skye's arm reassuringly. They both gazed at the sleeping newborns in silence. "How are you with computers?"

Skye shrugged. "Okay, I guess."

"A little birdie told me you're better than okay."

"Would that little birdie be Aspen?"

"She said you figured out the passcode to get inside her bedroom when I was delivering Hope at the hospital."

"That was just a lucky guess."

"Well, I have a job for you. It's complicated, and there's a huge learning curve, but I think you can handle it." Tora pushed up her sleeve to show Skye the touchscreen on her watch. "This is what controls the entire sanctuary: electricity, tunnel torches, entrances and exits, temperature regulation, the alarm system—everything. Michael and I each have one." She unzipped a side pocket on the laptop's carrying case and withdrew a watch identical to hers. "He's the only Shroud I've ever trusted enough to give this to"—she handed the watch to Skye—"until today."

"Wow." Skye gazed at it reverently. "I don't know what to say. You really trust me with this?"

"I do. But there's a lot of information to cover. It's going to take some time to review." She pulled her laptop out of the case and flipped it open. "Are you up for this?"

Skye grinned. "You bet I am."

CHAPTER TWENTY-SIX

Still airborne, Aspen had been flying for about an hour and a half and guessed she was at least two-thirds of the way there. She was passing over Rutland when she felt a presence above her. She turned her head slightly to see what it was and realized, too late, that a hawk was diving straight toward her. The hawk was swooping in for breakfast and she, in her little bird body, was on the menu. Judging from the speed of its approach, she couldn't outfly the hawk—it was much larger and faster than she was. She didn't have time to take cover anywhere as it was now just feet from her, talons extended. Her only defense was to shift in midflight.

She assumed a hawk's body and watched as her likeness slowed its descent, retracted its talons, and regarded her quizzically. It flew alongside her for long seconds before veering off in another direction, seemingly convinced that breakfast would have to be found elsewhere.

She shifted back into a bay-breasted warbler as soon as the coast was clear, hoping she was high enough off the ground for the sudden change to go unnoticed by anyone below. It was important that she maintain the body of this smaller bird. A larger bird, like a hawk, was sure to grab the SEA's attention.

Flying was a lot easier than she'd ever imagined. She was actually starting to enjoy herself a little. At a steady altitude of five hundred feet, her view was spectacular.

She had never spent much time in Vermont. The landscape was truly breathtaking. Pristine white snow blanketed the ground and clung to the bare branches of maple, oak, and birch trees. Towering pine trees with snow-covered needles jutted up into the skyline like proud older siblings.

From her vantage point, Vermont resembled a wintry wonderland. The feeling of freedom was intoxicating. All things felt possible. Everything was within her grasp. This war that the president insisted on waging seemed finite and incomprehensibly foolish from up here. Flying, she decided, put all things in perspective. Every Shroud should be able to fly. She felt a sudden longing to share this incredible experience with Tora.

She flew on for another fifteen minutes and arrived at what she assumed was her destination. A twenty-foot-high electrified fence, topped with barbed wire, encircled the entire property. She'd sensed the electrical current in the air from over a mile away. It vibrated through her body like loud music.

Increasing her altitude slightly, she flew along the property's perimeter to familiarize herself with the layout. The building in the center of the property was massive. At twelve stories high, it was wider than it was tall. The corners of the building were rounded, giving it an odd oval-shaped appearance. Every surface of the building, including the roof, was covered in mirrored glass. SEA personnel almost certainly had a crystal-clear view from inside the building, but all Aspen could see from the outside was her own reflection.

After several sweeps from above, she realized there was no place to safely land on the building without being noticed. Maybe her best bet was to land on the ground outside the building, search for an entry point, and go from there. She started her descent and caught sight of three black Suburbans with tinted windows. They were all flying the American flag.

The vehicles slowed to a stop in front of the gate. Two armed guards flanked the first Suburban in line, unlocked the gate, and swung it open to allow the vehicles entrance. Instinct told her this was her chance. The plan was risky and full of holes, but she couldn't waste time perfecting it. She realized this is where she and Tora were different. Tora would be reining her in right now, cautioning her against doing anything rash.

Without giving it further thought, she folded her wings and dove toward the ground. The sudden acceleration gave her an adrenaline rush. She extended her wings at the last second to land softly on the ground behind the last Suburban in line.

That was fun. Now what? She couldn't simply hop onto the roof and hitch a ride inside. The guards would definitely take notice of an avian passenger, no matter how small. She needed to hide under the car, which meant she had to climb into the car's undercarriage somehow. Time to come up with another animal fast.

The guards were approaching the last car now. She watched their boots make tracks in the snow and heard men's voices asking for identification. Still in bird form, she hopped under the car and out of view. She looked around, thinking.

If she shifted into a mouse, she'd be too short to reach the car. Squirrels were good climbers. She'd certainly seen enough squirrels in her life to be able to shift into one. She extended her wings and hopped along the ground until she felt her body grow heavier and longer as fur replaced feathers. She glanced down to take stock of herself, relieved to see the fluffy squirrel tail exactly where it was supposed to be. She reached up and pulled herself into a crevice, hugging the car's metal undercarriage as it pulled away.

Skye absorbed every bit of information Tora threw at her. The girl's intellect far surpassed that of most kids her age. She suspected Skye would be stiff competition in a battle of memory.

Tora closed her laptop. "Show me how to override the torches in tunnel eight, section K."

Skye swiped at her watch face until she came to the appropriate screen. A few taps later, she was exactly where she needed to be to control the lights in that part of the sanctuary.

Tora nodded. "What about the door in tunnel fifteen, between chambers two and three?"

Skye didn't even look up from her watch as she swiped and tapped faster than Tora ever had.

"And if you wanted to increase the temperature in here by a few degrees?"

"I already did that a while ago. I was cold. Hope that's okay."

Tora smiled, leaning over to give her a sideways hug. They'd already reviewed battle scenarios and safety precautions. Skye had kept up with no problem. She reached into her pocket and withdrew the same type of earbud she had given to Aspen. "From now on, I want you to wear this at all times. I'm giving one to everyone here. This will allow us to stay in contact 24/7, no matter where we are in the sanctuary. Aspen has one. I'm wearing one, too. See?" She moved her hair aside to reveal the earbud.

"It's so tiny. I can barely see it," Skye said, pushing her own earbud in place.

"Just tap once to turn it on, twice to turn it off. Like this." Tora demonstrated, and Skye imitated the gesture.

"Will I be able to hear Aspen when she gets back?"

"You'll know she's back the same moment I do."

"Cool." Skye removed her earbud and studied it. She frowned, looking back and forth between her watch and the earbud.

"Is something wrong?"

"We're the only ones here, right? Just Alpha Genesis and the newborns?"

Tora nodded. "Everyone else was evacuated." She saw Skye's wheels turning. "Why? What are you thinking?"

"With the SEA on the way, wouldn't it be better if each of us could open the doors ourselves? That way, none of us would get stuck. Everyone would be able to move around the sanctuary freely and not have to depend on you, me, or Michael."

Tora nodded. "That would be preferable, but there aren't any keypads near the doors. My father and I didn't want to run the risk of someone hacking their way in."

"You installed a voice recognition system in each chamber, right?"

Tora nodded again, remembering the voice messages she and Aspen had left for Skye her first day here.

"Do you have more of these earbuds?"

"A lot more. Why?"

"If you let me borrow your laptop, I can program the system to recognize the voice of everyone in Alpha Genesis, so every door in the sanctuary will open when we tell it to. All I would need is a voice sample. I saved the recording that Aspen made for me the other day, so I can program the system to recognize her, too. I think it's safer that way. If something happened and you couldn't get back to entry point twelve, she'd be stuck outside. This way, she can open the door and let herself in."

Dumbfounded, Tora stared at Skye.

"Sorry." Skye shook her head and cast her eyes to the floor. "It's a stupid idea, isn't it?"

"No, it's a *brilliant* idea. You may have just given us the edge we've been looking for. What do you need from me?"

"Your laptop."

Tora handed it over without hesitation.

"What's your passcode?"

"Ice queen."

"Before today, that's pretty much how I thought of you." Skye met her gaze and smiled. "But I like you much better this way."

"Me, too," Tora admitted with a wink.

"You'll have to hide the earbuds on both sides of every door in the sanctuary," Skye went on. "I'll write the code from here while you're doing that." Her fingers were already flying across the keyboard. "There are a lot of doors in this place." She glanced up. "Maybe you should ask Oscar and the pack to help you."

Convinced she was talking to a mini-Aspen, Tora decided to do just that. She kissed Skye on the forehead and hurried out of the bedroom to find Oscar and his pack. She didn't know how much time they had until SEA soldiers arrived, but something told her there wasn't a second to spare.

❖

Aspen hung on for dear life as the car pulled into an underground garage and the doors sealed shut behind them. Two men climbed out from the SUV and opened the rear door. A third pair of shoes—much shinier than the other two—joined them. She looked on in disbelief as the tip of a black cane made contact with the ground, just inches from her hidey-hole under the car.

This had to be the man she had come for. Gaylord Cobbledick.

Hank was right. She should search for his parents and give them a good talking-to.

Men from the other two Suburbans walked over and waited near the man with the cane. Six bodyguards? Talk about overkill. He was obviously important to the SEA and, quite possibly, a target for assassination. But since Shrouds were too busy hiding and trying to stay alive, she couldn't help but wonder from where the threat was coming. What Shroud in their right mind would attempt to assassinate a high-ranking SEA official? Other than her, of course. Except she wasn't there to assassinate him. She was there to gather intel, return with reinforcements, and abduct the sonofabitch. Her plan did sound pretty insane, now that she thought about it. Even so, she was committed to seeing this through and giving Alpha Genesis the bargaining chip they needed.

With six bodyguards surrounding him, how the hell was she going to follow her quarry without being seen? If she let him go into the building without her, chances were she'd never be able to find him again in the time allotted. *Think, Aspen. Think.*

Harry Potter's invisibility cloak sprang to mind. Something like that sure would come in handy right about now. Shaking her head to stay focused, she tried to plan her next move.

"Prestwick, will you fetch me my trench coat, please? It's just right there on the back seat."

Aspen listened as the rear door opened. Prestwick's shoes disappeared as he climbed inside. He was back in a flash, trench coat in hand.

"Here you go, sir."

"Thank you." The trench coat fell to the ground. As the old man knelt to pick it up, the strangest thing happened. He waved a hand under the car and held the pocket open for her to climb inside.

Telling herself she was crazy for following the old man's lead, she released her grip from the car's undercarriage, shifted into a mouse, and scurried into the pocket in the amount of time it took him to sneeze. He was clearly stalling to give her enough time. But why? Once inside, she felt the coat being lifted as the old man stood.

She was jostled around in the pocket as she imagined he was sliding each of his arms into the coat. "There, that's better. Let me see if I have some tissues." He reached into the pocket and gently touched Aspen with the tip of one finger. "I'm afraid I must have left them at home."

"I'll get some inside for you, sir. If you'll follow me."

Aspen remained as quiet as a mouse. Careful not to snicker at her own joke, she held on for the ride as they stepped inside an elevator. Instead of going up as she'd anticipated, the elevator began a slow descent.

Her mind raced with plausible explanations for this new development, but there was only one that made sense. The six men surrounding Gaylord weren't bodyguards as Tora had thought. They were there to keep the old man from escaping. He had to be a Shroud. How else would he have known she was hiding under the car?

But why would the SEA keep one Shroud alive while murdering countless others? Unless they believed he was more valuable than a Shroud. The only thing more valuable than a Shroud was a Myriad. In the government's view, their success in exterminating Shrouds from the population was all but guaranteed if they had a Myriad under their control.

Had she just played into their hands by willingly offering herself up to the enemy? Her heart hammered inside her small body. She thought of the newborns, Oscar, Tora, Skye, and the rest of Alpha Genesis. Everyone was counting on her. She closed her eyes and took a deep breath to prepare herself for what lay ahead.

❖

"That's the last one," Tora said to Skye. Armed with tubes of rock adhesive, she, Oscar, and the rest of the pack had split up to install earbuds at every single door inside the sanctuary. The earbud's gray color was perfectly camouflaged against the jagged surface of the tunnel wall. After she gathered her materials and turned back to inspect her handiwork, even she couldn't spot it.

"Copy that," Skye said, true to her role as mini-Aspen. "If all of you could stay where you are for just a minute…" Tora heard fingers typing furiously on a keyboard. "There. That should do it. Go ahead and test it out. Oscar, you first."

"What command should I use?"

"Open sesame," came Skye's reply.

Tora, Oscar, and his pack had a good laugh. Tora knew if Aspen had been there, she'd be proud of her newfound protégé.

Satisfied the new voice command system was up and running, they agreed to meet back in chamber one.

CHAPTER TWENTY-SEVEN

Aspen heard the sound of elevator doors opening, followed by footsteps on linoleum. A man's voice sounded above her, "Your coat, sir."

"Yes, of course. Thank you. Can you find me some tissues, please?" The old man sneezed repeatedly as he slipped a hand inside his coat pocket.

Aspen quickly hopped aboard, hoping he would take care not to squeeze her too tightly. She was just as quickly deposited into a different pocket—a suit pocket, she guessed. His body heat radiated through the fabric like an electric blanket.

"Here you go, sir. We'll be right outside if you need anything."

"Thank you, Prestwick."

She heard a door close, a desk drawer open, a TV switched on. She recognized the voice of a CNN news anchor. The old man walked across the room, closed another door, and turned on the overhead fan. "This is the only room that's private. We don't have much time," he whispered, reaching into his pocket. She hopped into his hand once again. He withdrew her and gently deposited her onto the floor. "Shift now, please, so we can talk."

She shifted to human form and stood before him, face to face. They were inside a modest-looking bathroom.

His Charlie Chaplin hat, cloud-gray moustache, soft wrinkles, and intelligent blue eyes lent him a distinguished look. "You're a Myriad," he said with a broad smile that reached the crow's feet around the outer corners of his eyes. "My goodness. I never thought I'd see the day." He removed a white glove and extended his hand. "Felix."

"Aspen." When their hands connected, she saw him as a massive lion with a thick dark mane. Much larger than Tora's lioness, he circled her proudly, muscles rippling with every stride. He sized her up with bright yellow eyes—the truest sign of a Myriad.

"Felix," she said aloud, stepping back. She remembered the story Beckett had shared about Great-grandpa Amos's best friend, who also went by the name Felix. But that was impossible. That would make Felix over a century old. This man couldn't be more than seventy. "You wouldn't be Amos's friend, by any chance?"

His eyes lit up. "Like a brother to me." The old man regarded her warily as he replaced the white glove on his hand. "How do you know of Amos?"

"He adopted Henry, that little boy you saved. Henry was Beckett's great-grandfather. Beckett and his son are…" She paused, trying to find the right words. "Well, they're part of *my* family now."

Felix smiled even more broadly. "I have so many questions, but we must use our time wisely."

"I was told you go by a different name."

The old man shook his head and lowered his eyes. "Forced upon me after my capture. The government's twisted sense of humor, I'm afraid."

At least she wouldn't have to go looking for the old man's parents now. One less thing to do. "If you're Amos's friend, that must make you, like"—she tried to do the math in her head but failed—"*really* old."

He laughed quietly. "A hundred and twenty-eight last month. Myriads are blessed—or cursed, depending on how you look at it— with an unusually long lifespan. The government led me to believe I was the only Myriad left. The others are in stasis—"

"There are others?"

"Used to be eight of us. When I refused to do the government's bidding…" He cleared his throat with tears in his eyes. "Four left now. As long as I do what they ask of me, they're kept in stasis. If

I refuse to cooperate, they die. And any hope for Shrouds surviving this war dies with them."

"Are you sure they're still alive?" she asked, feeling sorry for the old man and the agonizing predicament he'd been faced with all these years.

"They're kept here, five floors below us. The SEA allows me to look in on them once every month." He withdrew a gold pocket watch, flipped it open, and checked the time. "My next visit takes place in an hour."

Her new mission became clear. She had no idea how they'd pull it off, but of one thing she was sure: she wasn't leaving until every last Myriad was freed. She set a hand on his arm. "I think it's time we rescued your friends."

"Family," he corrected her. "We share a bond deeper than any I've ever known." He slapped his pocket watch shut, adjusted his grip on the cane, and regarded her. "I have a plan. But first, I need to know what your gifts are."

"Afraid I come up short in that department." She told him about the vaccine she'd received as a kid.

He removed his white glove once again. "Give me your hand. I'll tell you what gifts you possess."

❖

Tora was the last to return to chamber one. She deactivated her earbud and stepped through the closet.

Skye glanced up from the laptop screen. "I've been monitoring the cameras like you taught me. Still no sign of the soldiers," she reported.

"Where are the newborns?" No longer curled up together on the bed, they were nowhere to be seen.

Skye closed the laptop and set it on the bed. "I thought they were with you," she said, standing.

Tora felt every drop of blood drain from her face. Did the SEA steal the newborns from right under their noses? How was that even possible?

Skye gave her an elbow in the ribs. "Kidding. Jeez, lighten up. They're right behind you."

She turned to find eight pairs of baby animal eyes staring up at her. Like stealthy little ninjas, they had somehow gotten around her without her seeing them. They were now slightly larger and more developed. They all looked healthy and strong.

"You're too easy." Skye laughed. "Aspen wouldn't have fallen for that."

Feeling her competitive nature flare up, Tora raised an eyebrow.

"She's too smart." The girl caught herself and looked sheepishly at Tora. "What I meant to say is, you're book-smart, but Aspen's street-smart."

"Nice save." Tora draped an arm around her. "And you're a combination of both." She looked down at her watch as it vibrated furiously on her wrist. A high-pitched shriek soon followed that reverberated through her bones. She locked eyes with Skye, and they both tapped their watches to silence the alarms.

"Soldiers have breached the cabin entrance," Tora said.

Studying her watch face, Skye dismissed the alert and brought up the camera in that section of the tunnels. "They're in the tunnels now, on foot."

Felix took a step back, his blue eyes wide with wonder. "You possess the rarest of any gift bestowed to a Myriad."

"The ability to eat seven doughnuts in one sitting?" she joked.

He just stared at her.

"Okay, eight. But that was just once."

"Manipulation of time," he said, shaking his head as if to bring himself back to reality.

"*Back to the Future* is my favorite movie." She waited for him to share what her gift really was. "You're kidding, right?"

"I'm afraid not."

"Are you saying I have my own personal remote control over time? That I can rewind and fast-forward at will?"

"You can't go backward. No one can. But you can move forward in time and then return to the present, which, I must say, is most useful in our present circumstance."

She failed to see how such a gift could benefit them in rescuing the four remaining Myriads. "Even if I knew how to make that work—which I don't, by the way—how does that help us?"

"By looking forward, we can work backward," he said with a wink.

"Riddles hurt my brain."

He cast his gaze to the floor and thought for a moment. "The very second we make a plan, you'll move forward into the future to check the results of that plan. If you find failure, then we'll adjust the plan accordingly. You'll move forward into the future once again, and so on and so forth. We'll keep at it until you confirm our ultimate success. By using this simple process of elimination, we'll know which plan to implement."

Simple was hardly the word that came to Aspen's mind. Just thinking about time travel was giving her a headache. But she was willing to try just about anything if it meant saving the lives of Felix and the other Myriads. "How do I get this time travel thing to work?"

"That's the easy part."

"I beg to differ."

"The hard part will be coming up with a plan that works. We won't be able to talk once we leave this room, so we'll need to do this here."

Doing her best to move past the seemingly insurmountable obstacle of time travel, she pitched her idea. "I'll travel in your pocket as a mouse. You'll release me wherever the others are being kept. Once you and your prison guards leave, I'll shift into human form, get each Myriad out from stasis—however that's done—and go find you. Then we'll all work together to get our asses out of here and live happily ever after."

"Well done. Succinct and to the point," he said, glancing at his watch. "Now for the easy part."

Aspen realized she was about to put her faith in a Shroud she knew nothing about. She took a deep breath to steady her nerves and found herself craving a Butterfinger. King-size. She sighed. "Tell me what to do."

❖

Tora led Skye and the newborns into the main room of chamber one. The entire Alpha Genesis team was seated around the fire, drinking coffee. "The tunnels have been breached," she announced.

"Showtime," Tony said, driving his fist into the palm of his hand.

Oscar stood from the massive circular sofa and pierced Tora with the unyielding gaze of an alpha. "Bring up video surveillance," he said, his voice calm, his demeanor relaxed but alert. "Let's get a good look at these soldiers, see what we're up against."

Tora nodded, wishing Aspen wasn't so far away right now. She tapped her watch to raise the television screen from the floor, zoomed in on the soldiers, and counted them. Four.

Despite the labyrinth of tunnels with endless twists, turns, and forks from which to choose, the soldiers were steadily making their way toward chamber one with alarming speed and navigational accuracy. Armed with assault rifles, they were using weapon-mounted flashlights to illuminate the tunnels. But what made Tora's heart beat double-time were the fully encapsulated Level A personal protective suits they were wearing. Each suit was equipped with a self-contained breathing apparatus. She knew from her hazmat training that Level A suits offered the greatest protection from toxins.

"We've been invaded by yellow space men," Hank said, squinting.

Skye stepped closer to the screen. "Those canisters they're carrying have biohazard symbols on them." She looked to Tora. "That's bad, right?"

"Great. They've graduated from bullets to chemical warfare." Hank nervously fidgeted with the ball cap in his lap. "How are we supposed to defend ourselves against that?"

"We have Level A PPE suits with respirators in chamber five." Tora kicked herself for not thinking of them earlier. PPEs should have been stocked in every chamber. "There's enough for everyone here."

Oscar set his hands on his hips. "Do all the chambers in the sanctuary share the same air filtration system?"

She shook her head. "No, but the tunnels do. We'd have to go through each chamber in numerical order to get to chamber five," she reminded them.

Skye was still studying the screen intently. "If the soldiers release whatever they have in those canisters while we're traveling between chambers, we're all goners for sure."

Oscar cast his eyes to the floor in thought. "I guess we have some decisions to make," he said finally, looking up. "We'll make them as a family. Everyone's vote counts."

The newborns were sitting in rapt attention, their eyes on Oscar, as if waiting for him to go on.

"Option one: we stay put, do nothing, and hope the soldiers aren't successful in their attempt to break in. Option two: we put a little distance between us and them and relocate to chamber two now, before they get any closer. Option three: some of us go to chamber five, get the gear, and double back here." Oscar looked around at the group. "Those are the three options that give us the best chance for survival. Let's vote. Those in favor of option one, raise your—"

"There's a fourth option," Tony interrupted. "Some of us shift and take out the soldiers in the tunnels before they break into chamber one and launch their chemical attack. Like Aspen wants, I'll try not to kill anyone." He shrugged. "But I may not have much of a choice."

"That's a suicide mission," Oscar said firmly, the note of reprimand clear. "I will *not* send anyone on a suicide mission."

"You don't have to," Tony said. "I volunteer." He looked at Tora. "If you cut the lights in the tunnels so the soldiers can't see me coming, I'll take out as many as I can."

Miller, Oscar's second-in-command, set a hand on Tony's shoulder. "I'll go with him, boss."

Each member of Oscar's pack stepped forward. "We'll all go, boss," Beckett said.

"You know I'd never send you out there." Oscar scowled. "Not like this."

Miller nodded. "I know you'd never send us. That doesn't mean you shouldn't."

He and Oscar locked eyes.

"Look around, boss. Makes the most sense for *us* to go," Miller said. "This is a job for the pack."

"Then I go, too," Oscar said, standing up straighter.

"You can't." Skye came up beside Oscar and hugged his arm. "We need you here."

"She's right, boss. We're willing to do whatever's necessary to protect you, the newborns, and everyone else here. This is the only shot our people have for any hope of a future."

Tora hated to admit it, but Miller was right. It had to be done. Oscar knew it, too. She could see it in his eyes. But she could also see the agony there. He would never send his own pack on a suicide mission. She recognized the dilemma for what it was. He'd rather die than watch his pack sacrifice themselves.

"We don't have much time," she said, stepping between Oscar and his men. "If you're going to do this, you need to do it now." She glanced at the video feed on the screen. The soldiers were making steady progress. "Four of you, Team One, leave through the front entrance—the door you came in when you first arrived. The other four, Team Two, you leave through the back. I'll monitor your progress on the screen and guide you through the tunnels. Since you won't have your earbuds once you shift, I'll lead you with the lights. It'll be subtle, so you'll have to pay attention. I'll also cut the lights along the way to give you cover."

"Copy that," the pack said in unison.

"You don't take orders from Tora." Oscar tore off the Spider-Man earmuffs and threw them across the room. They struck the rock wall with such force that they snapped in half. "You take orders from me." He stepped forward, almost nose to nose with Miller. "This plan stops here. Now."

Miller held his ground. He met Oscar's gaze with equal ferocity. "We're not your pack anymore. This is *my* pack now. I'm in charge.

That"—he pointed to the newborns and the rest of Alpha Genesis behind Oscar—"that's your pack. You're *their* leader now. So lead them."

All pack members exchanged eye contact and gave almost imperceptible nods. They waited as Beckett hugged his son, Liam, one last time. Then, under the direction of their new alpha, the pack shifted in the blink of an eye. Miller led Rivera, Derby, and Barnes to the front door of chamber one. Beckett, Rivera, Kennedy, and Malenko trotted off toward the door in Aspen's bedroom closet.

With tears in his eyes, Oscar watched them disappear.

"Where do you want me?" Tony asked, turning to Tora.

"I'm sending you out the front door, ahead of Team One. You're our first line of defense."

"First line of defense, huh? I like that." He smiled proudly. "Hey, when Aspen gets back, tell her I know she'll make one hell of a leader. She was my best recruit at the academy." With that, he shifted into a tiger and bounded off to join Team One.

Eight wolves and one tiger. Working together, Tora predicted they would do some serious damage.

CHAPTER TWENTY-EIGHT

Following the old man's advice, Aspen took a deep breath and exhaled. The same blue particles of light that had appeared at each newborn's blessing returned with a fury. They spilled from her mouth and danced in the air around her.

Aspen reached out, palms up, and gathered the light in her hands. She molded and shaped it into a glowing, pulsating sphere. *Imagine what you've just planned and then ask the question, How does this journey conclude?* Felix had instructed her. She asked herself that very question and, as she did, expanded the sphere by pulling her hands apart until it was large enough for her to step inside.

A mild buzzing sounded in her ears as a steady low-level vibration coursed through her body. She watched the scenery change as she was transported to a point in the future. It was like being held underwater for the briefest of moments before popping to the surface for air.

Looking around, she began taking inventory of her new surroundings. She was surprised to see herself sprinting down a long corridor in sleek panther form. The other Myriads followed closely behind her, their human appearance cloaked by their primary animal. She counted—all four were there. The only one missing was Felix's dark-maned lion.

She was the first to reach the end of the corridor and stopped short, apparently realizing she had led them to a dead end. Nothing but walls and windows. Instead of stopping, the Myriads behind her increased their speed and, one by one, jumped through the plate glass window with a resounding crash. They shifted into birds before they hit the ground and darted off into the sky.

Aspen looked down at the other end of the corridor as an army of security guards approached with Felix in the lead. Intrigued, she noticed immediately that Felix's cane was absent. A balding man in an expensive-looking suit and tie had Felix at gunpoint. He looked to be the man in charge. She heard him as he barked an ultimatum at Felix: use his powers to apprehend Aspen or die.

"Go!" Felix shouted. "Now!" The words were barely out of his mouth as the man in the suit pulled the trigger. Felix dropped, lifeless, to the cold linoleum.

She watched her panther leap through the window and shift into the same bay-breasted warbler body she had used to journey there. Her eyes returned to the balding man as he kicked Felix's body out of the way, his expression devoid of compassion, his soul devoid of humanity. Prestwick took a knee beside Felix with tears on his cheeks.

Looked like Felix was the only one who didn't make it. She was determined to get everyone out alive, especially Felix. After all these years, he deserved to have his freedom restored.

The solution was simple: she'd just have to go back to the drawing board and start over.

Tora divided the television screen into fourths to monitor Tony, Team One, Team Two, and the soldiers at the same time. Since both teams were now in animal form, she'd have to open the doors remotely. "Skye, on my mark, I want you to open the door for Team One," she said without taking her eyes from the screen. She checked several cameras in the vicinity to make sure the coast was clear. "Now."

She watched as Tony and the wolves from Team One stepped into the tunnels. Tony pulled ahead of the wolves and quickly began closing the gap on his way to the soldiers.

"On my mark, open the door for Team Two." She checked the tunnel cameras in the immediate area. "Now," she told Skye, looking on as the wolves from Team Two entered the tunnels.

She looked over at Michael and Skye. "Come stand beside me. Michael, you'll lead Tony with the lights. Skye, you'll lead Team One. I'll take Team Two. We want to time it so Tony gets there just a few seconds before the others."

"Copy that," Skye said, already swiping through the screens on her watch.

"On it," Michael said, doing the same.

They all watched in silence as Tony stealthily approached his quarry, his massive paws silent on the tunnel floor. Tora swiped to the screen that controlled the speakers in the tunnels. She still remembered the day her dad had gone back and forth about whether or not to add them. Installing speakers along miles and miles of tunnels was both expensive and labor-intensive. She remembered questioning his decision, wondering if the money might be better spent elsewhere in the sanctuary. She suddenly found herself grateful for his extravagant spending habits on state-of-the-art equipment. The advantage of having this particular sound system, she knew, was that it worked both ways.

She glanced over her shoulder at Hank. "I need you to growl into my watch."

"That's a new one," Hank said, shifting into a formidable-looking grizzly.

She didn't dare ask Oscar. His eyes were glued to the TV screen. He was too busy watching what would likely be the last moments of the lives of his men.

Tora held out her watch as Hank obliged with a ferocious growl that reverberated through the rock floor under her feet.

Just as she had hoped, the four soldiers stopped dead in their tracks and swung around to confront the phantom bear behind them. Waiting nearby, Tony now had his opening and sprang into action. Instead of killing a soldier as Tora had expected, he galloped down the line, simultaneously knocking the rifles from their gloved hands and tearing at their protective suits with four-inch claws. Tony was smart. He was giving the wolves behind him a fighting chance by disabling all four soldiers. Without weapons or flashlights, the soldiers were easy prey. Their suits compromised, they were now just as susceptible to whatever was in those canisters.

Four wolves sprinted in, scooped up the rifles with their teeth, and darted out of sight before the soldiers knew what hit them. They were now cast in total darkness. Since all video cameras in the tunnels were equipped with infrared, Tora and the rest of Alpha Genesis had a clear view of the soldiers. She waited to see what their next move would be as Tony crouched nearby, his striped tail flicking from side to side.

"Weapon's gone, and my suit's torn." The tallest of the four soldiers ripped off his helmet and facemask and threw them to the ground.

"Mine, too."

"Same here."

"Anyone hurt?"

"Can't see shit, Sarge, but I think we're all okay."

"Anyone missing their canister?"

Each soldier frantically reached behind his back to feel for the canister attached to his backpack. Tora heard a collective sigh of relief as they realized all of the canisters were accounted for.

"How do we know the canisters weren't compromised, along with our suits?" the tall one asked with a note of panic.

"'Cuz we'd all be dead right now, dummy," someone else answered.

"Roll call," their sergeant barked.

Each soldier called out in alphabetical order.

"Grubbs."

"Lattimore," the tall one said.

"Steiner here, sir."

"Anyone's suit *not* torn?" The sergeant was greeted with silence. "I'm calling HQ to tell them we've been compromised. They'll have to send another team." He removed his yellow gloves and tapped a button on his headset. "Falcon 866 has been compromised. Retreating now to the entry point. Request pickup."

He waited, listening. "No casualties, sir. We've been disarmed and our suits have been compromised...Yes, all canisters are still intact, sir...Proceed with the mission? But our suits...Yes, sir. Copy that. Over." He tapped the button on his headset to disconnect the call. "Mission's still a go," he told his men.

Lattimore sighed. "But that means—"

"We're dead men walking," Steiner finished, shaking his head in disbelief. "Come on, Sarge, this is crazy." He shoved his helmet under one arm and held it like a basketball. "We won't even make it to the nest before one of those freaks takes us out. We'll all die for nothin'."

"We have our orders, Steiner."

"Lattimore's got a kid at home, Sarge. And I got one on the way," Steiner pleaded. "Never thought I'd die before he was born. Shit. My wife's gonna kill me."

"I can't believe this." Grubbs set his hands on his hips and began pacing in small circles. "I'm going to die a virgin."

Everyone suddenly grew quiet. They all stared in Grubbs's direction.

"You're twenty-two years old, man. What the hell have you been doing all this time?"

"Saving myself."

"If you were saving yourself for Jesus, then today's your lucky day."

Lattimore and Steiner had a good long laugh at Grubbs's expense.

"Nice." Grubbs ran a hand through his hair. "Thanks for your support, guys. Really appreciate it."

Tora couldn't help but smile. This was the opportunity Aspen had said would present itself. She just prayed Tony and the wolves were on the same page.

She watched Tony shift into human form and raise his hands in surrender. He stepped closer to the four blinded soldiers and glanced up at the video camera. Hoping she was making the right decision, she followed his lead and switched on the tunnel lights.

❖

The old man hadn't instructed Aspen on how to return to the time she had left. He'd assured her she would know what to do and had simply advised her to follow her instincts. He was right. Instinct took over as she exhaled once again. Breathing the blue light directly into her palms this time, she had already molded it into a sphere by the time she was finished exhaling. But instead of expanding it and stepping inside, she simply let it go as she thought about returning to Felix in the bathroom. Before she knew it, she was standing with the old man once again, as if not a second had elapsed.

Cane in hand, he blinked once, twice, studying her. "Did you leave and return already?" he asked, clearly perplexed.

She nodded. "What's with the cane? You don't need it to walk."

"My father left me this cane. All the men in my family have carried it for generations. It's the only possession the government allowed me to keep."

Her cop instincts kicked in. She smelled an omission. "What aren't you telling me?"

Felix raised an eyebrow. "You're very astute for such a young Myriad." He rubbed the cane's golden horse head handle. "I'll tell you in a moment. But first, I need to hear the results of your time jump."

"Everyone made it but you." As she described the man who'd shot him, Felix's expression remained unchanged.

"That's Vickers. He runs the show here."

"You don't look surprised," she said.

"I'm not. His grandfather's the one who gave me the name."

She thought about Prestwick. Having only heard him from the confines of Felix's pocket, she finally had a face for the voice. "Prestwick held your hand at the end. He looked upset."

Felix nodded. "Prestwick has been with me for years. Always respectful. He works for the SEA, but he's a good man."

She remembered Vickers's voice as he ordered Felix to use his powers on her. More than a little curious, she asked, "What are your gifts?"

He sighed and cast his eyes to the floor. "I release a light that incapacitates. It renders an individual unconscious—a coma of sorts." He hung his head. "Stasis, if you will."

It took Aspen a few moments to grasp the full weight of his confession.

❖

Tora held her breath as she watched the screen.

"I'm unarmed," Tony said, lifting his hands higher.

The soldiers took a collective step back. "Don't come any closer," their sergeant warned.

Tony heeded the warning. "Heard what HQ is asking you to do. Wanted to offer you an alternative."

"What...kill and eat us now?" Grubbs asked with a look of stark terror.

"We don't want to kill you. And we definitely don't want to eat you." Tony grimaced.

"What then?" their sergeant barked. "What the hell could *you* possibly offer us?"

"A chance to live out your lives," Tony answered. "The chance to see your families again." He looked at Steiner. "The chance to be there when your son comes into the world."

Steiner shook his head. "He's trying to trick us, Sarge."

"If I was going to kill you, I'd have done it already." Tony lowered his hands. "I was a cop on the surface. A good cop. I was one of you."

"You were *never* one of us," Steiner spat.

"I was. Still am," Tony insisted. "We're not much different than you. We have families, too—people we care about, humans included. As a cop, I would've laid my life down for a human without giving it a second thought."

The soldiers exchanged glances and shifted uncomfortably.

"You're free to go," Tony said. "We'll light the tunnels to guide you back to the surface. You'll have safe passage the whole way through. You have my word on that." He turned to walk away.

"We can't go back," the sergeant called out after him.

Tony turned. "Why not?"

"These things are on a timer," he said, pointing to the canister on his back. "They're going off, whether we want them to or not."

"Then take your packs off. I'll lead you to a safe zone."

"The canisters are sewn into the packs. Each pack is secured to the back of the suit. Removing our suits will only trigger the canisters to release sooner."

Grubbs drew back. "How come you didn't tell *us* that, Sarge?"

"HQ didn't tell me till after we'd already geared up. Didn't think it'd be an issue because the suits were supposed to protect us." Sarge held up his shredded sleeve and looked at Tony. "You the one who did this?"

Tony nodded.

"What the hell are you?" Lattimore asked, poking his fingers through the long gashes on his own sleeve.

"A tiger."

"Cool!" Grubbs's boyish smile caught Tora off guard. "That's what I'd wanna be."

Sarge slapped Grubbs on the back of his head. Hard.

"Sorry, Sarge. Just sayin' *if* I was one of them, that's the animal I'd have chosen."

"How much time do we have?" Tony asked.

Sarge pushed up his bulky suit sleeve to check his watch. "Thirty-eight minutes."

Tora addressed Tony through the earbud, "Ask him what's in the canister." She suspected they were carrying a nerve agent of some kind.

"What are we up against?" Tony asked.

"Z-23—a nerve agent with a hundred percent lethality in under one minute. SEA created it. There's no antidote." Sarge hesitated. "They'll send a team of four soldiers every two hours until they receive confirmation that the mission was a success."

Tora squeezed her eyes shut and shuddered at the SEA's callousness. For a moment, she actually considered leaving the soldiers there to die. But then she remembered Aspen's words:

We need to lead by example and show those soldiers we're not the monsters the government is saying we are.

Ready to do what needed to be done, she opened her eyes and looked at the screen. "Get those soldiers here as fast as you can. I think we can save them." It was a long shot, but it just might work. She owed it to Aspen to try. She'd have to worry about the other teams of soldiers later, if she somehow managed to navigate her way through *this* crisis. One crisis at a time.

Tony studied the soldiers' bulky suits. "Can you guys run in those things?"

"Yeah. Why?"

"Tora has a plan."

"Who's Tora?"

"The doctor who's going to save your helpless human asses so Grubbs here won't have to die a virgin."

"See? Even the Shroud thinks you're a freak, Grubbs."

"Thanks for pointing that out, Steiner."

CHAPTER TWENTY-NINE

Aspen could hardly bring herself to believe what the old man was saying. "You're responsible for putting the other Myriads in stasis?"

Felix nodded, reluctantly meeting her gaze. "I was young and afraid to die when the government captured me all those years ago. Doing what they asked to save my own skin was the worst mistake of my life—one I can never atone for."

"I don't understand," she said, still trying to wrap her mind around what he'd just shared. "Why don't you just use your gift to fight against them?"

He lifted his trouser cuff to reveal a black electronic device hooked snugly around his ankle. Green dots lit up and danced in a continuous circle around the top of the anklet. "This inhibits the use of my power against them. Everyone I come into contact with here is equipped with something similar. It renders my power ineffective against anyone who's wearing it."

"Can you use your power on someone who's not wearing the anklet?"

"Yes, but I made a vow to myself that I'd never use it again, regardless of the circumstances."

After what he'd done, she could certainly understand why. "Can you shapeshift with that thing on?"

"No."

"Then we'll need to get it off."

"Impossible. Vickers has the only key."

"Okay. Then we'll need to come up with another plan—one that doesn't involve you shifting or using your power."

"You said everyone else escaped unscathed, including you?"

"Right, but—"

He met her gaze, resolute. "Then that is the plan we stick to."

She shook her head. "Just give me a minute, and I'll come up with—"

"I've been waiting too long for a chance to make things right. I won't put these Myriads at risk again to save myself."

"I know I can find a way to save everyone. Just give me some time."

"Time we can't afford." Felix took her by the shoulders. "I'm ready to make this sacrifice, Aspen. Let me."

Tora watched as the wolves led the way to chamber one. Tony brought up the rear, still in human form.

"You're bringing the soldiers here? To chamber one?" Hank asked, looking more than a little concerned.

"They'll remain in the tunnels, just outside the door."

"You sure everything in here is airtight? Properly sealed?"

Tora set a hand on Hank's shoulder and nodded. "I'm sure."

Oscar finally looked away from the screen long enough to meet her gaze. "What's the plan, Doc?"

"Hope," she answered, peering down at the white tiger cub. "She can make a protective shield around those canisters."

"But you heard what he said, right?" Hank asked. "The canisters will go off if the soldiers try to remove them."

Mrs. B pushed her glasses up with one finger. "And if Hope creates a bubble around the canisters, the soldiers will be inside that bubble. They'll all die."

Skye stepped forward. "Maybe we should let them die."

Tora's momentary shock was quickly replaced by awe over the girl's genius solution. "You've never revived more than one person at a time. Do you think you can do this?"

Skye frowned and looked down at the floor. "I don't know." After several tense moments, she met Tora's gaze, her bright green eyes filled with the focus and determination of a born leader. "I'll give it everything I've got."

For the first time since they'd met, Aspen looked at the old man—really looked at him. The government had captured him over a century ago. Living inside an organization that was actively killing off Shrouds, waking each morning with the knowledge that he'd sacrificed his fellow Myriads to save himself, not being allowed to shapeshift or use his gift to help his people—all of it had worn him down. He was tired. She suspected Felix's will to live had been extinguished long ago. "Is there anything you want me to tell the Myriads?" she asked.

The old man smiled sadly. "Just tell them I'm sorry." He held up the cane. "This is the only way to undo what I've done. Tapping each Myriad with this cane will release them from stasis. The only problem is, it can't be me."

"You've been carrying that thing around all this time, knowing you couldn't use it, just hoping for a miracle?"

"And my miracle came along in the form of a mouse." He smiled—the first genuine smile she'd seen from him. "It only took a hundred and something years. I guess patience really does pay off."

There was a soft knock at the door. "Everything okay in there, sir?"

The old man didn't skip a beat. "The simplest tasks take much longer when you're my age, Prestwick." He flushed the toilet to maintain his cover.

"Just wanted to give you a heads-up, sir. We're leaving in thirty minutes for your visit down below."

"Very well. I hope to be done by then." He gestured at Aspen to keep quiet with a finger over his lips as he held his pocket open. Taking her cue, she shifted into a brown field mouse once again.

❖

Tora wondered if her expectations of Skye and Hope were too high. They'd had no time to practice or prepare for this at all. She realized she was putting everyone here at risk to save these soldiers. Including the precious newborns.

Skye took a seat on the floor beside Hope and draped an arm around the white tiger cub's shoulders. The pair gazed into one another's eyes. Tora watched, amazed, as Hope's eyes grew momentarily brighter before returning to their usual golden hue.

Skye looked up at Tora. "I think our powers are stronger when Hope and I are together. I should go out there with her."

Oscar stepped forward. "I don't think that's a good idea, kiddo."

Tora's gaze lingered on Skye. Putting the girl in harm's way made her feel sick to her stomach. Despite her best efforts, she had already grown quite attached to Skye.

Skye looked from Tora to Oscar. "I'm pretty sure we'll be okay, as long as we're together," she assured him.

Pretty sure wouldn't cut it with Aspen when it came to the girl's safety. Tora knew Aspen would never forgive her if something happened to Skye. Worse, she'd never forgive herself. She suddenly found herself in a dilemma. Her instincts were doing battle with her rational mind. In the past, logic always won out—hands down, no exceptions. But today, her instincts were compelling her to trust the girl's judgment and move forward with this plan.

Tora despised three things in life: taking risks, asking for help, and flying by the seat of her pants. She almost laughed out loud as she realized she was about to do all three. Looked like Aspen was starting to rub off on her.

She glanced at the television screen as the wolves approached. Tony and the soldiers jogged to a stop. All of them were now just outside the door to chamber one.

Sarge checked his watch. "Twenty-two minutes remaining," he announced.

"What now, Doc?" Tony asked, looking up at the camera.

As Tora spoke through the earbud, the wolves returned to human form and listened in.

Tony ran a hand over his face, silent as he processed her plan. He turned to address the soldiers. "Some weird shit is about to go down. I don't have time to explain everything, so just go with it."

Sarge set his hands on his hips. "What the hell does that mean?"

"I'm saying, you'll just have to trust us."

"While you and your dog friends go inside where it's safe?"

Tony took a long moment to answer. "The pack will go inside, yes. My people need them to help defend this sanctuary from humans. But I'm staying here. With you."

Sarge narrowed his eyes. "So if things go south—"

"They *will* go south," Tony admitted. "That's kind of the plan. We're all going to die. But there's a very special Shroud inside there"—he pointed to the chamber's steel door—"who can bring us back to life."

All four soldiers looked stunned.

"I know it's a lot to take in, but this is the only way."

"You're really not going to leave?" Sarge asked. "You'd *die* with us?"

Tony nodded. "Can't say I'm especially excited about it, but, yeah, we'll take this leap of faith together."

"Are you insane?" Sarge shook his head. "We came here to kill you, man. That was our mission—to destroy every living thing down here."

"I know that."

"Then why the hell are you doing this?"

Tony shrugged and cast his eyes to the floor. "Because Lattimore needs to see his kid again, and Steiner should be there to meet his baby." He looked up. "But mostly because I don't want Grubbs to die a total loser."

The tension finally broken, everyone laughed.

Even Grubbs couldn't help but crack a smile. "Thanks, guys. Once again, I appreciate the support."

Sarge extended his hand. "What's your name, man?"

"Tony," he said, reaching back. "Tony Carrillo."

"Good to meet you, Tony Carrillo. Name's Bartholomew Antonius DeAndre Bergedorff-Schumacher."

"That's a mouthful."

"Everyone just calls me Sarge."

Tora watched them, keenly aware how fast their clock was ticking but also aware that what was happening between them was important. This was the first stepping stone toward building a relationship with humans.

Snug in the old man's pocket, Aspen listened intently as he joined Prestwick and, presumably, the other guards in the corridor. She heard multiple shoes tapping on the floor, but she couldn't tell how many guards were accompanying Felix. The only one who talked to him was Prestwick.

They stepped inside the elevator and descended farther into the unknown depths of the building. Prestwick mentioned a football game from the night before. He and Felix debated if the star quarterback would last the season with rumors of a knee injury. It was clear to Aspen that a mutual fondness and respect existed between the two. She was glad Felix had someone like Prestwick by his side. She got the feeling Prestwick did what he could to look out for the old man.

A robotic voice announced that they'd reached subfloor eight. She heard the elevator doors slide open.

"I'll take it from here," Prestwick said.

"Vickers said we're supposed to stay together at all times, sir," one of the other guards replied.

"I'm your commanding officer," Prestwick shot back. "Are you questioning me?"

There was a brief silence. "No, sir. We'll wait here."

"We'll be back in five minutes."

Aspen heard more walking, a badge swiped, a series of electronic beeps that she could only imagine was the sound of a code being entered on a touchpad, the *swoosh* of a door opening and closing, and, finally, the old man's voice. "This is out of the ordinary, even for you Prestwick. Is everything okay?"

"We have your bathroom bugged, sir," Prestwick whispered. "So far, I'm the only one who's heard your conversation."

"What are you planning to do about it?" Felix asked, his tone wary.

Aspen considered shifting at that moment to step in on the old man's behalf. But something told her to stay put and listen.

Tora stood in front of the door to chamber one with Skye and Hope behind her. With one last look at the formidable door, she turned to address the unlikely superhero duo.

The tiger cub met her gaze with golden eyes.

Tora took a deep breath. "Remember, I'm staying inside chamber one. I'll watch everything from over there." She pointed to the screen in the main room. "I'll talk you through this, step by step, over the speakers."

"Copy that," Skye replied. Her unnaturally bright green eyes wielded a keen intellect and a purity Tora never before had the pleasure of knowing.

She felt herself getting cold feet. What she was about to do could very well turn out to be the biggest mistake of her life. "And don't forget, Hope must also put a shield around you."

Skye nodded. "She will."

Tora gathered the girl in her arms for a tight embrace and kissed her forehead. When she bent down to do the same for Hope, she was rewarded with a loud purr.

Standing, she entered the code. The heavy steel door slid smoothly aside with a *whoosh*, and the outer door began to crank open, inch by inch. The sound of metal scraping against rock was nearly deafening in the silence.

Tora locked eyes with the soldiers as Skye and Hope traded places with the wolf pack.

❖

"Here," Prestwick said. "This will unlock your ankle bracelet."

"How did you get this?" Felix asked.

"That doesn't matter. We don't have much time—"

"It matters to me," Felix insisted.

"I slipped it from Vickers's office after I heard what Aspen said. I can't let him kill you, sir."

"I can't accept this, Prestwick."

Yes, you can! Aspen wanted to scream from Felix's pocket.

"Without the device," Prestwick went on, "you can shapeshift and escape with the others."

"And what happens to you if I do that? It'll be obvious that you're the one who helped me escape."

"I don't care about that, sir."

"Well, I do."

There was a brief silence. Aspen sensed they were at an impasse.

"Put me in stasis," Prestwick said. "Then it'll look like you escaped on your own."

"I could *never*—"

"Just hear me out, sir. Put me in stasis, and then come back for me. Remember the name John Gruger. He works intelligence here. He's a sympathizer, too. He'll help you find me and get me out."

"Then what, Prestwick? Your life will be all but over. You couldn't go back to your home, your friends, your family. Where would you go?"

"With you, sir. I can help you and your people win this war. I know I can."

"I could never ask that of you, son."

"No matter what the government has done to you, you've always been kind. I don't believe the things they say about Shrouds. If your people are anything like you, then they're good through and through. You deserve to be in this world as much as humans, if not more. After I met you, I realized I was on the wrong side of this war. I'd like to change that, if you'll give me the chance, sir."

CHAPTER THIRTY

With the pack on her heels, Tora hurried back to the main room to keep Skye and Hope in her sights on the big screen.

"Rescue squad's here," Tony announced.

"*That's* the rescue squad? A teenage girl and a...cub?" Sarge asked, bending down to get a closer look at Hope.

Skye stepped in front of him, barring his view of the cub. "You're not allowed to touch her."

Sarge stood, towering above Skye. "What's your name, young soldier?" he asked gruffly.

"I'm Skye. This is Hope. And I'm not a soldier. I'm a Shroud."

"Nice to meet you, Skye." He extended a beefy hand. "I'm Sarge. And I *am* a soldier."

"I know." Skye made no motion to return the handshake. "You came down here to kill us," she said matter-of-factly.

Nodding, Sarge ran a hand over his face. "I regret that now."

"Because you're afraid to die?"

He shook his head. "I'm not afraid to die. We all have to do it sooner or later. I'd just prefer it was later." He laughed dryly and thought for a moment. "What I regret is not deciding for myself if your people are as much of a threat as our government says you are."

Seemingly satisfied with his answer, Skye finally extended her hand.

A soldier and a young Shroud shaking hands. Tora never thought she'd see the day.

"Hope and I will do everything we can to save you. You have my word." Skye stepped aside as the white tiger cub shifted into a dove.

❖

Making up the old man's mind for him, Aspen climbed out from his pocket and quickly shifted into human form.

Prestwick jumped back in surprise. "That will take some getting used to," he said.

She nodded at Prestwick and turned to Felix. "We could use his help in this war. I know you vowed never to use your power again, but this is the right thing to do for our people. You owe us at least that much." It was a low blow, but she wasn't beyond guilting him into compliance if doing so ended up saving his life.

The old man narrowed vibrant blue eyes. "No matter what happens, you *must* return for Prestwick."

"You have my word."

"You'll need this." Prestwick handed his badge to Felix and pointed across the room. "Today's code is 0724. There's a back elevator down the hall and to the right. We're on subfloor eight. Take the elevator to the eleventh floor. That floor's empty because it's under construction." He looked at Felix and held out his hand. "May I do the honors, sir?"

Felix handed him the key.

"Working with you has been the best part of my life." Prestwick knelt, unlocked the device, and slipped it off. "You're the closest thing to a father I've ever known."

"And I'd be proud to have you as a son."

Aspen found herself getting a little choked up as the two men hugged.

Prestwick withdrew his 9 mm from his belt and tried handing it to Aspen.

She looked down at the gun but made no move to take it. "We won't be needing that."

Prestwick holstered his weapon. "Ready when you are," he said, stepping back. "See you on the other side, sir."

Felix released a ball of red light from his palm. She watched as the light expanded and slowly enveloped Prestwick. The old man handed Aspen his cane, stepped over to Prestwick, and gently guided his body to the floor as he slipped into unconsciousness.

It was clear that Prestwick was loyal to the old man and, perhaps, to Shrouds in general. Anyone who would willingly consent to stasis with an unknown outcome was a hero in her book. Prestwick would make a great addition to Alpha Genesis.

She looked around. No sign of the Myriads. She'd expected to see pods with live human bodies inside, but it looked like this room was used for storage. She was anxious to free the Myriads and get the hell out of there. "Where are the others?"

The old man stood. "This way."

Tora watched as the soldiers counted aloud and then shed their yellow suits in unison. Just as Sarge had warned, the canisters began releasing their deadly gas at once. Tora couldn't see the invisible gas, but the effects were almost immediate.

She held back tears as Tony and the four soldiers collapsed on the tunnel floor, clawing at their throats and gasping for clean air. Her eyes darted to Skye and the white tiger cub—still standing. The shield Hope had put around them was working.

Struggling to keep her own composure, Tora addressed Skye through the speaker. "Are you feeling any effects from the nerve agent?"

With tears on her cheeks, all the girl could manage was a shake of her head as she glanced up at the camera.

"Good." Tora tried to sound more confident than she felt. She didn't know how long Hope would be able to sustain the shields. The canisters were no doubt still leaking their poisonous gas. All tunnels in the sanctuary were now compromised. This next step would be tricky—bringing everyone safely inside.

Hope had already created shields around Tony and each of the soldiers. At Tora's direction, she had also created one around the outer door to protect chamber one.

Tora thought back to when Hope had demonstrated her ability in the kitchen. It seemed only *shielded* people and objects could pass through Hope's barrier. She just hoped that still held true.

With a deep breath and a silent prayer, Tora opened both doors to chamber one, locked eyes with Skye, and waited. Nothing. She felt no effects whatsoever. The shield was holding.

Hope shifted into a dove once again and created a shield around each pack member. Tora stayed put and watched as the pack hurriedly retrieved five bodies. Once safely inside, she sealed both doors shut and led them to a back room for decontamination.

Aspen followed Felix down a short hallway. He swiped Prestwick's badge and entered the code. The door unlocked, and they stepped inside.

The four Myriads were lying on military-style cots—not inside the futuristic pods Aspen had envisioned. There were no leads or monitors attached to them, no nurse standing nearby. They didn't even have pillows under their heads or blankets to keep them warm.

"No one watches over them?" she asked, feeling her anger at the SEA swell to seismic proportions.

"Nobody needs to. That's the beauty of my gift," Felix said sarcastically. "Inducing stasis is like being frozen in time, indefinitely."

"Remind me never to get on your bad side."

The Myriads appeared to be sleeping—two men and two women. All looked to be in their early to middle twenties.

Felix held up his cane and pointed the golden horse head handle in the direction of each Myriad. The same red ball of light that had draped itself over Prestwick emerged from each of their bodies. He extended his arm as the light returned to the palm of his hand and disappeared inside, briefly setting his hand aglow in a fiery blaze.

The Myriads opened their eyes and sat up. They looked around the room in confusion.

"No time for introductions." The old man stepped toward them. "You've all been in stasis for over a century."

"Felix?" The man with a long scar on his cheek stood from the cot. "Is that you?"

Felix nodded.

"You look old," he said, frowning. "What happened?"

"I'll explain everything later. For now, it's important you follow Aspen's lead. She's one of us, and she's helping us escape."

Without another word, she led everyone to the elevator, swiped Prestwick's badge, and pressed the button for the eleventh floor. "By the way," she whispered, "we're not killing anyone today. If we can help it."

Darkness and silence greeted them as they stepped off the elevator. She set her sights on the window at the end of a long corridor. They were halfway there when she felt a tingle on the back of her neck. Not bothering to turn and look behind her, she knew Vickers was there with some of his men. "Shift now!" she yelled, hoping the Myriads' ability to do so hadn't grown rusty over the years.

To Aspen's surprise, everyone but Felix shifted into a bird. He cast a quick glance at his fellow Myriads and then over his shoulder before shifting into a dark-maned lion.

With a resounding roar that reverberated through her entire body, he galloped down the corridor toward the plate glass window as shots were fired from behind, one after another. She watched as the bullets pierced his body, too many times to count. Still moving, he reached the end and leaped up, using the bulk of his weight to break through the glass.

The four Myriads ahead of Aspen flew to their freedom— through the hole that the old man had cleared for them by sacrificing himself.

She watched, helpless, as the lifeless body of a mighty lion landed on the ground eleven stories below. Bullets ricocheted around her as she extended her wings and soared through the air, called by instinct to join the Myriads already waiting for her in the sky above.

Tora looked on as Skye extended her arms into the enormous white wings of an owl. Head bowed, feathers aglow, she began to work her magic. A sound like ocean waves crashing ashore filled the small room.

One by one, the soldiers stirred and replenished their lungs with clean air. The only one who remained still was Tony.

With Skye, Hope, and several members of the pack by her side, Tora led the soldiers to the main room of chamber one. The question of what to do with these men hadn't entered her mind until now. She couldn't release them into the tunnels—the air wasn't safe—so bringing them to the surface wasn't an option.

Lattimore, Steiner, and Grubbs took seats on the circular sofa and warmed themselves by the fire. The only one who remained standing was Sarge. An awkward silence ensued as every Shroud in the room stared at him, including the newborns.

Easily six foot five, Sarge's massive structure rivaled only one other's in the room. But unlike Michael's innate gentle nature, Sarge looked ready to wage war on a moment's notice. Hard brown eyes filled with tears as he addressed the group. "Tony Carrillo sacrificed his life today to save me and my men. I didn't know him long, but he was funny and brave…and someone I would've liked to call my friend. I'll never get the chance to thank him for what he did." He leaned over and whispered something to the three soldiers beside him. They all nodded.

Straightening, Sarge turned to the group once more. "We'd like to stay and help you fight. If you'll have us."

Tora could hardly believe what was happening. Aspen had been right all along. This was how they were going to win the war.

❖

With a heavy heart, Aspen led the four Myriads on a long trek back to the sanctuary. She couldn't believe Felix was gone. She'd never had the chance to tell him about the sanctuary or the newborns.

Something told her he would have made a wonderful addition to Alpha Genesis.

They perched in the trees and looked on as soldiers in yellow hazmat suits finished packing up and piled inside their Humvees. It was clear they were making a hasty retreat—no doubt set in motion by the news that four powerful Myriads had escaped from their prison nearby.

She took immense satisfaction in watching them scurry, but the hazmat suits had her worried. Taking such precautions could mean only one thing. Her stomach somersaulted as she watched the last vehicle flee from the scene.

The Myriads followed her as she glided to the ground and returned to human form. She activated the earbud. "Tora? You there?"

"Aspen?"

It was Skye. Thank God she was okay. "Soldiers just left. They were all wearing—"

"Don't come in the tunnels," Skye warned. "They attacked us with nerve gas. The air's not safe."

There was a sudden and painful lump in her throat. She was afraid to ask. "Is everyone okay?"

"Aspen, it's Tora. Tony didn't make it. Everyone else is fine, but there's a lot to fill you in on."

Tony was gone. Poor Tony. She squeezed her eyes shut and spoke through the tears that welled up against her will. "Oscar? The newborns?"

"All fine. Hope and Oscar are coming to get you. She'll make a shield around you to protect you from the nerve gas."

It felt indescribably good to hear Tora's voice again. Aspen glanced at the other Myriads. They had abandoned their human bodies for the well-insulated bodies of bison. She didn't blame them. It was freezing outside. The sun was already beginning to set on the horizon. "I have four adult Myriads with me. Can Hope make shields around them, too?"

"What?" Tora said. "How?"

"The SEA was holding them prisoner."

"Hope can make a shield around all of us." Oscar was talking now. "We're on our way to you."

"Good to hear your voice, Pop."

"Something you should know," he said grimly. "Spidey didn't make it."

"He died for the cause," Hank added.

"Can everyone hear this conversation?" she asked, suddenly embarrassed by her own tears.

All of Alpha Genesis answered at once, "Yep."

"We'll have some tissues ready for you," Beckett said.

"And a hug," Mrs. B chimed in.

"I'm in the kitchen, baking," Helga said. "There's some chocolate lava cake down here with your name on it."

"But we're all pretty hungry, so you better get down here." Tora cleared her throat. "Fast."

Aspen smiled through the tears. "Copy that."

CHAPTER THIRTY-ONE

Already aboard Air Force One, Timothy Decker accepted the call from Vickers and switched on his Bluetooth. To hell with pleasantries. "Did the four Myriads in stasis escape your custody or what?"

"Yes, Mr. President."

He balled his hands into fists. "How the *hell* did that happen?"

"Best we can tell, it was the Myriad, sir."

"The cop?"

"She somehow slipped out of the nest and found the old Myriad who was helping us. Looks like they worked together to free the others. The old one's handler is in a coma."

"And the old Myriad? Where's he?"

"Dead. Killed him myself."

"Good." One down. Five to go. Tim took a breath, steeling himself for the war ahead. "A private jet will pick you up and take you to the bunker. You'll have all of our top military strategists at your disposal. Looks like these cockroaches aren't going quietly, like we'd hoped."

Aspen looked on as the members of Alpha Genesis busily scurried about the kitchen. Even the humans had been assigned posts, blending in seamlessly with the controlled chaos of meal prep. Salad and pizza were on the menu for tonight.

She glanced at her watch as everyone took seats at the table: 7:02 p.m. Skye had already added eight place settings. Out of unspoken respect for their fallen comrade, Tony's seat remained unoccupied—flanked on both sides by the soldiers whose lives he'd saved.

Sarge cast a glance down the long table. "I see cheese, cheese, more cheese, onion, green pepper, green pepper and onion, mushroom..." He craned his neck. "Is that pineapple pizza down there?"

Those at the other end of the table nodded.

"Everything here but pepperoni, sausage, and hamburger." He sighed. "Did you guys run out?"

Skye spoke up beside Aspen. "Shrouds are strict vegetarians."

"Does that mean we have to be vegetarians, too?" Grubbs asked.

"It does if you want to be part of Alpha Genesis."

"Cool name," Lattimore said.

"Catchy," Steiner agreed.

"Soon they'll be asking for their own T-shirts with our logo," Hank said.

"We have a logo?" Mrs. B asked.

"We do now." Liam swept his blue hair aside. "I finished it this morning."

Grubbs raised his hand. "I'd like a T-shirt."

"You've got some nerve." Hank winked. "But lucky for you, I haven't placed the order yet."

Chocolate milk in hand, Sarge stood from the table. "To Alpha Genesis," he said.

Everyone raised their glass.

"Thanks to all of you—but especially Tony—these men and I will live to see another day. I vow to stand by you in battle for however long it takes to win this war and free your people."

"And stop eating meat," Skye added. "You forgot that part."

With a long sigh, Sarge's shoulders sagged in defeat. "Right. That, too."

Aspen smiled. It looked like these particular humans were going to fit into their group just fine.

❖

Aspen stepped out of the shower, dried off, and dressed in her pajamas. It felt good to be back in her old room. Even though she'd only slept here for two nights, she realized it already felt like home. Having access to the tunnels whenever she wanted made her feel less confined and gave her the sense of freedom she needed while living underground. She would always miss her life on the surface, but she knew this was where she belonged.

Skye had tidied up and changed the fur-ridden sheets before returning to her own bedroom next door. Everything was perfect. The only thing missing was Tora. Looked like they were back to the thirty-yard rule after all.

Tora had kept her distance throughout dinner and then ducked out after dessert. Aspen suspected she was obsessing over the sanctuary's air filtration system and already at work on decontaminating the tunnels for safe passage. Something told her Tora would always find a project to keep herself occupied. She shook her head, wondering how long her chosen mate would stay just out of reach.

Aspen opened the bathroom door, teeth brushed and ready for bed. She smelled Tora's perfume at once. Subtly intoxicating, it reminded her of marigolds and summer rain. Dozens of tea light candles cast flickering shadows on the rock walls. A beautiful piano melody sounded from the speakers. Tora stood from the bed.

"What's all this?" Aspen asked.

"I promised to give you whatever you wanted if you got back safely." Dressed in a red silk nightgown that ended just above her knees, Tora stepped over, took her by the hand, and led her to the bed. "I always keep my promises."

"Wow," she said, looking around the bedroom. "And all I was going to ask for was new Spidey earmuffs."

Tora laughed. It was the carefree laugh Aspen had been longing to hear from her since they'd met. She smiled and brought a hand under Tora's chin as she leaned in to kiss her softly on the lips. When Tora opened her mouth and invited her inside, she accepted.

They kissed slowly at first, with all the tenderness of two people falling in love. As the passion ignited between them, their tongues danced with more urgency. She unbuttoned Tora's nightgown and slipped her hands over Tora's breasts, down her stomach, over her hips, looking for the panties that weren't where they were supposed to be.

"I made things easy for you," Tora whispered in her ear as she slipped her nightgown off the rest of the way. "Your turn," she said, easing back onto the bed.

Aspen stood in place and let her eyes roam over Tora's body. She lifted her white tank top over her head, kicked off her pajama bottoms, and eased her body over Tora's.

They kissed and ground against one another for long minutes. Feeling Tora on the edge, she pulled away.

"Wait. Come back," Tora pleaded.

Aspen ignored the request and teased her way down Tora's body with her tongue. At last, she settled between Tora's thighs to sample the slippery sweetness that awaited her, instantly rewarded with cries of pleasure as Tora writhed beneath her.

"You better not have made me pregnant," Tora said, breathless as Aspen lay beside her.

She laughed as Tora climbed on top and returned the favor with a skill and ferocity that left her gasping.

About the Author

Michelle Larkin lives in the Boston area with her two young sons. She garnered material for her stories while working as an EMT, dog trainer, inventor, entrepreneur, and business owner. Her days now consist of hiking and biking, kissing boo-boos, building forts, and writing in the wee hours when the kids are asleep—a life she couldn't have dreamed was even possible and wouldn't trade for anything.

Books Available from Bold Strokes Books

Beautiful Dreamer by Melissa Brayden. With love on the line, can Devyn Winters find it in her heart to stay in the small town of Dreamer's Bay, the one place she swore she'd never remain? (978-1-63555-305-5)

Create a Life to Love by Erin Zak. When sixteen-year-old Beth shows up at her birth mother's door, three lives will change forever. (978-1-63555-425-0)

Deadeye by Meredith Doench. Stranded while hunting the serial predator Deadeye, Special Agent Luce Hansen fights for survival while her lover, forensic pathologist Harper Bennett, hunts for clues to Hansen's disappearance along the killer's trail. (978-1-63555-253-9)

Death Takes a Bow by David S. Pederson. Alan Keys takes part in a local stage production, but when the leading man is murdered, his partner Detective Heath Barrington is thrust into the limelight to find the killer. (978-1-63555-472-4)

Endangered by Michelle Larkin. Shapeshifters Officer Aspen Wolfe and Dr. Tora Madigan fight their growing attraction as they work together to destroy a secret government agency that exterminates their kind. (978-1-63555-377-2)

Incognito by VK Powell. The only thing Evan Spears is focused on is capturing a fleeing murder suspect until wild card Frankie Strong is added to her team and causes chaos on and off the job. (978-1-63555-389-5)

Insult to Injury by Gun Brooke. After losing everything, Gail Owen withdraws to her old farmhouse and finds a destitute young woman, Romi Shepherd, living in a secret room. (978-1-63555-323-9)

Just One Moment by Dena Blake. If you were given the chance to have the love of your life back, could you ignore everything that went wrong and start over again? (978-1-63555-387-1)

Scene of the Crime by MJ Williamz. Cullen Mathew finds herself caught between the woman she thinks she loves but can no longer trust and a beautiful detective she can't stop thinking about who will stop at nothing to find the truth. (978-1-63555-405-2)

Accidental Prophet by Bud Gundy. Days after his grandmother dies, Drew Morten learns his true identity and finds himself racing against time to save civilization from the apocalypse. (978-1-63555-452-6)

Daughter of No One by Sam Ledel. When their worlds are threatened, a princess and a village outcast must overcome their differences and embrace a budding attraction if they want to survive. (978-1-63555-427-4)

Fear of Falling by Georgia Beers. Singer Sophie James is ready to shake up her career, but her new manager, the gorgeous Dana Landon, has other ideas. (978-1-63555-443-4)

In Case You Forgot by Fredrick Smith and Chaz Lamar. Zaire and Kenny, two newly single, Black, queer, and socially aware men, start again—in love, career, and life—in the West Hollywood neighborhood of LA. (978-1-63555-493-9)

Playing with Fire by Lesley Davis. When Takira Lathan and Dante Groves meet at Takira's restaurant, love may find its way onto the menu. (978-1-63555-433-5)

Practice Makes Perfect by Carsen Taite. Meet law school friends Campbell, Abby, and Grace, law partners at Austin's premier boutique legal firm for young, hip entrepreneurs. Legal Affairs: one law firm, three best friends, three chances to fall in love. (978-1-63555-357-4)

The Last Seduction by Ronica Black. When you allow true love to elude you once and you desperately regret it, are you brave enough to grab it when it comes around again? (978-1-63555-211-9)

Wavering Convictions by Erin Dutton. After a traumatic event, Maggie has vowed to regain her strength and independence. So how can Ally be both the woman who makes her feel safe and a constant reminder of the person who took her security away? (978-1-63555-403-8)

A Bird of Sorrow by Shea Godfrey. As Darrius and her lover, Princess Jessa, gather their strength for the coming war, a mysterious spell will reveal the truth of an ancient love. (978-1-63555-009-2)

All the Worlds Between Us by Morgan Lee Miller. High school senior Quinn Hughes discovers that a broken friendship is actually a door propped open for an unexpected romance. (978-1-63555-457-1)

An Intimate Deception by CJ Birch. Flynn County Sheriff Elle Ashley has spent her adult life atoning for her wild youth, but when she finds her ex, Jessie, murdered two weeks before the small town's biggest social event, she comes face-to-face with her past and all her well-kept secrets. (978-1-63555-417-5)

Cash and the Sorority Girl by Ashley Bartlett. Cash Braddock doesn't want to deal with morality, drugs, or people. Unfortunately, she's going to have to. (978-1-63555-310-9)

Counting for Thunder by Phillip Irwin Cooper. A struggling actor returns to the Deep South to manage a family crisis, finds love, and ultimately his own voice as his mother is regaining hers for possibly the last time. (978-1-63555-450-2)

Falling by Kris Bryant. Falling in love isn't part of the plan, but will Shaylie Beck put her heart first and stick around, or tell the damaging truth? (978-1-63555-373-4)

Secrets in a Small Town by Nicole Stiling. Deputy Chief Mackenzie Blake has one mission: find the person harassing Savannah Castillo and her daughter before they cause real harm. (978-1-63555-436-6)

Stormy Seas by Ali Vali. The high-octane follow-up to the best-selling action-romance, *Blue Skies*. (978-1-63555-299-7)

The Road to Madison by Elle Spencer. Can two women who fell in love as girls overcome the hurt caused by the father who tore them apart? (978-1-63555-421-2)

Dangerous Curves by Larkin Rose. When love waits at the finish line, dangerous curves are a risk worth taking. (978-1-63555-353-6)

Love to the Rescue by Radclyffe. Can two people who share a past really be strangers? (978-1-62639-973-0)

Love's Portrait by Anna Larner. When museum curator Molly Goode and benefactor Georgina Wright uncover a portrait's secret, public and private truths are exposed, and their deepening love hangs in the balance. (978-1-63555-057-3)

Model Behavior by MJ Williamz. Can one woman's instability shatter a new couple's dreams of happiness? (978-1-63555-379-6)

Pretending in Paradise by M. Ullrich. When travelwisdom.com assigns PR specialist Caroline Beckett and travel blogger Emma Morgan to cover a hot new couples retreat, they're forced to fake a relationship to secure a reservation. (978-1-63555-399-4)

Recipe for Love by Aurora Rey. Hannah Little doesn't have much use for fancy chefs or fancy restaurants, but when New York City chef Drew Davis comes to town, their attraction just might be a recipe for love. (978-1-63555-367-3)

Survivor's Guilt and Other Stories by Greg Herren. Award-winning author Greg Herren's short stories are finally pulled together into a single collection, including the Macavity Award nominated title story and the first-ever Chanse MacLeod short story. (978-1-63555-413-7)

The House by Eden Darry. After a vicious assault, Sadie, Fin, and their family retreat to a house they think is the perfect place to start over, until they realize not all is as it seems. (978-1-63555-395-6)

Uninvited by Jane C. Esther. When Aerin McLeary's body becomes host for an alien intent on invading Earth, she must work with researcher Olivia Ando to uncover the truth and save humankind. (978-1-63555-282-9)

Comrade Cowgirl by Yolanda Wallace. When cattle rancher Laramie Bowman accepts a lucrative job offer far from home, will her heart end up getting lost in translation? (978-1-63555-375-8)

Double Vision by Ellie Hart. When her cell phone rings, Giselle Cutler answers it—and finds herself speaking to a dead woman. (978-1-63555-385-7)

Inheritors of Chaos by Barbara Ann Wright. As factions splinter and reunite, will anyone survive the final showdown between gods and mortals on an alien world? (978-1-63555-294-2)

Love on Lavender Lane by Karis Walsh. Accompanied by the buzz of honeybees and the scent of lavender, Paige and Kassidy must find a way to compromise on their approach to business if they want to save Lavender Lane Farm—and find a way to make room for love along the way. (978-1-63555-286-7)

Spinning Tales by Brey Willows. When the fairy tale begins to unravel and villains are on the loose, will Maggie and Kody be able to spin a new tale? (978-1-63555-314-7)

The Do-Over by Georgia Beers. Bella Hunt has made a good life for herself and put the past behind her. But when the bane of her high school existence shows up for Bella's class on conflict resolution, the last thing they expect is to fall in love. (978-1-63555-393-2)

What Happens When by Samantha Boyette. For Molly Kennan, senior year is already an epic disaster, and falling for mysterious waitress Zia is about to make life a whole lot worse. (978-1-63555-408-3)

Wooing the Farmer by Jenny Frame. When fiercely independent modern socialite Penelope Huntingdon-Stewart and traditional country farmer Sam McQuade meet, trusting their hearts is harder than it looks. (978-1-63555-381-9)